"Money Buys a Great Many Things . . . And a Great Many People . . . Or Haven't You Heard?"

Lord Alex's words stung Zanna deeply. He spoke of men and women bought—bought like her mother. She swung back to strike at him but he moved quickly, pulling her forward into his arms.

His lips came down on hers. Like an iron cage, they held her prisoner and she could not breathe, his tongue a bold marauding intruder into her unwilling mouth. And then his touch changed. Without ceasing, without pause, the firm strong fingers began to caress her shoulders and throat and the swell of her breasts. These were the lips she remembered, the achingly tender touch that had filled all her dreams.

Yet even while she drew him close, a doubt as soft as nightmist blew through her mind. I will never be the same if he does this. It will change me forever.

Winter Blossom

Cynthia Sinclair

A TAPESTRY HISTORICAL ROMANCE
from
CORONET BOOKS

Copyright © 1983 by Cynthia Sinclair

First published in the United States of
America 1983 by Pocket Books

Coronet edition 1984

British Library C.I.P.

Sinclair, Cynthia
    Winter blossom.—(A Tapestry historical romance)
    I. Title
    823'.914[F]   PR6069.I52/
    ISBN 0-340-36057-7

Printed and bound in Great Britain for
Hodder and Stoughton Paperbacks, a
division of Hodder and Stoughton Ltd.,
Mill Road, Dunton Green, Sevenoaks,
Kent (Editorial Office: 47 Bedford
Square, London WC1 3DP) by
Richard Clay (The Chaucer Press) Ltd.,
Bungay, Suffolk.

Winter
Blossom

Chapter One

"THE SHIP! HONORED MISS, LOOK BEYOND THE point and you can see the English ship!"

Zanna leaned out of her lacquered palanquin. Late afternoon sunlight dazzled her thick-lashed eyes and glinted dusty gold on her long black hair as she followed old Kenjuro's pointing finger. She could clearly see tall white sails rounding the treacherous rocks that divided Katayama Inlet from the Pacific beyond.

"The great lord Azuma once swore that no barbarian vessel could round that point without being torn apart by the rocks," Kenjuro was saying, excitedly. "But now see how confidently the English ships travel to Japan! Naturally, they come to visit the Katayama London Company and its director general, Rutledge-sama."

Kenjuro's voice was full of respect, and

Zanna's delicate features tightened with determination. "Honored director," she promised silently, *I'm going to do my best to please this Englishman!*

"Can you make out the English lord?" Her heart beat wildly against her ribs, but, outwardly calm, she allowed the old man to help her from the cramped palanquin and onto the pier.

Kenjuro shook his head. "Not yet, but you'll see him soon. The ship will come up fast around the point and then drop anchor in the inlet." He smiled. "Surely, you remember? When you were a child, we came together to this pier and watched the ships come in."

His friendliness caught at her heart. Since her return to the Great House in Katayama a week ago, there had been scant kindliness shown her. "That was a long time ago. It has been thirteen years since then," she said.

"But now Rutledge-sama needs your help in dealing with the foreigner, and you have returned."

"English lord," she corrected, gently. "Manager Kita insists that we all pay the deepest respect to Lord Alex Curtis." She nodded at the richly saddled horse tethered by the palanquin. "You're sure this is the best horse in our stable, Kenjuro? Lord Alex must have the best of everything!"

It was an effort to speak calmly, hard to speak at all. Tensely, she watched the ship, its sails bellied with wind, rounding the point.

2

Then, she could hear faraway shouting and the sails flapped down. Was Lord Alex shouting also? she wondered. She had no idea what he was like—young or old, kind or bad-tempered. She prayed he wouldn't be angry that she, instead of Rutledge, was there to meet him. If he was angry with her, she would have failed before even beginning her important duty. Zanna shivered, suddenly, in the cool sea wind.

Manager Kita had warned her about failing. This morning he had called her into the inner office of the Katayama London Company and had faced her grimly across Rutledge's costly, lacquered desk.

"You have been in the Great House for a week," he began without preamble. "Are you prepared to show gratitude and duty to our director general?"

Zanna had bowed. She had always been in awe of Manager Kita. He was the second most important person in the Katayama London Company. Thirteen years ago, when she and her mother had lived in the Great House, Kita had appeared thin and spare and sharp. He was still thin and hard, and his dark eyes were unfriendly as they looked her over.

"You must realize that you were brought to Katayama for a reason. Not long ago we received word that Lord Jasper, in England, is sending his nephew to inspect our Katayama office." He tapped his fingers on the lacquered desk. "You've heard of this?"

"The servants talk about it constantly," Zanna said. "The finest room is being prepared for the English guest."

"English *lord!*" Kita's eyes narrowed. "You will always treat Lord Alex Curtis with the greatest deference." He frowned. "I am not at all sure that you are the right person for this delicate business! In fact, I advised the director against relying on you. Unfortunately, you are the only one who speaks English well enough to be of any use."

Zanna said nothing. Kita's hostility did not bother her, but as he spelled out the importance of the task before her, she became more and more nervous. Lord Jasper, Kita said, was one of the richest backers of the British East India Company. His nephew had therefore to be pleased at all costs.

"He must be satisfied with the Katayama staff, be pleased with our company, delighted with our efforts in Japan! Then, he will make a favorable report to his uncle when he returns to England." He stabbed a thin finger at Zanna. "Do you understand your part in this? You are to please Lord Alex Curtis in all things. You will interpret for him when Rutledge-sama is not present. You will make sure that his lightest whims are attended to."

She said, distressed, "Kita-san, I don't know anything about English lords! Perhaps I'll blunder and offend him!"

He cut her off impatiently. "Lord Alex's visit coincides with our busiest time of year.

4

Today, Rutledge-sama is away from this office for the day, and news has come that the English ship has been sighted!" He jabbed his finger at her again. "This means that you will have to meet the English lord at the pier! You must please him! If you fail to do so, the disgrace will reflect on all of us."

The long, narrow eyes were now slits of concentration. The manager's voice had become low and intense. "You will explain to the Englishman, Zanna! You will be his intermediary, his liaison! You will do as he commands, even to scrubbing his back in the bath! As I have said before, you must not fail. Do you hear me, honored miss?"

The mockery in those last words had made her flush, and she had met his stare squarely. "Yes," she had told him. "Yes, I understand. And no, Kita-san, I don't intend to fail!"

From the vantage point of a full six feet, Alex Curtis swept the crowd on the pier with his spyglass. Where in hell was James Rutledge? Certainly, among all the short, dark-haired folk who had assembled to meet the *Anabella*, a tall, fair-haired English trader should stand out like an eagle among pigeons! Alex had been searching for Rutledge since the ship dropped anchor. Didn't the man realize that the *Anabella* had arrived in Katayama?

"Spotted the trader yet?" It was the skipper of the vessel, swarthy, bearded Captain Francis. When Alex shook his head, he added, "Well, if he was there on the pier, you'd spot him amongst the Jappos easy. Look at the monkeys. You'd swear they'd never set eyes on an English merchantman before."

There was contempt in the captain's tone, but Alex ignored it. He had pictured this moment of arrival often, first back in England, and later during the long voyage when the wind roared in the rigging and great spumes of salt water hurled themselves against the bow of the little English merchantman. This was Japan. This was Marco Polo's fabled Chipangu!

It was nearly twenty-one years since Will Adams, that redoubtable ship's pilot, had made landfall in 1600, and tales had filtered back to England from other British adventurers: stories of fierce samurai warriors with shaved foreheads and deadly twin swords; tales of profit to be made from Chinese silk and Japanese silver; hopes, always, that Japan could be used as a steppingstone toward the vast riches of the spice trade, in which the London Company had paramount interest.

"It's your first voyage," the captain was saying, "so I'll give you a piece of free advice, Mr. Curtis. Don't you trust these Jappos! They always grin, but you never know what's behind those grins." He licked his thick lips. "The Jappo women, now, that's quite another story. A piece of silver will furnish you with an armful of sweetness."

6

Alex grinned. Lord Jasper had warned him at great length about the lures of the flesh. "You're a young man," he had lectured, "and after a long ship's voyage, no doubt your blood will be hot. But remember! Reflect! It is business, not lust, that takes you to Japan. Take an example from James Rutledge, our director general in Katayama. In spite of temptation, he's remained single!"

"But, then, you'll be here on business," the swarthy captain was amending. "Do you plan to shake up the Katayama office of the London Company? Rumor says that Rutledge hasn't been doing as well as he should. Those Dutch merchants are faring better in matters of trade. God rot them!"

Ships' captains, Alex knew, were often privy to a great deal of information. "I've heard the Hollanders have a firm toehold in Japan," he began.

"Toehold!" The captain spat his disgust. "First, it was the Portuguese with their hold of Macao and their monopoly on trade with China. Now, it's the Dutch! They've got both feet in what should be England's business. These God-cursed Hollanders are everywhere, Mr. Curtis. They're in India and they're in Java and in the Moluccans. There's millions to be made in the spice trade, thank you! After all, didn't Sir Francis Drake bring home a fortune in cloves from the Moluccans? But, curse them, the Dutch East India Company is richer and more powerful than our

7

London Company, and those big East In-
diamen of theirs can rule the trade on the
seas." He leaned closer. "If you ask me, Mr.
Curtis, you need a director general who
can. . . ."

He broke off as one of the *Anabella's* crew
let out a shout. "We've got company," Captain
Francis growled.

A boat was being rowed toward them across
the inlet. In the boat stood three Japanese
men. They wore stiff, ceremonial trousers
over their robes, and their foreheads were
shaved. What hair remained formed a kind of
topknot at the back of their heads. All three
looked decidedly grim, and one kept his hand
on the handles of his twin swords.

"Samurai?" Alex asked.

The captain nodded. "They represent the
authority of the lord Azuma of Iwase. They're
here to make sure we really are a peaceful
merchantman!" He grimaced. "Now I'll have
to go and make my bows. You come, too, Mr.
Curtis. They'll want to see you."

The Samurai's visit to the *Anabella* was
brief. They treated the captain with cool contempt, but their interest sparked as they sur-
veyed Alex's inches. One of the warriors
barked something to Captain Francis, who
nodded, gravely. Then the samurai bowed to
Alex, who returned the courtesy, and snapped
out an order.

"What's going on?" Alex asked as the samurai ceremoniously left the ship.

The captain grinned. "He asked if you were nobility, so I said your father and uncle are great lords. That made all the difference, Mr. Curtis. The Japanese are cursed status-conscious! They're letting us disembark." He paused. "Another piece of advice, young sir. Never stand up to a samurai! They're as proud as the devil and mighty free with those swords. They'd cut you up quicker than look at you!"

Alex smiled. "I intend to keep well out of the way. I'm here on business, remember?" He wished that there were some way of returning to the earlier conversation about James Rutledge, but Captain Francis had moved away and was now giving orders that the longboat be lowered. Excitement surged through him. He was going to set foot on Japanese soil, and Rutledge could wait. And, when it came to that, where the devil *was* Rutledge?

He scanned the faces on the pier again as he and Captain Francis were rowed ashore. The pier was completely thronged with Japanese. Both men and women wore flowing, wraparound robes—kimonos, the captain called them—which fell in a straight line from shoulder to ankle and which were caught at the waist by a wide sash. The men wore their hair in topknots, but the women's dark tresses were elaborately coifed and ornamented. They held flowing sleeves to their mouths and giggled at the sailors' ribald greetings as the longboat touched the pier.

9

"Here we are, Mr. Curtis," the captain said. "Up you go, now."

After weeks at sea, Alex was grateful for the solid ground. As he stepped ashore, he was surrounded by a circle of short, olive-skinned people. Before he could think of what to do or say, he felt a light touch on his arm.

"Lord Alex Curtis?" a soft voice asked.

A slim Japanese woman stood before him, hands on knees, head and shoulders bent in a low bow. Her hair was not piled high like the other women's, but was pulled back from her face and held at the nape of her neck with a tortoiseshell comb. All he could see of her face was the ivory white of her forehead with its widow's peak of contrasting jet black hair.

"Lord Alex," she was saying, "I have been sent to guide you to the house of James Rutledge."

Now it registered that a Japanese woman was speaking English! There was a slight musical accent to her words, but the soft voice formed the words clearly. All he could think of to say was "Where *is* Rutledge?"

He noted that the slender shoulders in the pale kimono tensed at his words. "I am very sorry," she said, "but he is away on business. If you will come with me, I will guide you at once to the Great House."

She looked up at him then, and he caught his breath. Her pale face with its high, dark brows, tip-tilted little nose and generous mouth would have been striking in any con-

text. What held Alex, however, were her eyes
—wide, thick-lashed, silver gray eyes.

"Who are you?" he managed.

"I am Zanna. I am the—the unworthy
daughter of James Rutledge. It would be my
great honor, my lord, to accompany you to my
father's home."

Chapter Two

"DAUGHTER? I DIDN'T REALIZE JAMES RUT-ledge was a married man!" From behind the tall Englishman, Zanna heard a guffaw, and a swarthy fellow with thick beard and mocking eyes winked at her.

"No more is he, Mr. Curtis! But a man who spends nearly twenty years in these islands might be excused for taking a companion, eh? The girl's mother must have been better looking than most, at that!"

Zanna tried to pretend she hadn't heard, but a bitter swell of humiliation made her throw back her head instead of retaining the correct, humble position. The next moment, she was furious at herself. She had no right to take offense at what anyone said about her mother or herself! The only important thing was that she lead this English guest to the

Great House. But would he come? He was frowning, as if angered. Panic filled her.

"Please, my lord," she said urgently, and forced herself to smile into his scowl. "We have brought a horse for your convenience. We had thought you might not enjoy a palanquin ride. . . ."

She gestured to the narrow lacquered box nearby and breathed a sigh of relief as he smiled. "Madam, I doubt if I could get my legs into that contraption! A horse will be pleasant after so long at sea."

Her knees were trembling, but she bowed again and led him to where Kenjuro held the bridle of the horse they had brought. As they walked, the Englishman said, "I take it that your father's business keeps him away from Katayama a great deal?"

"He is a very busy person for the company, my lord." She gestured to the old man who was bowing deeply. "This is Kenjuro, Lord Alex Curtis. He is a very old servant of the director, and he welcomes you to Japan."

She stepped gracefully into the narrow palanquin, watched Kenjuro hold the horse still as Alex swung into the saddle. With infinite gratitude she felt the bearers of the palanquin take up the stout poles that held the lacquered box aloft, heard old Kenjuro's proud cry: "Make way for the palanquin and the noble English lord!"

It was done! So far, she had succeeded! Zanna realized that she had clenched her small hands into fists. Slowly, carefully, she relaxed them. She closed her eyes and leaned back against the swaying palanquin. *Merciful Buddha,* she thought, *thank you! Now, if only Rutledge-sama is at the Great House when we get there....*

"Lady Zanna?"

Her eyes flew open and, looking through the open door of the palanquin, she saw that he was riding beside her and watching her. She shook her head. "Oh, no, my lord. I'm Zanna, not Lady anything!"

His laugh was deep, pleasant. "And I'm just Alex, I'm afraid. My uncle Jasper is a lord, and my father is a knight. My older brother, Griffin, will inherit the title, not I."

"I don't understand. If your father is a knight...."

"Titles go to the oldest boy in the family," Alex explained. "As the second son, I must make my name and my fortune elsewhere. Truth to tell, poor Griff doesn't have much of a fortune, either, as he's learned to his sorrow."

She frowned, trying to follow the rapid flow of English. "Is he a poor man?" she asked.

"Not poor, no, but not rich enough to make a difference. He loved a neighbor squire's pretty daughter, but the wench married a richer man." He laughed again, but this time his laugh had a hard edge to it. "Money and land—this is what the woman wanted. Perhaps she's right. Money and power are everything in this world."

She wondered if she understood all he said,

14

and ventured to glance up at him. Until now she had been so afraid of doing or saying something wrong that she hadn't noticed much about him except his willingness to follow her to Rutledge-sama's home. Now, she was surprised at the breadth of his shoulders, his tallness, his erect carriage as he rode. She had always thought Rutledge to be the tallest man in the world, but this Englishman was even taller. She could see the ripple of muscle under his dark-red velvet doublet as he rode beside her, the taut power of thigh and long leg. And there was his coloring, too: the deep gold of his hair, the midday blue of his eyes. It was so different from what she was used to, and yet right for him. He was as vivid, as powerful as the sunset through which they rode.

She found herself saying, "Perhaps it was not her fault, my lord. The lady may have loved your brother, but women cannot always do as they wish. Not in Japan, at least," she added, hastily. "It may, of course, be different in your country."

He was silent for a moment, and she feared she had offended him. He, watching her, wondered again at the delicacy of her beauty. Everything about her—features, voice, movement—was graceful and yet controlled. He had seen a flash of angry spirit in those great gray eyes a while back when that damned fool of a sea captain had insulted her mother. Was there fire under the snow-cool grace of her?

"The lord of Katayama has a large fief," she was telling him. "Rutledge-sama lives in a small town not far away. We are on the road there now." She held up a small hand in warning. "We come to an unhappy place now. We will travel through it as quickly as we can."

She saw him narrow his eyes as he realized what she meant. Didn't England have places of execution? she wondered, as the bearers and old Kenjuro quickened their step to get through this dolorous spot. Though she knew that murderers and thieves had to be executed publicly, Zanna always hated the sight of corpses left hanging on wooden crosses outside the town limits. She was relieved when she could point to the town ahead.

"It's a small place," she said. "I am sure that it will seem even smaller after the cities you have seen in England."

He made absent comment. The place of execution had unsettled him, had made him remember what the captain had said about dangerous samurai, and had brought back his uncle Jasper's warnings. In fact, Jasper had warned him of this just before the *Anabella* had sailed.

"The Japanese are a proud race," Lord Jasper had said. "They attach a great deal of importance to their honor, or 'face,' as it is called. Don't ever insult a Japanese! Never cause a Japanese to lose his self-respect!" Then, he had added, "I'm sending you to Katayama, Alex, not just because you are my

16

nephew and ambitious for a fortune in the spice trade. Who isn't? No, it's because you've got a knack of dealing with people. You'll please your Japanese hosts. If you can get the ear of the authorities and plead our company's case, lessen the influence of those cursed Hollanders. . . ."

A low, tolling sound broke through his thoughts, and he looked up in surprise. Zanna smiled. "That is the temple bell of Kin-dō-ji, on the hill," she explained. "It marks the sunset. And now, here is our town."

The sun had nearly set, and bands of crimson and gold streamed across the narrow streets of the town. Modest homes, shingled and tiled in grays and dark brick reds, lined the streets. Each home was surrounded by a wall, and over the walls Alex glimpsed tall pines, the tops of green, waving bamboo. Some distance from these homes were shops with brightly painted curtains fluttering at the doorways. Children laughed over their games, dogs barked, a woman called. The tranquil air was full of the smells of wood smoke, dry fish, cooking.

"Is it different from an English town?" Zanna asked, as Alex looked about him.

He nodded. "It's cleaner, for one thing." He sounded surprised, pleased. "There's no garbage in the streets, no slops being emptied out. And look at that old fellow sweeping the street!"

Zanna's smile caused a deep dimple to form momentarily in one cheek. "He's not sweep-

17

ing the *street,* Lord Alex! He's sweeping the gateway to Rutledge-sama's Great House."

Alex widened his eyes. The Great House, with its tall, stout walls, its considerable grounds, was well named. "This is where the trader lives?" Alex whistled. Zanna felt a leap of pride. So far, the English guest was impressed! He seemed even more impressed when old Ji-ya dropped his broom and threw open the gates, shouting for the household to gather in welcome. By the time the palanquin had followed Alex's horse through the wide-flung gates, all the household servants and the office staff were on hand to bow their respectful greetings. At the head of all was Manager Kita, surrounded by the head clerks, clerks and apprentices. Kita shot Zanna a small look of approval. So far she had done well!

Her work was not over, by any means. Alighting from the palanquin, she translated Manager Kita's speech of welcome, then interpreted Alex's thanks and greetings. Under Kita's watchful eyes, she next led the Englishman into the Great House, kneeling to remove his leather boots so that he could step unshod onto the polished, woven tatami mats of the inner house. As they walked down long corridors of polished wood, she watched him anxiously. Did this house seem too plain? Would he find his suite of rooms adequate?

"This is the Bamboo Suite, Lord Alex," she explained, as she ceremoniously slid open the ornate wood-and-paper doors of the best suite in the Great House. The principal room was twelve mats in length, and a small anteroom led into the austere loveliness of a Japanese garden. For the convenience of the foreign guest, this room held a Western-style table and chair, a desk for writing comfort. However, the scroll in one corner, decorated with bold calligraphy, was pure Japanese.

"It's very grand." He smiled, to try to make her look less troubled. Why was she so concerned about his reaction? Did that hatchet-faced Kita have something to do with her uneasiness? "It's much finer than anything in my father's home."

Zanna bowed, relieved. "Rutledge-sama will be here to greet you at dinner, Lord Alex. Meanwhile, a bath has been prepared for you. A servant will guide you there when you have changed into these." She indicated some folded, comfortable-looking robes in a wicker basket by the door. "The maid will also fetch tea and cakes for your refreshment. Is there anything else you need?"

There was nothing. She went to her knees and bowed in the ritual manner, her forehead touching her fingertips. Then, sliding the paper screen doors behind her, she called to Mitsuko, one of the maids, and instructed her to care of the English guest's bath.

"So I'm to take care of him." The maid's tone, as well as her words, was mocking, and it rankled her. Zanna's head had begun to throb from the strain she had been under, and this servant's sarcasm was the last straw. She

19

lifted her chin, and something deep in her gray eyes flashed.

"Yes. Those are Kita-san's orders and those of Rutledge-sama. Do you have anything to say about them?" she demanded, her soft voice holding steel. For a moment, the servant woman stared, and then she bobbed her head and scuttled away, muttering. Zanna closed her eyes. *Now, why did I do that?* she wondered. *I have no right to give orders here. The Great House is not my home. And, oh, my head does hurt!*

Rubbing her temples, she walked down the polished wooden corridor to her own room. Compared with Alex Curtis's chambers, this was a tiny place, only five mats wide; but it was cheerful with the red-gold of the setting sun, and the paper-and-wood doors were open to a small, private garden. The outside air was cool and fresh, and Zanna gratefully stepped down onto the single stone step to breathe in the fragrances of pine and spruce and the clean, cool, healing scent of running water.

After a few moments, Zanna stepped off the stone and into the garden. She walked around the small pool of red fish and water lilies, and bent to draw in the perfume of white and scarlet roses James Rutledge had imported from England many years ago. Today, the bold, crimson roses reminded her of Alex Curtis, with his vivid coloring and dark-red surcoat. Gently, she touched the velvet petals and found herself smiling.

He had been kind, she thought. He had smiled at her and called her "my lady," as if she were a true daughter of the house. Suddenly, Zanna's eyes went wide. Suppose he hadn't believed what that crude man had said back at the pier? Suppose he really thought she was Rutledge-sama's honored daughter? "I must tell him," she said out loud. "I cannot deceive him!"

"Miss. . . ."

She turned quickly and saw Mitsuko. There was nothing sarcastic or condescending about the servant woman now. Her cheeks were red with distress, and she stood twisting her hands in her apron.

"Why aren't you helping the English lord bathe?" Zanna asked.

"I tried, but. . . ." She made a helpless gesture. "He shouted at me and told me to get out! At least, that's what I think he was saying. I was terrified, so I ran away!"

Zanna's eyes went wide with horror. It was an unspeakable breach of etiquette! Kita's words from the morning came back to her: "You'll please the English lord in all things. Even scrub his back in the bath. . . ."

"These foreign barbarians are all mad," Mitsuko was grumbling. She gave Zanna a sly look. "Why don't *you* go see what that one wants? It makes sense. You can understand their language!"

She was as good as implying that Zanna was no more than a servant in the Great House. Quickly, Zanna subdued the sudden twisting anger and nodded. "I'll go, yes," she said, with a quiet dignity that silenced the woman. Then, she left the garden and hurried down the corridor toward the heavy wooden door of the bathing room. There, she paused and gathered courage before calling a low greeting. "Forgive my intrusion," she said, and slid open the door.

There was a muffled curse from the great, half-sunken wooden tub in the center of the room. Steam rose from the hot water, and more displaced water splashed onto the latticed wooden slats that covered the wet stone floor. "What the hell is the meaning of this?" Alex demanded.

She felt like sinking through the floor. She could see the thunderous frown on the Englishman's face as he sat, chest-deep, in hot water. Broad, boldly muscled shoulders tensed as she took a tentative step forward.

"I humbly apologize for the maid," she said. What had the foolish woman done to enrage him? she wondered. "Can you tell me what is wrong, Lord Alex? Please help me to understand."

He was making an effort to keep his temper. "Is it customary for a man to have an audience while he takes a bath?" he demanded.

"To have an. . . . But someone is needed to pour cool water over the head and perform other services." She was shocked. No wonder the Englishman was upset! There he sat in that scalding-hot tub with no one to pour a dipperful of cool water over his head and cool him! Hurriedly pushing back her sleeves, she moved across the damp, steamy slats and plunged a wooden dipper into a bucket of cool water. Then, lifting it, she poured it carefully over Alex's head and shoulders. "Is that not better?"

For a moment he stared at her, and then he laughed, ruefully. "I fear we have different customs," he said, and the anger left his eyes.

"We have offended your customs?"

Noting her dismay, he shook his head. "Nothing worth mentioning." He had forgotten, and so quickly, too, Lord Jasper's directive not to insult his Japanese hosts or cause them to lose self-respect! But, Alex thought, it was damnably difficult to remain polite when sitting mother-naked in a wooden tub while a beautiful woman poured water on his head. The humor of the situation touched him, though, and he grinned. "If you'll forget it, Zanna, I will, too. Truthfully, in England men and women bathe themselves. No one's—er, assisted me since I was a babe."

Zanna had a momentary vision of Alex as a child. Then, the image disappeared and in its stead came reality: the tall, well-muscled body with broad shoulders and golden-crisp hair that curled across powerful chest and waist and down over the flat planes of belly, strong-muscled thighs. Her cheeks felt hot. What was the matter with her? She was used to seeing men and women naked in the bath. That was natural. What she was thinking about this man was not!

Aloud, she said, "Please, honored lord, explain more about your different customs. It's important that we understand in order to please you. Whatever you desire will be done at once."

"There's nothing I need; you've been very kind." What he *desired*, however, was something else again! He reflected again on her softness, her delicate control. What would she look like without that robe? Her bared arms were soft and rounded, and her body would be like that, too: sweetly rounded breasts with rosy flowers of nipples, a curve of waist and then rounded hips. He realized suddenly that he wanted Zanna desperately, and that his body's response to her was highly visible in the water. He thought frantically of some way to be rid of her, and said, "Perhaps afterward we could talk. If you don't mind, I'd like to finish my bath alone. After a long time cooped up in a ship, I find it a luxury to be by myself."

Her face cleared, and she bowed and moved quickly to the heavy wooden door. There, she stopped. "Honored lord, do you come from England near Sussex?" she asked. "That is where Rutledge-sama lived before he came to Katayama."

He shook his head. "No, we live to the north. But the countryside is much the same."

"I hear it is beautiful," Zanna said, wistfully. "My mother told me about it. She says that when it is spring, as it is here in Katayama, there are white and pink flowers all over, and

WINTER BLOSSOM

green hills covered with mist. It sounds just a little like Isudai, where I grew up."

He was surprised. "Didn't you grow up here? In Katayama?"

Zanna hesitated, then shook her head resolutely. Here was her chance to correct whatever misunderstandings Alex might have about her status in the Great House.

"No, honored lord. You see, I'm not a real daughter of this house. My mother, Oyuri, was the first companion Rutledge-sama had." When he remained silent, she added, "My father and mother parted when I was not yet five. We went back to her brother's house in Isudai. My mother always made me speak English to her, though, and she insisted that everyone call me Zanna, for 'Suzanna,' instead of by my Japanese name. She was sure that the director would someday call her back to Katayama, but when I was eleven, she died."

Alex felt the sadness in her voice. What she told him inspired him with no liking for the Katayama director. Still, Rutledge had behaved no differently from other men. Men took willing women to their beds and gave little thought to the resulting bastards. He himself had bedded many a wench with much pleasure and no qualms. He frowned as he asked, "But after your mother's death you returned here?"

"Oh, no." She was very matter of fact. "I was recalled only last week. Since I speak English, it was felt that I might be useful."

25

She lifted her head to look directly at him. "Kita-san and Rutledge-sama hope that—that you will not object to using me as a guide and interpreter, Lord Alex."

She was obviously afraid that he might refuse, and her mouth had a barely concealed tremble. Yet her gray eyes were honest and direct and asked no quarter. He was oddly touched by her courage. No doubt about it now, he thought. Rutledge and that manager of his had threatened her with damnation if she didn't make herself indispensable to the foreign guest.

"I will be delighted to have you as an interpreter," he said, and caught his breath at the dazzling beauty of her smile. "Only, please call me Alex, Zanna—or would you prefer I called you by your Japanese name?"

She shook her head. "I hardly know my Japanese name. It is Suzuran; I was named for a flower that blooms early—a winter blossom."

Winter Blossom—a snow flower, he thought, and something tender and strangely gentle warmed him when she smiled again. And yet, at the same time, he had to fight an impulse to reach out for her, to gather her tightly and fiercely into his arms.

As if catching his thought, she flushed suddenly. "Forgive me for interrupting your bath," she murmured. Then, without another look at him, she slid open the door and quickly stepped outside. There, hands clenched, she fought to gain control of her rapid breathing, the erratic beat of her heart. *What is the matter with me?* she wondered. *He said nothing. He did nothing. He only looked at me, and I may have imagined that look! He is an English lord and an honored guest and I—I cannot think of him in any other way!*

Chapter Three

"KITA TELLS ME YOU'VE DONE WELL, ZANNA."
James Rutledge's face was almost as flushed
as the ruby colored glass from which he
sipped precious brandy. "He says that you
handled the Englishman perfectly."

Zanna bowed, wishing that the unsmiling
manager was not watching her so closely.
There was an assessing gleam in his eyes that
was discomfiting. They were in Rutledge-
sama's own suite in the Great House, the
rooms decorated totally in the European fashion, with a carpet over the tatami mats, high
chairs and a table, and beyond all this a
four-poster bed. Kita stood behind the director
general's chair, a spare, black figure against
the bright hangings that covered the walls.

"I am grateful you returned so early,
Rutledge-sama," Zanna said. "The English
lord wants to meet you very much."

28

"And so he shall, when we dine." Rutledge took another draft of the brandy. "There's little time, now. Go and dress, Zanna. You will dine with us."

Zanna was sure she hadn't heard right. "You mean I will serve you," she said, hedging.

"In England, men and women sit down at table together. I want the Englishman to feel you're his social equal; it will serve our purposes better." Rutledge's barrel chest expanded against the folds of his rich green doublet, and he hooked his thumbs into the jeweled belt of his fine breeches as he added, "Put on your best kimono, Zanna. We'll dine within the hour, in the Chrysanthemum Room."

Of course, Lord Alex would have more use for a translator who was not a mere servant. But there was a difficulty. "Rutledge-sama," she stammered, "I'm ashamed to say that this kimono I am wearing is the best I have."

Kita's voice was dry, somewhat amused, as he made the reply, instead of the director general. "I've already attended to that, girl. You've bathed already? Then go to your rooms and change. When the servants announce dinner, go to Lord Alex's room and guide him to the Chrysanthemum Room."

Bowing, she left Rutledge's rooms and heard the sound of the two men's laughter. She was sure that they were laughing at her expense, but she did not mind. So far, she had not failed in her duty. If only she could continue to please the Englishman! At this thought he seemed to fill her mind, not as an honored guest but as a man; and she saw him, heard him, felt his presence. *It is only because I have never seen a man like him before,* she told herself, but could not reason away the leap of her pulse as she recalled the power of his lean, muscled body and the unexpected warmth of his smile.

"So there you are!" Startled from her thoughts, Zanna saw that the maid, Mitsuko, was standing in the corridor in front of her. She carried a folded kimono in her arms. "Kita-san says you're to put this on," she added impudently, thrusting the garment at Zanna.

The kimono was lovely and looked costly, with its pattern of dark blue and silver plum blossoms. The formal obi, or sash, that went with it was a heavy, silvered brocade. Had Kita-san bought this for her? Zanna wondered, astonished.

"I'm to help you to dress," Mitsuko was saying. "I have work to do serving the evening meal, so you must hurry." She pushed open the screen doors to Zanna's quarters, adding, "You want to make a good impression tonight, don't you?"

There was something sly in the woman's voice, but Zanna was too bemused by the expensive kimono to pay much attention. She ran her slender fingers lightly over the silk of the fabric, remembering. "Mother used to own kimonos like this," she murmured, half aloud. "But she didn't take any with her to Isudai."

Mitsuko said nothing, but began to undo the heavy, complex sash around Zanna's waist. Silently, Zanna submitted to being disrobed. First the sash, and then the kimono, and then the undercollar were removed. Mitsuko clicked her tongue. "Your skin is as white as sugar," she said, with grudging envy. "Most women need to spend an hour painting their faces with rice powder, but in your case that's not necessary." Her eyes moved assessingly over Zanna, taking in the swell of her high breasts under the white crepe chemise, her slender legs draped in the multicolored under-petticoat. "No wonder," she muttered.

"What are you saying?" Zanna was becoming impatient. "You said yourself that you were here to help me dress. Please help."

Muttering to herself, the maid adjusted a new undercollar that matched the elegant kimono. Then she held the garment up so that Zanna could slip her rounded white arms and shoulders into the long, flowing sleeves. When the six yards of stiff, brocaded sash had been arranged in its intricate folds about the girl's waist, Mitsuko sniffed. "You're taller than most Japanese, but the kimono fits well enough."

Zanna knelt before the long, narrow mirror in a corner of the small room and began to recomb her hair. She fastened it in a simple knot in back of her head. "You should have your hair done fashionably and use an ornament or two," Mitsuko commented. "Maybe you'll get one as a reward for being nice to the English lord."

Before Zanna could respond, there were footsteps in the corridor outside her room. "The evening meal is ready," old Kenjuro's voice called. "Mitsuko is needed to help!"

Zanna hurried to fetch Lord Alex and found him dressed and waiting. He was standing by the sliding doors that opened to the garden beyond. The air was full of the scent of peonies and the heavy fragrance of wisteria from a vine that grew against the narrow wooden veranda that ran the outer periphery of the Great House. When he turned to face her, she saw that the deep blue of his doublet matched the color of his eyes, and that the fine lace of his shirt brought his sea-bronzed skin to sharp relief. More than these, she saw pleasure in his eyes as they swept over her. In the new kimono, she was pleasing to look at!

She spoke quickly to cover her confused pleasure. "I've come to escort you to dinner, my lord. Rutledge-sama is back and will dine in the most formal room in the Great House, the Chrysanthemum Room."

She stopped because he was shaking his head at her. "I asked you to call me Alex, if you remember!"

"I cannot do that. You see, it would seem a great insult to you, and with Rutledge-sama and Kita-san there—please give me permission to call you Lord Alex."

"Whatever you name me will seem sweet." He had meant it as a compliment, one of those graces he'd picked up easily along the way. But she smiled as if he truly meant it, and the smile made him catch his breath. In her new kimono she looked dazzlingly beautiful, and Alex thought, confusedly, that his words had seemed to fill her face with light. He was grateful when she turned to guide him down the polished corridor.

"I must warn you that this will be a truly Japanese dinner, Lord Alex. Sake will be served. This is a hot rice wine that goes very quickly to the head on an empty stomach. You will also be expected to eat with *hashi*, long wooden sticks. It's not easy to use them."

She was surprised when he said, "I practiced using them during the voyage from England. I tried to prepare for your customs," he added somewhat ruefully, "but obviously I wasn't aware of all of them."

He was thinking of that scene in the bathing room. Zanna fought an urge to duck her head in embarrassment. "Here is the Chrysanthemum Room," she announced, going down on her knees to formally slide open the screen doors.

Apart from the low Japanese table, the room was uncluttered with furniture. Two men, Kita and a big, barrel-chested European, were seated at the table, one on either side of a cushion set deferentially before a magnificent scroll painting that hung in a flower-decorated alcove. The paper-and-wood screen doors of the room were open to a formal garden of carefully swept sand, bamboo and pine.

"Mr. Curtis!" The broad-chested man was coming across the room, hand outstretched. Alex looked down into gray eyes that were the shape and color of Zanna's own, but there was no other resemblance. The bold, sharp features had none of Zanna's delicacy. "I trust it wasn't a bad voyage?"

"Not with such a welcome at the end of it." Alex glanced at Zanna, who had now entered the room and was kneeling just behind a fourth cushion, placed on Rutledge's left. So she was to eat with them!

"For you, the seat of honor by the *tokonoma*," Rutledge was saying. He indicated the beautiful scroll in the alcove. "I'd planned to have you eat some good, English beef for our supper, but my manager, here, said that would not be appropriate. When in Japan, do as the Japanese do. Eh, Zanna?"

Zanna bowed a little nervously. It was hard to catch all the words of rapid English. She glanced quickly at Alex Curtis, and saw that he was watching her. Aware of her attention, he now smiled, and the smile took the edge from her tension. Careful to be most correct, she settled herself on the cushion beside Rutledge and waited for further instructions.

Kita now leaned over. "You look very appealing tonight, Zanna," he murmured. She bowed her thanks. "The dress suits you very well."

34

"It was your kindness that made the dress possible," she said, gratefully, and once more noted the odd, assessing look in those narrow black eyes.

Mitsuko now brought in the first course of the formal Japanese feast, and another maid carried in small porcelain flasks of the warmed sake and small, shallow sake cups. Rutledge indicated that Zanna was to pour the potent rice wine.

"To your health, Mr. Curtis! To the health of your uncle," Rutledge said heartily. "May your stay with us be pleasant and satisfying."

He drained his cup and held it out for more. So did Kita. Zanna filled the cups and looked at Alex, who gave her a small shake of the head. Evidently, he was taking her warning about the sake to heart, and instead of drinking began to praise the food before them: the two soups, one clear and one cloudy with soybean paste; the dishes of grilled fish; the array of crisp salads touched with vinegar, sugar and ginger; and, among the more elaborate dishes, a bamboo basket heaped with fish, vegetables and huge, sweet prawns cooked in light batter.

Rutledge apologized for the lack of meat on the menu. "The Japanese don't eat beef," he told Alex. "Buddhism teaches against it, for one, and then the people feel that only social outcasts would eat the flesh of domestic beasts like horses and cattle. However, I'll see to it that our breakfast is more civilized. We'll breakfast as Englishmen should, Mr. Curtis. Or Alex—if I may?"

Zanna saw a thoughtful look in the Englishman's eyes as he thanked his host. "And tomorrow perhaps you'll favor me by letting me visit your office. If it's as magnificent as your house, it will be worth the trip from England."

Was it her imagination, or did Rutledge-sama look discomfited? Zanna wondered. "Now, Alex, you mustn't expect any ostentation in our place of business. The Japanese are a strange people. They expect the director general to live far beyond his means. I wouldn't have the respect of the average merchant in this area if I didn't keep up appearances, and hence this Great House." He lowered his voice and shook his head. "Unfortunately, expenses are heavy! You would be shocked to learn how heavily we must pay for the right to trade in this country."

"To the Tokugawa shogun, you mean?"

"To him—and then there are the tithes to be paid to Lord Azuma and his samurai. Katayama is one of Azuma's fiefs."

"This is a man I want to meet," Alex said. He was leaning forward in sudden eagerness, and his arm brushed against a full flask of sake. Zanna reached out quickly and caught it before it fell, and as she did so, her fingers brushed against Alex Curtis's hand. At the touch, his eyes came to her with an intense awareness, and Rutledge smiled.

"Zanna," he said, "our guest will find us lacking in entertainment. In England, there are minstrels to sing and dance for special guests. Perhaps you will dance for us."

Zanna felt a flood of raw shame. "I'm sorry, Rutledge-sama. I—wasn't taught to dance." She saw the director's frown and hurriedly added, "If you wish, I could play the flute. My uncle taught me how."

"Bring the flute," Rutledge commanded one of the maids. He added, "We don't want Lord Alex to think we're barbarians, do we?"

"Far from it." Alex registered Zanna's embarrassment and felt deeply for her. He wished he could say something to ease this moment for her, and was angered at her father for being so heavy-handed. No doubt customs in Japan were different, but the girl had feelings! "I find Japan fascinating," he went on, and found that he couldn't take his eyes off Zanna's face.

"A mixture of beauty and brute force," Rutledge agreed. "You were speaking of meeting the daimio Azuma. He lives about four days' journey from here, in Iwase. That's his principal fief." He paused. "It will be difficult to arrange, but I will try to get an audience for you. Perhaps, as Lord Jasper's nephew, you can convince him to allow us freer trading privileges."

"The sort of privileges enjoyed by Hollanders now," Alex was beginning, when the maid returned with Zanna's flute. It was a slim, bamboo instrument, and Zanna took it hesitantly.

"Do you wish me to play now, Rutledge-sama?"

"Yes. We are well fed and comfortable, and music would please us." He motioned her to stand against the backdrop of the garden, which glimmered faintly in the moonlight. "Play anything you like, though I must warn our guest that Japanese music may not suit an English ear."

Zanna glanced at Alex, who nodded reassurance. "I have a friend who professes to play the bagpipes," he said. "He's a Scot, like our King James. After hearing the pipes, anything will seem musical."

Zanna lifted the bamboo flute to her lips and began to play. Self-conscious at first, she blew only soft notes into the hollow reed. But as the familiar music filled her lips and mind, she forgot her shyness in the gentle, sad beauty of the piece she played. She closed her eyes, remembering her uncle's home in Isudai and the great rolling shape of the hills with the white curtain of mist at dawn. She could hear the free songbirds and smell the wildflowers, and could touch the sun-warmed grass beneath her feet. For just a few moments, the music conjured all these things, and then was gone as Rutledge and Kita clapped.

"That was well done!" Rutledge praised her. "I didn't realize you were so skilled, Zanna."

Zanna blinked rapidly, pulling herself back from her memories to the present. She glanced at Alex, who was clapping, too. He did not compliment her as Rutledge did, but she could see the approval in his eyes.

"What was the name of that song?" Kita was asking.

She shook her head. "I'm not sure. It's just something that I learned in the mountains." Learned, or had taught herself, or had come from her heart. She looked down, embarrassed. "It was a very bad song, but it is the best I know."

Kita's black eyes had now swiveled to Alex Curtis. "Our guest must be tired," he said in Japanese, and then in badly accented English added, "You rest, for tomorrow. Tomorrow, is work."

"Unless you'd enjoy a walk through the garden first," Rutledge added. "The Great House is so built that it's surrounded by gardens. Zanna will show you how to reach your room if you wish to walk in the outdoors before you retire."

He rose to his feet as he spoke, and both Kita and Alex rose also. "That is a kindly thought," Alex said. "After this good food, it will be wise to walk a little. But Zanna may be tired, and I would not want to inconvenience her."

"No inconvenience at all! The girl will be glad to do what you ask of her," Rutledge said heartily. He shook hands as he added, "I'll have your shoes brought around so you can step right into the garden here. One thing about the Japanese, Alex, my boy: they believe in hospitality and the comfort of their guests."

By the time Alex's good-nights were completed, the shoes had been brought and Zanna was waiting, shod in simple sandals, to help him put them on. He declined her service with a jest. "You will spoil me, madam. First help with the bath, then with my shoes. I'll end up unable to do anything for myself."

She looked hesitant, then smiled at the joke. "I doubt if that ever could be, Lord Alex." Then, she frowned. "I am never sure when you are joking. It is difficult to follow your speech, and I don't know when to be serious or when to laugh."

They began to walk in the fine garden. The sand glimmered silver in the moonlight and made him think of the vast and mysterious reaches of the sea. He glanced down at Zanna. There was a touch of mystery about her, too, and more than a hint of sadness. Abruptly, he asked, "What were you thinking about when you played the flute tonight?"

"I thought of Isudai, where my uncle lives." Her voice was so low he had to bend closer to hear it, and he caught the elusive fragrance of her—a delicate, subtle blend of flowers and spice. "There are songbirds there that sing so beautifully. I have tried to capture their songs, but I am not clever enough."

"It was a beautiful song," he said. She stopped and looked up at him, and again he saw that dazzling smile with its deep dimple. "Beautiful," he repeated, and now he was not thinking of the song. Hardly thinking, he reached out and picked a peony that nodded its heavy head beside them, and put it in Zanna's hands.

She felt the touch of his hands on hers, and her breath caught in her throat. A soft night breeze sighed through the rustling bamboo, and its coolness contrasted with the warmth of his nearness. She drew the peony closer to her, pressing it against her cheek, wanting to be nearer to him, aching for something she could not understand. Then, she felt his hands reach up and cup her face, and knew how much she wanted to be in his arms.

"Zanna." His voice was husky, as dark as the night around them. She yearned toward the strength of his hands, the powerful grace of the body she had seen so intimately and remembered so clearly. But when his hands left her face to clasp her shoulders and draw her closer, she pulled back. This man was Rutledge-sama's guest, she thought, almost desperately. An *honored* guest, an English lord! She had told herself all these things and she had already forgotten. She stepped backward, and the silken rustle of her kimono shamed her even more. Rutledge-sama had

honored her by trusting her to be translator for
Lord Alex. He had clothed her in this lovely
garment, let her eat beside him in the Chrysanthemum Room. She couldn't forget or ne-
glect this trust.

"You must be tired, my lord," she said, her
voice breathless in spite of her effort at self-
control. "You need to rest. The night is turning cool and—and perhaps it isn't good for
you."

Nor good for me, either, she thought, as she
looked up at him pleadingly. He frowned, and
then nodded somewhat abruptly as he turned
away from her. In a carefully controlled voice
he said, "You may be right, Zanna. There are
those in England who believe the darkness is
full of evil spirits and humors. I can see my
rooms now, so I'll bid you good night,
madam."

He raised her hand and, before she could
protest, kissed it. For a second, she felt his
breath, his warm lips. Then he lowered her
hand and bowed. "Good night, Zanna."

For a moment, the promise of fire had flick-
ered beneath the silky surface of Zanna's
mien. As she turned to go he subdued with
difficulty an almost uncontrollable urge to
gather her into his arms. That would be
a fine beginning, wouldn't it? Lord Jasper
would surely relish learning that his nephew had seduced James Rutledge's daughter!

Alex saw Zanna pause, turn back and look

over her shoulder for a fleeting instant before disappearing into the shadows of the garden. He swore under his breath. Perhaps there *were* spirits in this Japanese night. It was as if he were bewitched by the strangely lovely woman with the gray eyes.

Chapter Four

LONG BEFORE SHE SAW ALEX CURTIS THE NEXT
morning, Zanna heard his voice. She'd been
hurrying along the corridor, carrying an English teapot full of the hot Japanese tea the
director general liked with his breakfast; but
Alex's voice made her stop on the threshold of
Rutledge's rooms.

"I slept very comfortably," he was saying.
"This Japanese custom of piling soft bed
quilts on the floor is admirable. I'm surprised
you've kept your four-poster bed all these
years."

He had slept well! She herself had lain
awake for a long time, the giddy memory of
his touch spreading like slowly widening rip-
ples within her restless body. She had remembered, over and again, the yearning she had
felt to be held in Alex's strong arms. The

longing had become so strong that she had been frightened. Finally she had subdued her unruly emotions, or thought she had. Now, just the sound of his voice caused her hands to tremble.

Forcing them to stillness, she went into the room and bowed in answer to Rutledge's easy greeting. "Good morning, Zanna. You've taken good care of our guest, I see. He looks well."

She could not help looking at Alex. A thick bar of early sunlight had turned his hair to gilt and limned the hard planes of his face with gold. He returned her gaze unsmilingly, and she could not read the look in his eyes.

"I'm glad you slept well, my lord," she murmured.

"Thank you." To her relief he sounded completely matter of fact, as if last night had never been. "I slept so well I'm ready for the London Company's business this morning."

Rutledge nodded his approval. He was busily engaged with the breakfast heaped before him, a breakfast consisting of a brace of fowl, eggs boiled in the shell, loaves of the white bread that only the cook of the Great House knew how to bake. "It will be a busy day, Alex. And, though I myself will act as your interpreter, Zanna will keep us company. Since she will have to translate for you when I am not able to accompany you, she must get used to her work."

Zanna had expected that she might be

45

asked to accompany them, but she was unprepared for the leap her heart gave against her ribs. Perhaps Alex saw it, for he glanced at her before reaching for a portion of bread.

"You are not breakfasting, Zanna?" he asked.

"The girl eats in the Japanese way. Soybean soup and rice at this hour, ugh!" Rutledge gave a little shudder, adding, "There are things I miss terribly in this country, and breakfast is one of them. I also miss an English countryside in May, and the way a good English tavern smells and sounds. Ale and an armful of woman." He licked sensuous lips. "Not a dark, small, slant-eyed wench but a full-hipped, fair-haired English rose. By God, this I miss!"

Alex found himself frowning. This wasn't the kind of talk a man should indulge in before his daughter. Worse, it awakened the passion he had subdued with such difficulty last night.

"You mentioned that my meeting with Lord Azuma might help us trade more freely," he said. "Have there been new restrictions imposed on the London Company?"

Rutledge made a wry face. "The Portuguese devils have been here the longest, and they have powerful allies among the Japanese nobility. The Dutchmen have money and muscle behind them. Our 'restrictions' are that we don't have enough important connections!" He leaned forward. "However, this may change. There are certain avenues I'm exploring, and perhaps we may find a weapon to use against our principal rivals, these poxy Dutch!"

Alex was surprised at the tension in Rutledge's powerful, burly body and at the coldness of his gray eyes. "What is this mysterious weapon of yours?" he asked, curiously.

"I can't tell you yet. Time enough to talk about plans after you've inspected our Katayama office." He began to wash his fingers in a fine lacquered bowl on the table, and turned to Zanna. "We will be leaving in a short while. Since you are to come with us, you had better ready yourself for the day."

The office was not far from the Great House, and a disappointment after the impressiveness of the director general's estate. Still, it was large enough, and was surrounded by a forbidding outer wall of stone. Just inside massive wooden gates waited the London Company's employees, headed by Manager Kita. Though all of them were in obvious awe of the English lord, Zanna saw their curiosity as they peered at her, the director general's bastard daughter.

Zanna knew there was no point in taking offense. As Rutledge had said, she would need to accompany Lord Alex, and she must get used to the looks and startled comments. However, impudence was another matter. When one of the underclerks, a youth with a thin face and bold eyes, made a lascivious gesture toward her, she turned and faced him squarely.

"You!" Her voice, normally soft, had an undertone of steel. "What is your name?" she continued.

The underclerk swaggered a bit, hitching the sash of his kimono higher over his hips and glancing at his fellow employees. "I'm Shosuke," he said, and there was a sneer in his voice. "We know who *you* are."

Now, there was a soft snigger from the other underclerks. The older clerks looked shocked, and one of them glanced at the doorway to the inner offices, where Rutledge, Manager Kita and the Englishman had disappeared.

"Yes, I'm sure you do." Zanna raised her eyes and gave the impudent fellow a long, level look. "I also happen to be in Rutledge-sama's employ. I am the English lord's translator and his voice is my voice." The soft voice hardened as she added, "You will please remember that while I am here in this capacity you will do exactly as I say."

Shosuke tried to brazen it out, but her eyes held his steadily. To him the strange, silver eyes were unnatural, perhaps possessing the evil eye. He muttered a charm under his breath and hastily turned away. Her soft tones called him back. "Did you hear what I said?" Zanna asked.

"Yes. Yes . . . honored miss." Hurriedly, Shosuke and his fellow underclerks went back to work, and after a moment Zanna turned toward the inner office. Outwardly calm, she felt her heart beating wildly. *I should be used to this*, she thought, bitterly. After all those confrontations with the people in Isudai—but she was not used to it. Perhaps she would never get used to this feeling of being alien and alone.

"Zanna!" Rutledge's call made her hurry through the inner-office door. Inside the office, Kita had set another chair at the director general's great, lacquered desk.

Rutledge was saying, "Anything here is yours to examine, Alex. Ledgers, here. They're in English, so you'll be able to follow them. Here are letters and records of transaction. Some are in Japanese, but Zanna will be able to translate the rest. The girl can read and write her own language, and she can even write a little English."

"By your leave, I'll take some of the ledgers and records back to your home this evening." Alex's eyes swept the office with purpose. "Right now I'd like to see your warehousing facilities, James. That, and I'd like to meet your employees."

He spoke with great courtesy, the guest deferring to the host; but Zanna knew that there was an undertone of command there and that Rutledge also sensed it.

"Whatever you wish will be done," he said, and gave Kita orders to lead the way to the warehouses in back of the office building. "I warn you, Alex, that they may be in some uproar. Some of the goods going back to England on board the *Anabella* are being loaded, and the goods to be traded are being brought onto shore."

"That would be the best time to observe," Alex said, politely. To Zanna's mind, there was a quiet intensity about the English lord now. She thought he had forgotten all about her; but as she followed him out of the inner office, he turned to let her pass before him, and in the narrow doorway her shoulder brushed against him. It was only a fleeting touch, but somehow it conveyed all the leashed electricity of last night. He bent low so that only she could hear him as he said, "I heard you speaking in the outer office, Zanna. Did anyone trouble you in any way?"

"No," she said, and made the mistake of looking up at him. The deep blue of his eyes held her, drew the truth from her. "It wasn't anything," she amended. "I'm used to dealing with underclerks."

Before he could ask another question, Kita was pushing open the heavy wooden doors that separated the office from the warehouses. There were two large storage areas, both fronting the street for easy access to the pier. In one was piled incoming goods: English machinery, clocks. In the other warehouse were Japanese lacquer, silver, copper.

"This represents months of hard trading," Rutledge was saying. "When you meet the merchants I deal with, you'll see just how hard."

Alex nodded, but he was wondering how the London Company in Katayama could operate on such a slim volume of trade. True, much of the company's trade goods could be on board the *Anabella* by now. He asked for a cargo manifest and frowned down at it. "Is this all that is sent back to England?" he asked Rutledge.

The burly man spat. "God curse the Hollanders, yes," he said. "Until we deal with them, they'll steal goods and prospects from right under our noses." After a moment, he remarked, "I have added a new line of goods to those I have already sent back to England."

He gestured to Kita, who brought forward something wrapped in purple silk. He held it out to Alex with a formal obeisance, and Rutledge continued, "You're of knightly family, Alex. Give me your opinion on this."

Alex unwrapped the silk, and Zanna saw the thoughtful expression on his face give place to surprise and pleasure. What he held was a magnificent Japanese sword.

"How does it feel?" Rutledge was smiling, and well pleased as Alex drew the blade from its ornate scabbard and tested it, swishing the arrogant steel through the air. "It's finer than any European sword, isn't it?"

"Indeed. And you're adding these to your list of goods traded with the Japanese?" Alex returned the steel to its scabbard and hefted it in his hands. He seemed reluctant to give it back.

"So I am. Lord Jasper would be pleased, I

51

think." A smile touched the director general's thick lips. "I want you to accept this sword as a gift." As Alex began to protest, he raised a large hand. "It is customary in Japan for a host to offer gifts to his guests. Besides, it's just as well for a man to be armed in these dangerous times."

"Then I accept with thanks. But I thought that the shogun brought peace to the country."

"Things are *better,* but you'll always have brigands and cutthroats. Besides, there are the *ronin,* masterless samurai who can be the very plague." He nodded at Zanna. "Perhaps while you're in Japan you may go to Isudai and meet the swordsmith who crafted your blade. He's Zanna's uncle. His sister, Oyuri, was my first woman here—companion, they call it. I paid her a handsome stipend when I sent her back to Isudai, and I've remained on good terms with her brother."

Under the flowing sleeves of her kimono Zanna clenched her hands so tightly that her nails pierced the skin. The unthinking words and indifferent tone in which they had been uttered hurt deeply, in spite of anything she might try to say to justify them. *Rutledge-sama,* she thought, *if you'd heard mother calling for you in her last illness, you wouldn't talk about her as if she were some prostitute bought for a few coins!*

She hadn't realized that Alex was beside her, and that he had placed a hand under her

52

elbow. There was no passion in his touch, now—just a warm, sure grip that somehow pierced her misery and eased the sting of the hurt. "I think it's time I met the employees of the London Company," he was saying. "I want to talk to them all, and perhaps Zanna could interpret for me." The grip on her elbow tightened. "After all, if she's to translate for me, she has to get used to her work."

The interviews with the employees took up the rest of the day. Rutledge had eagerly agreed to let Zanna act as interpreter, and she stood at Alex Curtis's elbow and faithfully translated everything that was said. She was grateful for something to do, something on which to concentrate her entire mind. She did not want to think of the words Rutledge had used in talking about her mother, or to realize that it was foolish of her to be shocked or hurt. She had known, all along, that her mother had been the director general's *companion*, not the woman he loved. But still, she had hoped. Perhaps because her mother had loved Rutledge-sama so much, she had even dreamed that deep in his heart there had been some love, some respect, something!

She succeeded in keeping away all thoughts of her mother until the work of the day was over. Then, wearily, she accompanied the others back to the Great House. There she received, with infinite gratitude, word that Rutledge did not want her presence at the evening meal. He and the English guest would dine alone and discuss the business of the London Company.

Zanna decided to take a nap. But though she was drained, her mind jumped like a netted fish and would not let her rest. "I paid her a handsome stipend when I sent her back to Isudai," Rutledge-sama had said, as if that wiped out five years of loving and living together. Zanna knew that Oyuri had lived for the director general each day of those five and a half years. Being away from him had killed her.

Unable to lie still any longer, Zanna went to the sliding doors of her room and stood looking into the garden. It had turned dark, and a half-moon was riding in and out of ragged clouds. The night air was touched with wood smoke and she could hear the liquid trill of a night bird. The beauty of that wild call made homesickness twist and turn within her like the point of a knife.

"Zanna?"

She caught her breath at the sound of his voice so near and could not answer for the leap of her pulse. He called to her again, and she said, "Yes, I'm here, my lord."

"I wasn't sure." She could hear him approaching across the fine sand. "I've been writing a report to my uncle all evening," he told her, "but it became cursed hard work. I came into the garden and heard a bird singing. It reminded me of your flute." He paused.

"Then, I saw you. Why aren't you resting after your long day's work?"

"You yourself must be tired," she said, politely. Her pulse was still unsteady as she added, "You must rest well, my lord. You will need your strength in the next few days. You are to meet the merchants Umezono and Yamaguchi."

There was a bamboo bench beneath the shade of a wide-branched pine. Alex sat down on it thoughtfully, looking up into Zanna's shadowed face. "Do you know either of these men, Zanna?"

She started to shake her head, then hesitated. "I haven't met them, but I know something *about* them from listening to the clerks at the office today. They were talking when Rutledge-sama announced you were to visit them both. From what they said, Umezono-san is short and fat like the god of wealth. He is supposed to be very jolly and laughs a great deal, but that is all pretense. Inside his head he is cold and hard and watchful, and will take profit whenever and however he can."

"And Yamaguchi?" The moon was sliding from behind the clouds and he watched her face intently. The great gray eyes were serious, shadowed by more than the darkness.

"Yamaguchi-san looks, they said, like a dried-out grasshopper. He has the appearance of a bitter and cruel man, but apparently he's just the opposite. Though a shrewd man of business, Yamaguchi-san is said to be honorable." Her hesitation grew more pronounced. "I—remember Yamaguchi-san's wife from long ago, before my mother and I moved back to Isudai. She was one of the few ladies who spoke politely to my mother even after Rutledge-sama found a new companion."

He made no comment but sat thoughtfully on his bench, his head tilted back to look at her. Finally, he said, "So these are the men I'm to deal with tomorrow. I'm glad you told me about them, even though your father will be with me." Her small start of protest must have been obvious, for he added, "He *is* your father, after all."

She was shocked. "Even when I was a child I wasn't allowed to think of him in that way. He has always been Rutledge-sama, director general of Katayama. I owe him my *giri,* or greatest duty and loyalty, for—for supporting my mother and me all these years."

He looked ready to speak again, then seemed to change his mind. "Will I be meeting any more merchants tomorrow?"

She was grateful that he was not pursuing the painful subject of her relationship with Rutledge. "Not tomorrow, my lord, but I'm sure there will be many other merchants with whom you must deal. Umezono-san and Yamaguchi-san, however, are the most important."

"Are they from samurai family?" he asked, and she smiled for the first time that evening.

"You are joking, Lord Alex! Merchants are

not samurai. In fact, they are thought of to be below the farmers who grow rice for the people. Though Lord Buddha teaches that each man can find salvation from his occupation, merchants are often greedy and cunning and grasping."

"I did not know this. It is not like that in England." Alex frowned as he remembered his half-written report to Lord Jasper. He knew he should return to it, but Zanna's presence in the half-moonlight kept him where she was. "Tell me more about this country, Zanna. Tell me about Isudai."

She was surprised. Why did he want to know about Isudai? But then, of course, he had been given a fine sword made by her uncle and was probably interested in sending such swords to England. "It is a mountainous area," she explained. "Isudai itself is a village at the foot of a mountain." In spite of herself, her words came more quickly as she spoke of the familiar place. "The people mostly grow rice, except for my uncle, Yasutomo. He is a swordsmith, and so was his father before him. He would have taught his son, but my aunt and her baby boy died in childbirth. I always put flowers on their graves when I climbed the mountain."

"And did you climb the mountain often?"

She nodded, suddenly as eager as if the beloved mountain were before her. "Oh, yes. I think I was the best climber of all of them—boys *and* men, as well as women! My uncle

57

said that I was half goat." She laughed suddenly—a small, clear laugh that rippled in the darkness like a falling star. "I was a terrible girl, my lord. I could climb trees as well as the boys, and I was very good at fishing and fencing with a bamboo pole."

"You're fond of your uncle." He was sorry he had said this, for the light that had turned her gray eyes silver died.

"He was kind to my mother and me." Her tone told him that there hadn't been many who were kind. "He accepted us back into his household when we were sent away from Katayama."

In his heart, Alex damned Rutledge. "It could not have been easy," he said, and felt the inadequacy of the words. She smiled without amusement.

"No," she said, and then, after a pause, "but my mother never lost hope that we would be recalled. Each time Kenjuro came with money and news from Katayama, she'd be so eager and she would hope. At least the money Kenjuro brought helped her die comfortably."

The garden was very still except for the wind rustling through the bamboo. Zanna could hear the sound of Alex's breathing and her own. It felt as if the world had slowed for a moment. *Why am I telling him this?* she asked herself. These memories she had not shared with anyone, not even Uncle Yasutomo. Yet she could not stop herself from going on. "My mother loved Rutledge-sama very much, and being away from him killed

58

her. That is when I started to climb the mountain. I could not sit by her and see her pain."

"Didn't you have any friends?" Alex broke in. She shook her head in a matter-of-fact way.

"At first the people in Isudai called me Foreign Devil, because of my eyes." She hesitated. "Later, they called both mother and me other names."

"I'm sorry." He realized how insufficient the words sounded, but he meant it desperately, the more so when he saw the determined way in which she squared her slender shoulders.

"You needn't be, my lord. As I said, I was good at fencing with a bamboo pole! After I became as tall as I am, no one was ready to call me names to my face." But behind her back had been another matter. And even when the people in Isudai had accepted her, there were always strangers from other villages, other mocking voices and cruel words. She had learned to live within herself, relying on no one, not even kind Uncle Yasutomo. She had taught herself to amuse her mother, to play the flute, to walk deep into the heart of the Isudai mountain. All of what she had said had been locked deep within her heart—until tonight.

"I was often alone as a boy, myself," he was saying, as if he understood some of her thoughts. "There were places on my family estate which were secret to everyone else, and there I would go to read or listen to songbirds.

I would try to snare the birds in cunning traps, but I never managed to catch one."

"I did once . . . ," she began, then stopped.

"Tell me about it." He reached out and took her hand, drawing her down on the bamboo seat beside him. She realized how cold her hands were because of the warmth of his. "You're frozen," he said, frowning, and took the other hand as well, holding them pressed between his large, strong ones.

"Just before my mother died, I managed to trap a songbird." The words did not come easily, but the warm pressure of his hands seemed to be drawing them hesitantly forward. "I made a bamboo cage for it and took it to her room. She loved the songs it sang, but by evening the bird's songs were not as strong. She said. . . ."

Zanna stopped. It was as if something tight and hard were pressing against her heart. She looked into Alex's eyes and made herself go on. "She told me to let the bird go, then. She said she couldn't see a free thing caged as she herself had been caged."

For a moment he said nothing, and then his hands tightened about hers and he drew them to him so that they rested against his hard chest. She could feel the beat of his heart against her palm. "Poor blossom of winter. Fortune has played an unfair game with you," he said. She shook her head, ducking it to hide the tremble in her lips, and heard him whisper some unintelligible comfort. The next moment, he had drawn her against him. For a moment she rested against his warm, hard body. Then she pulled away.

"My lord, please. . . ."

She had no time to speak again or even think before his mouth had descended on hers. What was he *doing*? she thought in sudden, disoriented panic; and yet at the same time her bewilderment at this totally alien gesture was mixed with an uncontrollable surge of desire. The firm, warm lips on hers were moving surely, controlling her mouth, controlling her breath, compelling her obedience. Under their sweet pressure her own opened, and she felt the strange excitement of his tongue probing the warm secrets of her mouth. She wanted to press herself harder against him, and unwittingly her body moved, nestling closer to the powerful strength of him. Under the robes she wore, her body seemed to be on fire, her loins heavy with a liquid heat that pulsed with the beat of her blood. Her breasts against the soft fabric of her clothing seemed swollen, the nipples taut, aching, yearning. When he moved his hands down over the front of her kimono, she felt the throb of their response.

"Sweeting," he murmured, his lips leaving hers for a moment so that she could breathe again. She did not want the kiss to end, but his lips were tracing the line of her temples, kissing the hollows there, the line of her chin, moving to her slender throat. His hands slid down her arms, under the wide sleeves and against her bare skin. Surely, unhurriedly, his hands circled the rounded sweetness of her breasts, circled, caressing the sensitive mounds but not yet touching the aching nipples. Murmuring wordlessly, she cried out against this sweet torture, pressing herself against his sensitive hands. Now, feather-light, his fingers touched the swollen peaks of her breasts, and his mouth came down on hers, stifling her gasp of ecstasy.

Her mind was whirling, caught in the giddy whirlpool of the heat that was spreading, filling her, making her moan under his mouth as he caressed her. She could not think, but images darted through her mind. She breathed in the clean, male scent of him, the hardness of his finely muscled body. She remembered that body in all its perfection as she had seen it yesterday in the bath. She had been aware of him as a man, wanted him even then. Yes, wanted him shamelessly, as she wanted him now.

Her hair had come loose and was streaming down her shoulders and back in an abandoned flow of dark silk. He was pushing aside the edges of her kimono, kissing her throat, the cleft between her breasts. In a few moments her aching breasts would be coverless, defenseless against his mouth.

And then, what? Into the whirling vortex of Zanna's mind came a question, so insistent that it broke through her desire. *And then what, Zanna? Will he make you his companion during his stay here in Japan?*

She tried to will the question away, but it returned. Louder. Clearer. Together with it came the memory of how Rutledge-sama had looked this morning when he spoke of Oyuri. Oyuri, who had been trapped and caged by love.

"Alex-sama, please, we must not!" In her confusion she had spoken in Japanese, but the pleading in her voice was clear. So was the withdrawal of her, the tightening of the lithe, slender body in Alex's arms. He tried to draw her closer, but with surprising strength, she pushed him away. He could not continue to hold her without hurting her, and though all his senses were aroused, he let her go.

For a second she sat beside him, her exposed bosom heaving, her eyes wide and passionate and afraid in the moonlight. Then, she gave a little sound that was half gasp, half sob, and ran.

"Zanna!"

His voice pursued her, but she did not stop. She prayed that he wouldn't follow her. She had been afraid that he would not let her go, and though he had, he might follow. She could feel the pounding of her heart and knew that deep within her, deep where the molten core of her still cried for the nearness and hardness and strength of him, she wanted him to follow her. The aroused, taut nipples chafed against the soft cloth of her garments as she ran, pulling the folds of her kimono together.

Instinctively, she made for the shortest way to her room, but before she could reach the outer veranda, a man's yell stopped her. It was a yell of fear. "Oh, Lord Buddha and all the saints of paradise, help me! It's she!"

The voice was familiar and stopped her even in her headlong flight. "Kenjuro?" Zanna gasped. There was no sound, only a monotonous mumble of the Buddhist prayer repeated over and over: "Nam-ai-dā. Nam-ai-dā!"

"Kenjuro?" Zanna asked again. "It is you, isn't it?"

This time, there was an intake of breath and Kenjuro groaned. Zanna could make out the old fellow half-sprawled on the wood of the outer veranda. "What's the matter?" she demanded. "You look as if you've seen a ghost!"

"Please don't joke! I really did think I saw one. I thought you were she. . . ."

She began to laugh, then stopped. No wonder Kenjuro had been frightened! Her hair was loose and blowing in the night air, and her clothing disarrayed. What must he think of her! She said, "I'm sorry. I didn't mean to scare you. I was taking a walk in the garden and a night animal scared me, so I ran away."

It was the best excuse she could give, but he didn't seem disposed to question her. "My eyes are not good these days," he sighed. "Am I to blame? You looked like *her,* and wearing her kimono, too. . . ." He stopped, suddenly, and clapped both hands over his mouth.

Zanna looked at him with curiosity. "What

64

are you talking about? *Who* wore this kimono before I did?"

Kenjuro sighed and ducked his head. "I didn't mean to tell you. I not only have bad eyes but have a big mouth, as well! Oyuri-san, your mother, wore that kimono. The director general gave it to her when she came to this Great House. It was her favorite kimono."

So that had been the reason for Mitsuko's snide remarks the day Zanna wore the kimono for the first time! She had felt so pleased with the lovely robe, while the household laughed at her expense.

Kenjuro said, in a subdued voice, "I'm sorry, honored miss. I—I might as well tell you the rest since you know as much. Other companions of Rutledge-sama have worn the kimono, also. I have often thought that poor Oyuri-san would be angry about that, and tonight I thought she'd come to haunt us at last."

She did not know whether it was anger or pain that was so hard a lump in her chest. Now she knew it all. Half of her wanted to take the handsome kimono off and throw it away, never to wear it again. The other half wanted to go and cry her misery out at Rutledge.

And yet, she thought, *just now in the garden I acted like a companion myself! I behaved shamefully. If Rutledge-sama had seen me, I would have died of shame. How different am I, really, from the women who have worn this kimono before me?*

Kenjuro was peering at her worriedly, and she managed a smile. "Thank you for telling me, old friend," she said gently. "Knowing will make it easier for me."

And the dress will always remind me, she thought to herself, *of what will happen to me if I allow the English lord to have his way!*

Chapter Five

"HONORED MISS, PLEASE FORGIVE THE INTRU-
sion!"

Zanna put down her needle and looked up
with a smile as the door to her room was slid
open by Kenjuro. Her speech of welcome was
swallowed up in surprise as she took in the old
man's agitated appearance.

"The director general has sent for you,
Zanna-san," he told her. "At once!"

She felt a spasm of alarm. What could have
happened? Kenjuro was explaining, "Nothing
bad has happened, honored miss, but it's im-
perative you go down to the London Company
office. Rutledge-sama has been called away to
take care of a problem concerning a late shipment of lacquerware, and the lord Englishman is to visit with the merchant
Umezono in Hamabashi this noon. I've been

67

sent to fetch you so that you can be his interpreter."

Kenjuro finished his speech on a deep gasp and plopped down in the wooden corridor just outside Zanna's room. "I'm getting old," he complained. "When I was young, I could run back and forth from the Great House to the office without getting tired. *And* I used to carry you on my back as I ran, too!"

A sudden memory of herself clinging to Kenjuro's neck as he galloped down the streets made Zanna smile. "Kenjuro-san, please have some tea and rest. I can walk down to the office by myself," she said.

He protested at once. What was she thinking of? Wasn't she a young, unmarried lady? "You must not go unaccompanied like a common housemaid," he scolded, and she felt a sharp spurt of tears for his concern. Since that night when he had told her about Oyuri's kimono, he had watched her worriedly, she knew. When the other servants commented on the fact that she no longer wore the lovely blue and silver kimono, he had silenced them.

"Very well, then. I will arrange my hair and come at once." She saw him looking at her simple navy and white kimono, the one she had brought from Isudai, and smiled. "Rutledge-sama did want me right away, didn't he? I will not have time to change."

Kenjuro said nothing until they were on their way to the office. Then he said, "It's a shame, Zanna-san. I have thought and thought about it, and it is still a shame. Oyuri-san was a beautiful, kind woman. The director general had no right to treat her badly." She said nothing. "He had no right to recall you to Katayama to serve this Englishman!"

She touched his shoulder in mute thanks but did not comment aloud. She wanted nothing better than an excuse to run back to Isudai and the safety of her uncle's house. With all her being she dreaded being close to Alex again, and she felt panic when she recalled the guilty rapture she had found in his arms.

She had managed to avoid being alone with him the last few days. Although she often had been ordered to accompany Rutledge and his guest, she had stayed well out of Lord Alex's way. When she was summoned each night to play the flute, she always made sure that somebody else besides Alex was present. Last night, her heart had almost stopped beating when Kita had suggested she accompany the Englishman on a walk through the garden. She had been grateful nearly to tears when Alex himself said that he was tired and then suggested that Rutledge alone accompany him on the next day's outing, a visit to a prominent local merchant.

Zanna knew the day's itinerary, and it worried her terribly now. With Rutledge gone, she would accompany Lord Alex to the next town and Umezono's place of business. There would be talk and sake, and there would be the journey to and from Hamabashi. She and Lord Alex would be alone, and there would be opportunity for him to have his will of her. Zanna shivered, suddenly and uncontrollably.

As if he had read her thoughts, old Kenjuro spoke bravely. "I will come with you, Zanna-san! After all, someone must show you the way to Umezono-san's house."

Zanna's flood of relief ended as she looked at the determined old man and felt new despair. How could this thin, timorous old body stand in the way of Alex Curtis? Again, she recalled Lord Alex's arms and the strength of them, but she said only, "Thank you, Kenjuro. You are a true friend."

He sniffed. "You could use a few, that's a fact. Look, honored miss! There's the director general on his horse! Do you think the Englishman will ride or walk?"

Zanna did not answer, for she had just seen Alex standing beside the mounted Rutledge. There was a treacherous leap of her pulse as she caught sight of the tall, powerfully built body. She bowed formally, and his own bow was equally cool.

"Well, madam. It seems you have me on your hands again."

"It is an honor," she managed to say, coolly enough.

"Naturally, taking care of Lord Jasper's nephew is an honor!" Rutledge frowned as he took in her less than glamorous kimono. He did not comment on it, however. "I must ride at once to Fukuoka. Take care you serve Lord Alex well, girl."

She bowed again and watched the two Englishmen shake hands. Once, she thought, Rutledge must have looked as Lord Alex did now. She felt a sudden ache for her mother, and an unreasoning anger. She turned away and came face to face with Manager Kita.

Kita proved the antidote to all her rebellious thoughts. He was sharply practical and full of instructions. She was to make sure that Lord Alex didn't drink too much sake and agree to foolish terms set by the merchant. She was to take care to leave Hamabashi in time to get back to Katayama by sunset. "Remember that there are bandits on the roads, especially after dark," Kita continued, his eyes as darkly assessing as always. "Now, you must go! The Englishman's horse and the palanquin for you are waiting."

They began their journey in silence, Alex not adjusting the speed of his horse to the palanquin bearers' pace but going on ahead and leaving Kenjuro to trot at Zanna's side. She was glad of this. Perhaps, she thought hopefully, her resistance in the moonlit garden had disgusted him, and he was willing to leave her alone. However, as they approached Hamabashi she became concerned. No matter how she felt about Lord Alex, she must carry out her task as interpreter. She was wondering how to try to bridge the silence between them when she heard the sound of an approaching horse's hooves. Alex pulled his mount in to pace beside her palanquin.

"Since we seem to be approaching the town, it's time we discussed business matters," he said. His tone was even, and she took heart as she nodded. "I take it that hatchet-faced manager instructed you to make sure I made no wine-besotted deals that would beggar the London Company."

"How did—?" She raised startled eyes to his and saw his wry smile. "Yes he did, Lord Alex. I hope you aren't offended."

"Guzzling wine is not one of my prominent vices. Besides, I remember you once gave me advice to be sparing with sake." He seemed to be mocking her a little as he added, "I should remember to be sparing in other pursuits, as well."

"I do not understand. . . ." She shook her head, helplessly, and saw the light flare in his blue eyes. Her heart sank, and she thought, *He is not finished with me. He will not leave me alone!*

She drew back into her palanquin, almost like a small turtle pulling back into its shell. Beside her, she was very conscious of the tall Englishman on his horse. She was so aware of him that she could scarcely pull herself together when horse and palanquin bore them into Hamabashi, and down a busy dirt road to the establishment of the merchant Umezono. When he dismounted and held out a hand to help her from the palanquin, her hand trembled in his clasp.

To recover her composure she began to talk. "You'll notice that there are flags everywhere with the emblem of a flower. *Umezono* means plum garden in Japanese, so the merchant's sign is a plum blossom. I've been told that he is the richest merchant in these parts. That is why you have come to visit his establishment first."

The ritual of the occasion now enveloped them. First came the low-bowing Umezono. Behind him were his family: wife, daughters, son-in-law. There were also innumerable clerks, underclerks and apprentices supervised by an also-bowing manager. This entire cortege ushered the honored guest and his interpreter into the great, sprawling building, which doubled as home and place of business.

After a brief rest in the main room, where Alex, seated in the place of honor, was given tea and sweet cakes, he was escorted on a tour of office and warehouses. These last, Alex noted, were vastly different from those of the London Company. Umezono's warehouse bulged with the silver and copper he exported, with utensils and artifacts.

Alex made compliments and asked questions, with Zanna moving beside him like a well-trained shadow. It was not till the tour was nearly over that he realized he was waiting not for what she said but for the sound of her soft, delicately accented voice.

At one point she offered an aside: "It seems, honored lord, that Umezono-san's family learned the process of separating copper ore

73

from silver ore from a foreigner—a Spanish priest! I know that this is of no business value, but I thought you might find it interesting."

Alex was disturbed by her nearness as he nodded his thanks. He had been torn between pleasure and protest this morning when Rutledge had announced his need to travel to Fukuoka. For days, he knew, Zanna had avoided him, and he had kept out of her way. It seemed, on sober reflection, the only answer. Even if the girl was willing, the situation was untenable! He had almost told Rutledge that he could no longer accept Zanna as an interpreter, but then recalled her soft voice telling him about her childhood in the mountains. If he found her unacceptable, Kita and Rutledge would probably make life even harder for her than it was now.

"Please nod your head and look sympathetic, my lord," Zanna murmured beside him. "Umezono-san has made a remark about how difficult it is to make a living on the narrow margin of profits afforded by trading with the London Company."

How cool she looked, how poised! She was far too good, Alex thought, to be under the thumb of men like Kita and Rutledge. He frowned as he reflected that, so far, everything he had learned about Rutledge's directorship weighed against the man. He was self-indulgent, sluggish, a bad manager. No doubt his problems with the Dutch East India Company were bad, but surely under more aggressive leadership the firm could show a greater profit!

After the tour Umezono's wife and daughters served refreshments. They brought in bowls of noodles in a cold, clear sauce; bits of vinegared rice covered with slices of vegetables and raw fish; long skewers threaded with delectable bits of chicken and slivers of fresh ginger. Sake was served in abundance, and as the men downed the thimble-sized cups of hot wine, they began to fence about prospective trade. Obviously, the skill with which Alex conducted this side of affairs astonished his host.

"I have an idea that he did not expect you to have a good head for business," Zanna explained. "Now he sees that you do and respects you for it. He asks you why England has never tried to expand the London Company's trade beyond Katayama when the Dutch East India Company has branches all over Kyushu and parts of Honshu, too."

Rutledge's lack of management again, Alex thought. He could hardly say so, however! "Please tell Umezono-san that, with the backing of Lord Jasper, the London Company will begin to expand," he said. His message was clear: the London Company was an up-and-coming concern, and it would do well to establish trade with it.

When Zanna had translated, the merchant clapped his hands. At this signal, his wife came forward holding a smallish wooden box. She bowed several times to Alex and placed the box before her husband, who coughed and began a solemn-sounding speech.

"Umezono-san and his family would like you to accept this small gift as a memento of your visit," Zanna explained. She added uneasily, "Even if the object isn't to your liking, please express great gratitude."

But the carefully wrapped item was beautiful—a superbly crafted silver box made in the shape of a plum blossom.

"Tell Umezono-san that this is the finest memento I've ever been given. It and today will remain precious to me," Alex said.

Beside the magnificence of this gift Alex felt his presents were inadequate, but they still drew enthusiastic response. He had brought a fine French clock for Umezono, a jeweled watch on a gold chain for his wife. Lord Jasper had also written a long letter to the merchant that hoped for a new era of trade and good will.

Mindful of Kita's warning, Zanna tried to bring the afternoon to an end several times before their actual leave-taking just before sunset. As they bowed countless times and finally set off for Katayama, she glanced worriedly at the sky. The sun was rapidly lowering in the west, and the air was thick with dusty gold light. She would have liked to order the palanquin bearers to go quickly, but Alex was in no hurry. He chose to walk his horse beside her palanquin, keeping a leisurely pace in spite of her pleas for haste.

"After all that sitting and talking, it is good

to stretch my legs," he told her, and after some time she stood and walked with him.

"It does feel good to walk, my lord," she sighed.

"I forgot you are the champion mountain climber of Isudai," he said, and saw her features tighten at his words.

"It's best to forget those mountains, my lord." Her voice was cool, and so was the long look she gave him. For a moment, there was spirit in that silver gaze, and then the look became one of pleading. "Please, I would like very much to forget everything about that evening."

To his surprise, he thought he detected real fear in her tone. Did she fear he'd pull her to the side of the road and rape her? He was suddenly and unreasonably angry, but then he realized the position in which she had been placed—ordered to and from her real home in Isudai, forced to translate, play the flute, act as guide. *Poor Snowflower,* he thought, and again fought a complex urge to pull her into his arms. Whether to kiss or comfort, he did not know. "I find it hard to forget *everything,*" he said, and his voice was gentler. She raised pleading eyes, and he said, "What you told me of Isudai, for instance. There are no such mountains in England, but there are hills—green, sunlit hills that are shadowed with mist in the mornings."

"Yes, the mist in the mornings." She looked suddenly wistful, and his heart tightened. Suddenly, and without his conscious will, he was picturing her in a gown cut low across her creamy breasts, with her dress open in front to show satin petticoats of the latest mode. How lovely she would be, he thought as she added, "You must miss England, my lord."

"Yes, it's very lovely. Someday. . . ." he began, then stopped. He had almost said, "Someday, I will take you there." Instead, he managed to add, "Someday I will tell you more about it."

She nodded, then stopped, her head half-turned to listen. "My lord . . . , can you hear that?"

She could hear it, all right—the clip-clop of many horses cantering down the road. It spelled trouble. The palanquin bearers were no fools. Already, they had fled down the roadway and were making for the thicket of bamboo by the roadside. Kenjuro, following with Alex's horse, shouted a warning: "Honored miss! Someone's coming, and fast. We'd better get out of the way!"

"What is it, Zanna?" Alex asked. Then he, too, saw the cloud of dust behind them. Four horsemen, bent low over their pommels, were riding fast. "Samurai?" he asked.

Hadn't Kita ordered her to be back in Kata-yama long before sunset? Zanna's heart pounded with self-reproach. She nodded. "They could be *ronin*. These are masterless samurai, and some are lawless. Please, Lord Alex, we must get out of the road."

Alex glanced down at the deep ditch by the

roadside. Kenjuro was coaxing his horse into this cavity. "Whoever these *ronin* are, they can't expect everyone to hide in a ditch while they pass," he protested.

Now the riders were in clear view, shouting and hurrying their mounts along. Zanna saw a flash of a steel sword and her heart sank. These were *ronin!* In her anxiety, she caught Alex by the arm. "Please, my lord," she begged. "There is no point in stirring up trouble. The *ronin* will cut us down without a second thought!"

Before Alex could respond, Kenjuro gave a horrified cry. The horse he had led into the ditch had been frightened by the noise on the roadway. Now it galloped into the midst of the riders. Kenjuro tried to grab its bridle, but instead of subduing the horse, he was dragged into the melee of hooves and moving bodies. Zanna screamed and would have gone after him, but Alex caught her around the waist and pulled her with him into the ditch. For a moment a thick cloud of dust swirled in the air. Then the riders passed, their laughter borne back on the wind.

Zanna realized that Alex was shaking her. "Are you all right?" he was demanding. Nodding furiously, she pulled herself away from him.

"I'm all right. But Kenjuro. . . ."

The old man was huddled on the ground, unmoving. Crying his name, Zanna ran to him and sank down on her knees in the dust to press her ear against his thin chest. *Merciful Buddha be thanked,* she thought. He was alive!

"Just scared senseless." Alex's competent hands were examining the old man for wounds or breakage. "Those damned, arrogant bastards!"

A burst of laughter made him jerk off the words. Zanna, looking up the road, felt her blood chill. The four riders had halted near the bamboo thicket and were looking back at the havoc they had caused. They were pointing and laughing uproariously, and one of them was pantomiming Kenjuro's fall. Zanna heard Alex make a low, feral noise in his throat.

In an instant he was on his feet and striding up the road. "What are you going to do?" Zanna cried.

"Snowflower, can you catch the horse?" There was something deceptively gentle, almost silky in Alex's voice. She nodded, and he added, "Do so. I want you and Kenjuro to get on that horse and ride back to Umezono-san's. Tell him what's happened."

"It would do no good. The *ronin* would be long gone before we returned with help. Besides, they are masters with the sword. Umezono-san's employees would be no match for them." She paused, and felt a rush of anger as one of the *ronin* began to shout insults at the "foreign devil" and his "woman." "Even the law would not be able to do very much. They didn't *hurt* anyone, my lord. It's best just to ignore them. They've had their amusement and will go away."

"Get the horse and do as I say." Then he shouted. "You! Samurai!"

Zanna let go of Kenjuro and, jumping to her feet, ran to Alex's side. "You cannot do this! You cannot challenge four armed men!"

"The horse, madam." Now, the silkiness of his tone was grim, and she knew she must obey him. Still, she tried once more. "Please, Lord Alex. You must get back to Katayama safely. You are Lord Jasper's nephew and here as a merchant. Please remember!"

"If you insist on staying there, send Kenjuro for the horse and translate." He took a step forward, his hand on the Isudai sword. "You dirty eaters of dung and unclean carrion! If you're any kind of men, get down off those horses and try your hand with me. Or do you go in only for scaring women and old men?"

"I'm not translating that!" Zanna gasped.

"They get the gist of it." Alex glanced to where Kenjuro had managed to subdue the horse. "On that beast's back, madam, and go back to Hamabashi. Now!"

Zanna took a step backward. Even Kenjuro was pleading with her to hurry, but she could not move. The *ronin* had stopped laughing now, and one of them had started his horse forward. "Alex! my Lord Alex, he'll run you through!"

The three samurai watched as their companion began to canter toward Alex. Evidently, they were quite sure that one *ronin* could make short work of the foreign devil. The mounted man, shouting loudly, lifted his sword high, and Zanna bit back a scream. Then, she saw Alex's own blade flash from his scabbard, blood red in the sunset.

Had he drawn too late? The rider was almost on top of him! Then there was a blur of movement, as Alex leaped aside at the last moment. The *ronin* tried to wheel his mount around, but took one instant too long. In that second, Alex heaved the warrior from his saddle and flung him to the ground. "Do you like to eat dust, too, you excuse for a knight?"

The *ronin* tried to get to his feet, but his sword had been kicked aside and the wicked point of Alex's blade was pressed against his throat. "Zanna, get on that horse *now!*" Alex ordered, over his shoulder.

She began to obey him, then stopped. "Look out!" she cried. The other three ronin were spurring forward. Blades flashed eagerly. Zanna knew that three mounted men against one were almost impossible odds.

Without thinking, she sprang into action. Running in front of Alex, she threw wide her arms. "This is an honored guest of Rutledge-sama, director general of the London Company," she cried. "He has the protection of Lord Azuma of Iwase. Are you insane enough to attack him?"

"Girl, are you mad?" A steel-strong hand clamped down on her shoulder, pulling her back as Alex lifted his sword. But the looked-for charge did not come. The three mounted samurai stood muttering among themselves, and then shouted to their wounded companion. Warily, the man crept out of Alex's range and was helped into the saddle of one of his companions.

"What are they jabbering about?" Alex demanded tersely.

"They are saying that only a great fighter under the protection of some great lord would dare to challenge four mounted samurai," she said. She felt faint, nauseated. "Oh, Lord Alex, you might have been killed!"

He glanced down at her, frowning darkly. "And you might have been cut down, madam. I may be here as a peaceful merchant, but I draw the line at seeing women and old men terrorized by swaggering brigands." She shook her head wordlessly, and his tone softened. "I am angry at what you did, Zanna, but I have never seen greater courage than yours."

"We must go! We must hurry!" Zanna urged. Old Kenjuro had come limping up to them, leading Alex's horse. "They may return at any moment."

"If they do, I will deal with them this time," Alex said. "You and Kenjuro will ride this horse, Zanna. Your palanquin bearers have run away a long time ago."

Zanna began to protest, but found herself lifted into the saddle, with Kenjuro perched behind her like an unhappy monkey. "Honored miss," he protested, "it's disrespectful for me to ride a fine horse like this!"

Before she could answer, the sound of unexpected clapping some distance down the road reached their ears. Looking backward, she saw a newcomer approaching from the direction of Hamabashi. She was surprised to discover that he was a European and that he rode a fine, spirited horse.

"Now where in God's name did he come from?" Alex wanted to know.

Zanna noted that he kept his hand on the pommel of his sword as the stranger rode up. "That was well done," he said in heavily accented English. "I have wanted to see these high-and-mighty samurai cowed for a long time." He leaned from his horse toward Alex, extending a large, well-gloved hand. "I am Piet van Feinstra."

A Hollander! Alex's automatic response was perfunctory, and he studied the man carefully. Zanna could almost hear his thoughts. A threat to them? It seemed not. But, in that case, why hadn't van Feinstra come to their assistance a few minutes ago?

The Dutchman also seemed to read Alex's mind. He hooked his thumbs into his empty belt and smiled. "As you see, I'm a peaceful merchant, Englishman, and unarmed." He then turned to Zanna. "If I am not mistaken, you are the daughter of James Rutledge. I saw you at your father's home just after your arrival from Katayama." He bowed. "Give my respects to him."

After a few moments, van Feinstra rode away. Alex frowned as he watched the Hollander leave. "So van Feinstra knows your father," he murmured thoughtfully.

For some reason, Zanna felt defensive. "I only saw him at the Great House once. As a merchant, Rutledge-sama deals with a lot of people."

"Why would he deal with a Hollander?" Van Feinstra was sure to belong to the Dutch East India Company. And after all that Rutledge had said about the Dutch as trade rivals. . . .

He clicked his tongue and urged the horse forward. "We had better get back to Kata-yama," he said. "I think that it's time Rutledge-*sama* and I had a long talk."

Chapter Six

Zanna was told to appear at the evening meal, as Rutledge and his manager wanted to know everything that had occurred with the merchants in Hamabashi. She answered all their questions calmly, putting off the moment when Alex would bring up the subject of van Feinstra. Though he seemed entirely at his ease, Zanna knew that there was tension behind his offhand account of the confrontation with the *ronin*, and guessed that the Dutchman was the cause.

"Oddly enough, I also met another European," he finally said. "A Dutch merchant by the name of van Feinstra, who asked to give you his respects. I had not known you were on such friendly footing with a man from the Dutch East India Company."

Zanna saw the glance Rutledge gave his manager. Then, he sighed. "So you've met. I hadn't meant to tell you about van Feinstra for a while, Alex. Not until I was sure of the man."

"Sure in what way?" Alex asked courteously, but Zanna knew that the very gentleness of his tone was deceptive.

"He's one of the avenues I have been exploring." The director general's tone was a deep rumble. "I hope to use Piet van Feinstra to help the London Company. He has a great deal of helpful information."

"You want to use him as a spy." The contempt in Alex's voice was barely concealed.

"Call him what you like. He'll be useful to us, and that's what matters. Van Feinstra's disenchanted with the Dutch East India Company, it seems. They've promised him a great deal and haven't delivered, and he's looking for a quick profit so that he can start a concern of his own." Rutledge's voice was suddenly sharp. "You find all this distasteful?"

Zanna saw Alex hesitate, then nod. "I do. A man who betrays one's trust may do so again."

Kita now leaned forward. "He speaks as the son of a knight and the nephew of a rich lord," he said. "He doesn't know how roughly the Hollanders can play the trade game."

When Rutledge had translated this, Alex said, "So the sword you gave me some time ago was not only to use on lawless *ronin*?"

There was a glint in those blue eyes that added to Zanna's unease. Alex the courteous envoy of Lord Jasper had changed, in her mind, to a reckless Alex drawing his sunset-stained sword against the *ronin. He will be hurt,* she thought, and then wondered at the stab of fear that followed the thought.

The director general was talking again. "You're young and like taking risks. I find my way easier. We have come to blows with the God-cursed Hollanders before over trade, and I prefer espionage to a knife in my guts! If you have no objection, I intend to use van Feinstra and any information that will help the London Company."

With relief, Zanna saw Alex's somewhat reluctant nod. Now Kita changed the subject. She translated for Alex's benefit, hoping to distract him. "Kita-san says that you have done well both in battle and with the merchant, Lord Alex. He wants to know if he can see the gifts that were given to you."

A servant was dispatched to fetch the gifts at once, and the silver plum-blossom box that the merchant had given him was admired. "I think you've done more than well," Rutledge said, admiring the softly glowing gift. "Umezono isn't known for his generosity, and this is a most generous gift! Between business diplomacy and swordplay, you'll go far, my friend."

"It was mostly due to Zanna." She could not help the warm pleasure that his words caused her, and when he looked at her his smile was friendly and open. "If it wasn't for her cool head, I might have been used as target practice by those *ronin.*" He took the silver box from Rutledge and held it in his palm for a moment. "No doubt, had they run us down they would have kept this. You're right, James. This is a fine gift, worthy of a king—or queen."

Before she realized what he was about, Alex rose from his place of honor at the low table and turned toward her. He knelt beside her, bending down to look into her startled gray eyes. "Zanna, will you accept this gift from me? As a token of my respect for your intelligence and courage?"

She could not lift her hand in surprise or speak at all. She could only stare, foolishly, as he lifted her hand and put the box into her palm. It nestled in her hand, warm from his clasp. It was this warmth that brought her to herself. "I can't take this, my lord!" she protested.

"But of course you can. I can't think of anyone who could use it better."

Past Alex's shoulder, Zanna saw that Kita was staring, his mouth half-open in surprise. Rutledge, too, was silent. Alex said, "In England, it's an insult to return a man's gift. Isn't that so, James?"

"Eh? Yes, of course! You take it, girl; don't be a fool." The director general's voice was rough. "Most women would jump at such a chance."

Most women, Alex was thinking, but not Zanna. Her eyes were dazzled with surprise, and something else that made him clear his throat and return to his place at the table.

"And now," he said heartily, "enough of to-day's activities! What of tomorrow?"

"Tomorrow should be easier than today. You will visit Yamaguchi, another merchant from Hamabashi. Yamaguchi is a plain man and there will be less fuss." Rutledge nodded at Zanna. "The girl will go with you again, since she's done so well for you today."

Zanna stared at Rutledge in consternation. "But, honored director general," she began, "I thought you were to go with the English lord! I'm sure that you would be so much more skilled at such matters."

Rutledge hadn't even heard her. "You'll like Yamaguchi, Alex. He's an honest man, and the stuff he sells is of good quality." He smiled at Zanna, adding, "You look worried, girl. Don't be. All you need do is exert yourself in Lord Alex's behalf as you did today."

The praise gave her courage. She placed her hands on the floor and bowed until her forehead touched the backs of her hands. "Rutledge-sama, may I please be excused from accompanying Lord Alex to Yamaguchi-san's tomorrow? I beg forgiveness for any disrespect, but I truly feel that I may not do well for the London Company."

Both Kita and the director general stared at her. "What's the matter?" Alex asked, and she turned to him with swift, hopeful eagerness.

Before she could speak, however, Kita was speaking in brusque Japanese. "You dare to question the director general's instructions, girl? You are insolent! Of course you will go

90

with Lord Alex! Isn't that why you were brought here from Katayama?"

"I asked Zanna what was going on." There was steel in Alex's voice, and Rutledge raised both hands to soothe the situation.

"Nothing to concern yourself with. A little question of details." He turned to Zanna and said, "Kita is right, of course. There is no question about that."

She knew that his word was law, and she clenched her hands over the silver plum box in her hand. The warmth of it made her reckless. Almost desperately, she turned to Alex. "My lord, if you would only excuse me from accompanying you tomorrow! Or if you could give me time to—to serve you better." Her blood was leaping through her, not so much at this blatant disregard for Rutledge's orders, but because of the way Lord Alex looked. "Just one day, my lord," she whispered, and saw his concern reach out to her like a friendly hand.

"Of course you will have your day," Alex was beginning, when Kita leaped to his feet.

"Be silent!" he thundered at her. "Insolent, stupid, ungrateful girl! You will do exactly as you're told. Who do you owe your duty and loyalty to, you disobedient wench?"

He would have said more except that Alex's hand had clamped down around the neck folds of his kimono. "Don't talk to her like that," Alex said.

Kita tried to speak but could only gurgle. His sallow cheeks flushed red, and he beat at the iron fist that was choking him. "Alex, he didn't mean anything!" The burly director general was on his feet. "Let him go!"

"When he apologizes to Zanna." Zanna saw Alex's grip tighten a fraction, heard the almost gentle note in his voice. "Tell her you're sorry," he instructed Kita.

"But Zanna took no offense!" Rutledge was bellowing.

"*I* took offense. She is my interpreter, is she not? You said so yourself, James. And as such, she should be under my orders." Inexorably, the iron grip lifted the struggling Kita off the ground as Alex added, "Apologize, Kita-san."

Zanna did not know which way to look, but her eyes kept coming back to Alex's face. In the light of the Chrysanthemum Room, he seemed a man carved in hard bronze. "Please don't, Lord Alex," she managed to say. "I'm not offended. It was my fault. I—."

"I'm sorry!" Kita croaked at last in Japanese. Alex let go of his kimono, and he sank onto the mat, massaging his neck. He shot a look at Alex, and then at Zanna. His narrow black eyes flashed with an anger quickly subdued as they went opaque. "I've offended our guest without knowing."

"I don't care how you treat women in your own households," Alex was beginning, but Zanna could bear no more. The strain of the day suddenly filled her throat, almost choking her. Whispering her excuses, she bowed and hurried from the room. As she closed the door behind her, she heard the director general's conciliatory laugh.

"Alex, come, have some sake. Japanese customs are different from those in England, after all. And, tell the truth. Isn't it best to let a wench know her place?"

She did not wait to hear Alex's answer but hurried to her room. She had forgotten her place tonight, and she was frightened because she was not more ashamed. When Alex had made Kita apologize, she had actually been glad!

What is happening to me? Zanna wondered, bleakly. *What is Lord Alex doing to me? He's turning my entire life upside down.*

It was then she realized that she was still clutching the costly silver box in her hand.

An hour later, she knelt before Alex's fine suite and called softly for admittance. Her heart beat fast at the thought of what she must do. She almost faltered at the look on his face as he opened the screen door.

"Zanna!" he exclaimed, and smiled, the smile softening the planes of his face and warming his eyes. "I am glad to see you. I have been working at that report for my Uncle Jasper, and need your counsel."

The words undid her, and she could not say what she had come to say. Not at once. "How, my lord?" she asked.

He led the way back to the desk and drew a

paper from it. "Can you read? I recall Rutledge saying that you had some training in writing English."

She shook her head. "Only a little, my lord. I'm afraid this is too difficult." She frowned at the paper. "Although," she added slowly, "I think I can make out words. Isn't this word *merchant*?"

"It is. Sound them out, Zanna, and you will be able to recognize most of them." He bent closer to her, pointing out the words on the paper. For a moment her concentration distracted her, but then she realized that she was almost standing in the circle of his arms. She moved a little away.

"How can I be of help to you?" she asked.

"By helping me estimate the amount of goods Umezono keeps in his warehouse. I am unfamiliar with Japanese weights and measures, and must give a fairly accurate account to my uncle." He frowned. "It was a well-stocked warehouse, indicative of a vast amount of trade. The London Company should learn from this."

He had given her an opening. "Lord Alex, I am sorry for what happened tonight," she said. He looked up at her swiftly, about to interrupt, but she swept on. "It was very wrong of me. I have come to tell you that I have told Rutledge-sama that I will go with you tomorrow, of course. I am completely at your disposal."

"Did Kita have anything to do with your

changing your mind?" Alex asked. There was a hard glint in his blue eyes. She shook her head quickly and felt a little breathless.

"No, he didn't. I did not even talk to him. I felt ashamed."

He put down the paper on the desk with an irritated gesture. "Why, for God's sake? He brought it on himself by the way he treated you. As if you were a servant to order here or there against your will!"

It was not against my will, she thought. *That is the problem!* Aloud she tried to explain. "In a way, I *am* like a servant in this house. I must do my duty. The Lord Buddha teaches that a person's salvation comes from doing his or her duty well." Carefully, she took the silver box from her flowing sleeve and laid it gently on the desk. "I cannot accept this great gift for simply doing my duty, my lord."

The glitter in his eyes had changed. He said, "You are content being a servant? You'd let that dried-up Kita order you around? I thought you had more spirit, madam!"

To her own surprise, anger swept through her. "It has nothing to do with spirit!" she cried. "You don't understand our country, Lord Alex. This is the way we do things. We live by our rules. Even if they don't appeal to you, you should try to respect them!"

Alex could not believe it. She was railing at him for defending her! "All right," he snapped. "Have it your way. From now on,

Kita can abuse you all he likes and not a word from me."

Her gray eyes flashed silver and her soft chin was firm. "You're worse than he is, Lord Alex! Yes," she added, heatedly, "worse than those *ronin*. I know exactly where I stand with Kita-san and lawless brigands. But you! You are only thinking of profit and riches. You said so yourself! Yet you pretend to care—" She broke off, abruptly. She had almost said it all. She had almost said, "You pretend to care about me."

But he was too angry himself to hear the slip or the catch of her breath. "Yes, so I do," he said, coldly. "And for all your high-minded talk about loyalty and duty, you're in this for gain, too! Living in this fine house must be easy compared with climbing mountains in Isudai. And you've gotten that fine blue and silver kimono to wear since you arrived, and other fine things." He heard her gasp of outrage and pressed on. "Money buys a great many things—and a great many people. Haven't you heard?"

His words silenced her. She had cried out at him from her pain, and he lashed back with cruel words. He spoke of men and women bought—bought like her mother. She did not know how he had known about Oyuri's kimono, the garment worn by Rutledge's many companions, but he obviously did. And then tormented her with the knowledge!

"How could you?" she cried, and an anger

filled her, a raging torrent of hurt and bitterness and despair. Suddenly, she was no longer a young woman living in a fine house. She was standing on the slopes of the Isudai mountains, a girl tormented by a ring of leering boys. "Whore's daughter," she heard them laugh. "Bastard! Foreign devil's bastard. . . ."

With a little gasping cry, she swung back her hand and slapped him as hard as she could. The blow hardly connected, for he stepped back as swiftly as he had when he avoided the marauding *ronin*, and caught her hand. He pulled her forward, and, unbalanced by the blow, she fell into his arms.

His lips came down on hers. Not loving, not tender, but cruel and hard and bruising. His mouth insulted her and stifled the protest she tried to utter. Like an iron cage, his lips held her prisoner and she could not breathe. She felt dizzy, but she struggled angrily, beating at his chest with her hands, kicking out with both feet. Her unshod feet were ineffectual against his legs, and so were her fists.

"Kick, will you, hellcat?" he muttered. She drew in a gulp of air as he took his mouth again and tried to scream, but he clamped a hand down over her mouth. She felt herself being lifted up and flung down hard—so hard that she cried out on a single, gasping note. But soft quilts cushioned her fall. Quilts. His sleeping quilts! True panic filled all the corners of her mind as she tried to roll off the quilts and rolled, instead, against his solid hardness. "No," she heard him say. "Not so fast. I'm not done with you, yet!"

She opened her eyes and glared up at him, saw the dark blue eyes close to hers, and his mouth coming down against her once again. Then, he was ravaging her lips again, his tongue a bold, marauding intruder into her unwilling mouth. Unwilling, but forced to breathe, she gasped in his warm breath and felt herself giddy and faint. *Oh, merciful Buddha,* she thought, *I will faint if he continues.*

From deep in her throat came a small moan that was almost a sob. Far away she was conscious of his hands pushing apart the folds of her kimono, the soft undergarment. His hands were rough on her flesh—rough and angry. And then, his touch changed. Without ceasing, without pause, the firm, strong fingers began to caress her shoulders and throat and the swell of her breasts.

His kiss changed, too. These were the lips she remembered, the achingly tender touch that had filled all her guilty dreams. "Zanna," she heard him murmur against her, and the pressure of his arms eased.

She knew that she could roll away from him now and flee. She knew, yet could not go. Instead, her mouth yearned for the touch of his, the sweet texture of his caressing lips. His hands, circling, covering her yearning breasts, traced erotic fire over the taut nipples. She arched her back to meet his touch, to press closer against him, and her hands reached out to trace the contours of his face, the bold nose, the hard line of cheek and jaw, the powerful column of his throat.

She murmured his name, feeling giddy as he kissed her. "Snowflower," he murmured, his lips caressing the hollow of her throat, following the path of his hands, his mouth and tongue creating a trail of liquid heat that circled her rounded breasts and sought their peaks. Pleasure that was almost pain whirled through Zanna as he tasted the honey sweetness of her flesh. She pulled impatiently at the fine linen shirt he wore, eager to touch him, to feel the smooth-muscled strength of his back against the palms of her hands.

Impatient too, he pulled aside her robes and, unable to undo the elaborate fixture of her sash, pulled up with one eager gesture her long petticoat. His mouth moved downward to stroke her long, slender legs, while he traced the rounded perfection of her hips with sensitive fingertips.

"I knew you'd be like this, perfect like this," he murmured, and she heard the soft laugh he gave, the deep, satisfied purr of his voice. It was all a part of what his hands and his lips were doing—what her own mouth and body wanted to do. She no longer thought, but felt with all her senses. She felt the softness of Alex's bed quilts against her back, the hardness and heat of his body against hers as he continued his wondrous exploration. Above the whirl of her desire she heard his breathing, her own sounds of pleasure. They mingled with the trilling, liquid notes of a night bird in the garden outside, and a soft, sensuous breeze drifted into the room and touched her near-naked body like a caress.

Suddenly, she gasped aloud with a pleasure so intense that she seemed to be in a whirlpool of fire. She cried out his name as his lips traced slow flames up her inner thighs, and the passionate demand of his kisses was almost too much to bear. Now he came to her, kissing her, robbing her of her breath. Dimly, she realized that he had taken off his shirt, that she could feel his urgent flesh against her breasts and ribs and belly. She wanted him and ached for him, and already her hips moved against his in an instinctive rhythm as old as breath itself.

"Alex." She knew she could call him this now. It was as right as this feeling that told her she could never be again complete without him. She wanted to tell him what she meant, but she could not find the right words and could only repeat his name.

He drew a little away from her, and the desire in his eyes left her weak. "Zanna, I want to make love to you. Do you want this also?"

Could he not see that she wanted him, too? And yet, even while she drew him close to her, a doubt as soft as night mist brushed against her mind. *I will never be the same if he does this*, a shadowy voice whispered. *It will change me forever. Not because of our bodies joining, not that. There is something else. If I let myself love him. . . .*

For a fragmentary second she thought of her mother. She thought of the songbird she had released in Isudai. She thought of Kenjuro's frightened face when he thought she was Oyuri's ghost.

She hesitated, and Alex felt her distance. "Zanna?" he questioned. And, at that moment, they both heard the familiar voice by Alex's closed door.

"Excuse my intrusion," Kita was saying. "May I come in, Lord Alex?"

With a gasp, Zanna sat up on the rumpled quilts and began frantically to pull her clothes to rights. Alex put out a hand to stop her, but before he could do so she had ducked under his arm and pulled aside the outer doors that led to the garden. A sigh of sand, and she had gone.

"Do I disturb?" Kita called.

Alex swore softly and fervently. Then, not bothering to don his cast-off shirt, he walked to the screen doors and pulled them open. "Kita-san," he acknowledged.

The hatchet-faced manager was smiling. "I come apologize," he said, in his terrible English. "Offend guest tonight. I am sorry."

Christ, you have the worst timing in the world, Alex thought. Angrily, he glanced to the open outer doors and saw that Kita had followed his gaze. "It's all right," he said, abruptly. Then, he softened his words with a smile. There was no point in making an enemy of this man, who might abuse Zanna further. "I, too, was hasty. I am sorry for my hastiness, Kita-san."

"Ah." Kita showed crooked teeth in a grin. "Not good to fight over woman." He paused. "Zanna like mother. Good to look at."

"She's a beautiful woman, yes." In spite of his good intentions, Alex's voice tightened.

"Her mother was Rutledge-sama's first companion," Kita said. "Very beautiful, too." He shook his head. "Zanna not like her. Too proud."

Alex held on to politeness with difficulty. "I don't think we need to discuss Zanna," he said shortly. "If you will excuse me, Kita-san, it's late."

Kita nodded and turned to go. Then, he paused. "Not first time English lord take Japanese woman for companion," he said. "The young woman called Winter Blossom is proud —but sometimes men likes proud woman. Taming wild bird bring pleasure."

Alex controlled an impulse to seize Kita by his scrawny throat and strangle him. "It is not my intention to make Zanna or anyone else my companion," he gritted. "You can mind your own damned business!"

It was only after Kita had sauntered away down the wooden corridor and he had slammed his door shut that Alex heard what he had said. A few more moments alone with Zanna and Kita's words would have come true!

He thought of Zanna's slim, perfect body, the ivory and rose of her skin, the sweet, high breasts and the promise of the rounded hips. And she had wanted him to take her as much as he had wanted to still his passion between her beautiful thighs.

He looked into the quiet, dark garden. He needed only to walk across to Zanna's room, and he knew she would be waiting for him. He took a step down onto the cold stone step and then he stopped, Kita's words hissing in his ear. "You are not the first English lord to take a Japanese companion."

Companion. Whore. None of these words fit Zanna, and he shook his head to clear it. Now he could see not only her eyes silvered with passion, but the cool serious grace of her, the chilly control that masked the warmth and the sweetness.

Aléx leaned his head against the wooden door and thought: *She's right. When I've done Uncle Jasper's work, I'll be going back to England—with luck, wealthier from commissions on trade I've generated for the London Company here. But I'll leave her behind. What right do I have to ruin her?*

He closed the door and went back into the strangely empty room, his eyes taking in the rumpled bed, the silver plum-blossom box on

103

the desk. He remembered both her defiance and her compliance, and there was a tight constriction about his chest. *I have to forget her*, he told himself. *No matter what I feel, I can't make that girl into a companion.*

Chapter Seven

THE NEWS THAT RUTLEDGE AND THE ENGLISH
lord had been summoned to Iwase brought
enormous excitement to the Great House. Although it had been expected that Lord Azuma
would want to see Alex, the speed with which
the summons came was a surprise. After all,
the servants said among themselves, it was
only two weeks since Lord Jasper's nephew
had arrived in Katayama!

Zanna herself was grateful for the trip.
Alex's absence would be a relief from the
unbearable tension that had grown between
them during the last week—a tension grown
from Alex's coldness whenever he spoke to
her or referred to her in any way. His obvious
reluctance to be with her first shocked, then
hurt and puzzled her terribly. She could not
understand it. That night of Kita's humiliation, she had sat awake until dawn, expecting

Alex with every rustle in the corridor or in the garden. But he had not come. Instead, he had become remote and uninterested in her.

Zanna sighed as she carried a tray of sake to Rutledge's rooms. Mitsuko, the maid, had brought her this command of the director general's soon after their return from the day's business. "They're planning their trip," she had said slyly. "We'll soon have no English lord in this house. Not that I'll miss him as you will, of course."

Zanna knew that the woman was speculating over whether or not she had become Alex's companion. What the maid thought didn't matter, but the memory of being in Alex's arms was like a tight, hard pain in her breast. As she stopped before Rutledge's threshold, she wondered if she could ask Alex why he was so angry with her. Surely even confrontation would be preferable to this silence!

She called softly at the door, entered, and found the two men bent over a map.

"The journey will take two days," Rutledge was saying.

"James, I'm impressed with the speed with which you've arranged this audience with Lord Azuma. I've brought him several gifts from my uncle, of course, but from what you've said I take it that this daimio is one man who can't be bought with gifts." Zanna could hear the tense excitement in Alex's voice.

"He is a different kettle of fish from anyone else you've met in Japan," Rutledge agreed.

106

"He's known as a just overlord, but he brooks absolutely no dissension in his fiefs, and his judgment can be terrible." He looked grave, suddenly. "Actually, Alex, I didn't arrange this audience at all. It was he who heard of your arrival and summoned you. And don't expect to see him as soon as we get to Iwase, either. I've known him to let an entire delegation cool its heels for weeks before seeing them."

Zanna watched Alex nod and felt the knot within her harden. *Couldn't he look at me? Do I offend him so much?* she thought. As if he had caught her unspoken words, he lifted his eyes to hers. The chill in that blue gaze made her blink confusedly before dropping her own.

Terrified that her feelings had shown too clearly, she poured a cupful of sake and presented it to Rutledge, who tossed it off. "Only one cup. I must see Kita about many things." He tipped a wink at Alex. "You'll enjoy the trip, my friend. You'll see sights and people who will fascinate you, and the inns are decent. Plenty of good food and pliant maids who can massage away a man's aches and see to his *other* comforts."

Alex did not look at Zanna as he forced himself to smile at the director general. "You paint a picture that makes me eager to start."

"Stay a while and drink this sake," Rutledge advised. He crossed to the door, then halted. "Get the girl to tell you about the great road. She's gone as far as Isudai."

He left the room, and they could hear his heavy footfall punishing the corridor. For a moment there was silence. Then Alex said, "You think well of the great road?"

"It's a fine road." She poured him sake hastily.

He took the cup from her with fingers that might have been a stranger's. "I thank you," he said. The words were a dismissal so obvious that she bit her lip.

"Lord Alex. . . ." She stopped, saw him tense slightly as she added, "Can you tell me what I've done wrong? Have I offended you in some way?"

He could sense her discomfort and unhappiness, and steeled himself against the urge to turn and take her in his arms. *That way is too easy,* he told himself. *I must not think of her feelings but of her good.*

"Of course not." His voice was firm and courteously cool. "Why do you suggest that, madam?"

"You have been. . . ." Again, she stopped, trying for the right word. Why did he not look at her? Unconsciously, she took a step toward him, saw the muscle of his cheek tighten. Did he hold her in such distaste that he could not bear her to be close? But why, after that night?

"I have been very preoccupied with business," he said, finishing her broken sentence. "I am sure you understand, Zanna, that I am here not for my own pleasure but to be my

108

uncle's envoy. Now, I must think only of this trip to Iwase and Lord Azuma."

"Of course, my lord." But that was not the reason, and she knew it as surely as she knew the beat of her own blood. He was disgusted with her. He could not stand to be with her.

"Perhaps you are puzzling about what happened the other night." Now, his voice was oddly harsh. "I was angry when you turned on me and tried to slap me, and I didn't think. What happened should not have happened. I should not have used you—or tried to use you—as some common serving wench. My only excuse is that I have not had a woman for so long."

"I—see," she said. She could barely form the words. Now, she knew! His kisses and caresses, the ecstasy she had thought to be an outpouring of love, had been a simple animal reflex. He would have held and touched and kissed a common serving woman so—someone like Mitsuko, maybe! The thought made her physically ill, and the reasoned, logical thoughts fell against her mind like cold darts of wind.

"Of course, this won't happen again," he was continuing. "My mission is much too important to allow for—diversions, no matter how pleasant they are. You'll be completely safe from my attentions from now on, Zanna."

She nodded, automatically. She felt as if she were turning to ice—a fragile, brittle cold that could shatter at any moment. "Yes, honored lord," she said. "I understand, of course. Your mission for Lord Jasper is paramount in your mind. I'm sorry I caused you anger, caused you to deviate from it—."

In spite of her control, her voice broke a little. She did not see Alex's almost involuntary movement toward her as she turned toward the door. "I wish you a profitable trip, Lord Alex!"

Chapter Eight

THEY WERE ON THEIR WAY BY THE TIME THE
first dawn grayed the horizon. Large bonfires
had been lit in the courtyard of the Great
House, and the snap of green logs and curtains of smoke blended with farewells as Alex
and Rutledge, followed by two young apprentices leading pack horses, rode through the
gates.

It had begun! This was what Alex had waited for—a chance to meet with the great
daimio in Iwase and plead the London Company's case.

The path to power and wealth, Alex
thought, and found that his eyes had involuntarily turned to seek Zanna out. He spotted
old Kenjuro bobbing his head and calling the
traditional Japanese "Go, and return safely!"
with the others who had come to see them off,

but there was no sign of midnight-dark hair and gray eyes. Hurt or angry, she had kept away. Whatever might have blossomed between them was dead. *Thank God I won't have to worry about the wench again*, he told himself firmly.

"Ready, Alex?" Rutledge urged his fine mount beside Alex's. "The apprentices will want to ride breakneck for a while in their excitement," he warned. "But that pace will kill us, so be guided by me. I've made the journey to Iwase several times. It's a long ride to the boat that will take us to Shimonoseki."

Rutledge was right. The enthusiasm of the morning lessened as the day grew hotter. Riding on a dusty, often narrow road, they drew flies, gnats and hordes of curious onlookers. These last were the worst to Alex's mind. "Why do they gawk?" he asked impatiently when, on the outskirts of one village, they were practically ambushed by a throng of villagers who gabbled and chattered and pointed to Rutledge and Alex, while the children shouted in shrill, laughing voices. "Where is your vaunted Japanese courtesy now?"

"You can't blame them," Rutledge rumbled. "They have seen nobody with our coloring or features before. They don't even know where we come from. The children are calling us Koreans, which is about as far as their imagination will take them." He grinned at Alex. "Don't worry, lad. They're friendly."

"I hope so." Alex eyed the crowds a little

grimly. "There are many more of them than there are of us!"

By the time they reached the ferry that would take them across the waters to the inn, they were exhausted. After eating heartily, Alex was too weary to do more than seek his sleeping quilts. He slept soundly, but since his room was adjacent to Rutledge's, he woke once to hear the other man's deep laugh and a woman's soft voice. The sounds became a part of his own dream, and he believed he held Zanna in his arms. She was naked, as was he, her head bent back with the weight of her unbound hair, her softly rounded breasts bare and the rosy peaks inviting his mouth and tongue. She whispered his name and moaned, hips moving invitingly; but when he tried to take her, sheathe his want between her thighs, he found she was no longer there. Instead, he heard her voice soft in his ear. "Alex . . . Alex."

The sound of Zanna's voice became the insistent call of a servant-maid at the door. It was time to wake up and take up the road again. For a moment he let his mind dwell on his dream, and then he smiled wryly. Even in dreams, it seemed, he would never be able to possess her!

He met the director general for a quick breakfast of Japanese soybean soup and rice, and found it not quite as bad as Rutledge had made out. The older man seemed to be in great spirits, though his eyes were shot with red. "You should have sampled the wares of

Shimonoseki," he told Alex as they left the inn to a chorus of good-byes. He then winked at one of the prettier maids, who giggled and hid her mouth with her hand. "The wenches of this country are skillful and willing."

Like Zanna's mother? Alex caught himself wondering, then angrily pushed the thought aside. Why could he not think of anything but that woman? He began to ask Rutledge questions about their journey overland toward Fukuza. "When do we join the major highway of which you spoke?"

They came to it after a half-hour's ride, and Alex was impressed. This road was broad and well kept, draining off on both sides into carefully dug drainage ditches. Pine trees had been planted, and they saw several people tending to the trees. Others were carefully making repairs on the highway, smoothing over uneven spots and sprinkling water to keep down the dust.

"The roads actually divide Japan into districts, and by watching the roads the shogun can keep an eye on everyone who is moving or traveling in the country," Rutledge explained. He pointed to a wooden gate. "He does this by a series of checkpoints, like those. We'll show our summons from Lord Azuma here."

A great many people were gathered about the wooden gate. There were families traveling together, old people and young, a lady of obviously good family with her retinue. Her palanquin bearers sat aside, playing with

114

dice, while the rituals of the checkpoint could be observed. Rutledge glanced at the lady and clicked his tongue. "If I know these bastards who run the checkpoint, they'll make it a point to give that one a hard time."

"How so?" The way the lady carried her head reminded Alex of Zanna's almost unconscious dignity. "What has she done?"

"She? Nothing! But the shogun knows that the daimio's ladies are hostages for their lord's behavior. Nobody is allowed on the great roads without a reason in the form of a pass. A woman's pass carries information like status, occupation, a description. A woman can even be searched." He paused, then nodded to a teashop near the gate. "Let's get out of the sun and see if someone can be bribed to get us through the checkpoint faster."

Rutledge's money must have been good, or Lord Azuma's name potent. Within minutes, they were sipping tea while the crowd at the checkpoint goggled at them with curiosity, and shortly they were summoned by the checkpoint officials. Their summons from Lord Azuma was scrutinized, stamped; and bows were exchanged. They were on their way again.

They were about to mount when Alex heard singing behind him. He half turned and saw a group of women approaching the checkpoint. These women did not seem downcast or worried at the prospect of being questioned or searched. They wore richly colored hoods on their heads and bright kimonos. They were all exceedingly beautiful. One of them, a slender young woman with bright red lips and flashing almond eyes, came up to Alex and murmured something in a sly voice.

"What is she saying?" Whatever it was, the checkpoint was agog with interest. Women clicked their tongues and looked disapproving. Men roared and craned closer. The hooded young woman smiled even more and pressed herself against Alex.

"They're *bikuni*," Rutledge explained. He was grinning as widely as the other men at the checkpoint. "They are begging nuns."

"Certainly not nuns!" Alex said, and began to grin himself. In spite of his surprise, the skillful pressure of the hooded girl's body was evoking an insistent response in him.

"That's what they call themselves, at any rate. They started out as some sort of traveling order, and then—well! Now they are more than capable of producing paradise of another kind. Too bad we don't have time to linger here, Alex. The 'nun' with you is intent on sleeping with a foreigner. She is wondering about your—er—equipment and whether it functions in the correct way."

"I'm sorry I can't give her a demonstration." Laughing outright, Alex mounted his horse and followed Rutledge out of the now-open checkpoint gate. Before it closed again, he turned to catch another look at the pretty *bikuni* and saw, instead, the wellborn lady. She had risen and was walking slowly toward the officials' hut. In spite of the distance, he could see her dignity warring with apprehension. Suddenly, he remembered what Zanna had once told him about women not being in control of their lives. Instantly, the heat called forth by the skilled *bikuni* ebbed away. He had to restrain himself from turning his mount and spurring back to the checkpoint to offer the unknown lady his assistance and, if need be, his sword.

Rutledge raised an admonishing finger. "This is Japan," he said. "You know the saying? When in Rome. . . . It's wise to remember! The people here have ways and customs they've used for thousands of years."

"Does that extend to the bullying of women?" Alex demanded.

Rutledge shrugged. "Japanese women are naturally passive. They accept the bullying. It's a way of life! And even in England, aren't there plenty of women under the thumb of menfolk? A woman is a marketable commodity. The sooner she learns that the better." He pushed forward his thick lips. "Take this habit of a man's companions. Why would a woman consent to bed unlawfully with a man unless she's decided to live with the system and try to better her lot?"

"Did you feel that Zanna's mother thought like that?" Alex was angry at his own lack of diplomacy, but the question had slipped out. Rutledge did not take offense.

"I was very young when I took Oyuri. I kept

her too long—a mistake, young man. Women have instincts to build nests, and Oyuri was a born nester." He shook his head. "Even so, she understood that there were never to be ties between us. It was a business deal, you see. She knew I'd support her and her daughter even when she went to Isudai."

The long hours of riding were not tiring Alex today, and he gratefully realized that his body and muscles, inactive for so many days on ship and land, were growing hardened again. He was not even weary when they reached the day's destination, an inn at Fukuza; but Rutledge said he was exhausted.

"A good night's rest," he told Alex, "is what I need. Tomorrow we push on toward Iwakuni."

Nodding, Alex dismounted and was about to hand his mount over to one of the apprentices when he heard the noise of a crowd. "What's going on?" he asked.

Rutledge inquired briefly of one of the inn's servants. "A wrestling match, it seems. They call it sumo here in this country. Two huge muscle-bound wrestlers try to push or lift each other out of the ring," he explained, then added, "Would you like to watch?"

"Why not?" A loud shout had come from the crowd. "It seems as if someone's just been beaten."

Rutledge gave an instruction to the apprentices and followed Alex as he walked up to the crowd. "Be careful," he joked. "You don't want to be challenged. After two days in the saddle, wrestling is hardly something you'd enjoy."

As he spoke, some men and women in the crowd turned to take in the newcomers, and a young boy close to Alex said something in a high, shrill voice that caused Rutledge to frown. "Now what?" Alex demanded.

"He says you're the right size and shape to challenge somebody called Dai-suké. That's a nickname meaning 'big fellow,' so I'd politely decline the offer! Perhaps it would be wisest to get to our rooms."

Alex did not answer, for he was looking over the heads of the crowd and watching the contest before him. A circle had been drawn with charcoal on the hard ground, and in this makeshift ring two huge men, stripped to their loincloths, were heaving and straining. One of them was undoubtedly Dai-suké, Alex thought. The man was about five feet eight but so broad and muscular that he looked massive. With ease he seized his opponent by the belt of his loincloth and swung him around. Then, with a speedy, effortless movement, he threw him from the ring.

The crowd roared. "Dai-suké, Dai-suké, ichiban-da!"

"They're saying that Dai-suké is the top, the best," Rutledge interpreted. "Well, now you've seen sumo. Come to the inn, Alex, and we'll. . . ."

Dai-suké shouted something and pointed. Alex did not need a translation for the gesture or the word. The big wrestler was pointing

119

directly at him, and there was a mocking, crooked grin on his flat, brutish face. "I think I've been challenged," he exclaimed.

Rutledge groaned. "I was afraid of this! You're so tall and look so different to them that this Dai-suké would enjoy beating you!" He tugged at Alex's arm. "You're here to meet the lord of Iwase, not to get bashed and mangled by some fool of a sumo!"

Alex knew that the older man was right. He nodded and began to turn, but a flood of invective from the wrestler stopped him. The finger was still pointed, but the grin had turned to a snarl. He was clearly saying that the foreign devil didn't dare stand up to Dai-suké. To make matters worse, the crowd roared approval, and the child who had first proposed Alex as a contestant stuck out his tongue in derision.

"Alex, for God's sake!"

Dai-suké turned around, and waggled his bare rump in the direction of the Englishman. He slapped his buttock with one hand and made a rude noise.

"Will you hold my sword and doublet, James?" Alex's voice was suddenly gentle, so pleasant that Rutledge stared at him. Swiftly, he undid the buttons of doublet and shirt, flung them at Rutledge. Then, just as swiftly, he unshod his feet. Clad only in breeches, he stepped into the ring. "Now, you foul-faced brute," he said in that silky way.

Dai-suké hadn't finished. He stood and laughed heartily at Alex for several minutes.

He's doing this to get me so angry I'll lose my temper, Alex told himself. He smiled at Dai-suké instead, and heard a ripple of surprise from the crowd. One young woman made a gesture to her friends that was unmistakable. *This is not Dai-suké, but what a body!* her eyes said.

Dai-suké now lumbered to the center of the ring and squatted down, hands on hamlike thighs. Alex followed suit. From the side of the ring he heard Rutledge's instructions. He was to crouch, facing his opponent until the signal was given. And then. . . .

"For God's sakes, Alex, I hope you know what you're doing!" James Rutledge seemed almost hysterical, and Alex found himself wondering what in hell he was doing half-naked in a crude ring facing a brutish man-mountain. Then, there was no time to wonder, just a split second of staring into bestial, muddy-brown eyes, a moment's chance to calm himself, to call all the resources of his body into play.

"Now!" Rutledge was yelling.

Dai-suké, more used to the rules of sumo, moved first. Alex felt the man's viselike grip on his breeches, countered automatically by feinting, grabbing Dai-suké by his loincloth. Foot to foot, they strained and swayed. *I mustn't let him get me around the waist,* Alex thought. *That will finish me!*

Dai-suké made his move to grasp Alex, and the lighter, leaner Englishman pulled aside. The next moment, he had seized the wrestler by an arm. But though he had intended to flip him across his shoulder, Dai-suké was too heavy and too powerful. He swung around, grasping Alex from behind.

Blood pounded in Alex's ears, and through the pounding, like surf on a rocky coast, he heard the shouting of the crowd. The big wrestler was trying to get his head in a hammer lock. Thinking he must not let him, Alex put every ounce of his strength, every nerve and sinew of his will into one convulsive movement. With a hoarse yell, Dai-suké lost his footing and flew over Alex's head, smashing out of the ring and into the crowd. Alex had won!

"Alex, Alex, by God!" Rutledge, his face dangerously mottled, was kneeling beside him on the hard ground, and Alex realized he had slumped to his knees. His muscles had gone to water, his strength to smoke. "Man, man! You showed that brutal wrestler something to remember!" Rutledge continued. "How did you learn to fight like that?"

"From the men on my father's land. . . ." Sweat poured like rivers from him and he could hardly talk. *I was insane*, he thought. *That sumo could easily have mutilated me!* "I was lucky," he added.

"We're not going to trade on that luck." Alex was aware that many of the crowd had surged forward, muttering. He had beaten their champion and they were not pleased. "We'll get down to the inn straightaway. A hot bath . . . and tonight, a massage, Alex. I insist on

122

it. Otherwise, you'll be of no use tomorrow on the road."

Alex could not have agreed more. He staggered as he rose and, not bothering to put on shoes or shirt, followed Rutledge away from the crowd toward the inn. As he walked, he saw the apprentices gaping at him in awe, the inn servants whispering to each other with wide eyes. "You're going to become a local legend," Rutledge grinned. "Dai-suké is the strongest wrestler in Fukuza!"

His fame had already swept the inn, it seemed. Bowing with extra courtesy, maids showed them to adjoining rooms overlooking a garden enclosed by high bamboo walls. "I'm told that this room has a special bath attached," Rutledge explained. "If you'll be guided by me, soak in hot water at once." He grinned. "It was unwise to fight with Dai-suké, Alex, but I'll never forget how that mountain of a man sailed through the air!"

The bath welcomed Alex with hot water scented by the satin-smooth pine of the tub. He could have stayed in it forever, but, mindful of Rutledge's needs to wash, he forced himself to emerge at a decent time. Then, wrapped only in a comfortably loose Japanese *yukata*, or summer kimono, he went into his room. The sleeping quilts had not been placed on the floor, but the tatami mats were cool and fragrant. He lay down, pillowing his face on his arms, and closed his eyes. Perhaps he slept.

Instinct told him he was not alone. He had

not heard the soft sigh of the sliding door to his room as it open and shut, but he could sense another presence near him. Rutledge? But the heavy man could not move so softly, almost stealthily. A maid would have called at the door. Eyes open, muscles tensed, Alex lay silent, waiting. He had humiliated a local hero today. Had Dai-suké come himself or sent someone else to teach the foreign devil a lesson?

He heard the soft footfall near him, felt as a physical thing the shadow that seemed to flow across his back. Wait, he counseled himself. A little more, and then. . . .

He turned swiftly, coming to his feet in one lithe movement and lunging forward to catch the intruder by the arms. But the form in his grip was not hard and muscular, but soft, rounded, remembered. Its cry of surprise and fear was familiar.

"My lord Alex," she cried. "What are you doing?"

It was Zanna.

Chapter Nine

ZANNA STARED INTO ALEX'S HARD EYES. IT was her fault. She knew she should have tiptoed away when she saw him asleep, instead of coming into his room uninvited as she had. He had a right to be angry, but she had meant no harm. She tried to explain that now.

"I only wanted to cover you as you slept, my lord. The evening has turned cool, and after your bath you might have caught a chill."

He let go of her, but the hard, tight look in his eyes remained. "Where did you come from?" he asked bluntly. "Why are you here?"

Zanna felt as if she were falling from a high mountain, falling with the wind roaring in her ears and her breath stopping from the speed of her descent. Remembering their last conversation, she knew how badly he must think of her. She said, "I was ordered to, my lord, by Kita-san. There has been an urgent problem at the London Company in Kata-yama, and I was sent to tell Rutledge-sama of it."

He turned from her and faced the little fenced-in garden. How many hours had he slept? he wondered. It had turned pitch dark, and, as Zanna had said, there was a cool wind blowing into the room. "Why send you?" he asked abruptly, remembering the highborn lady at the checkpoint so many miles back. "Did you have trouble on the road?"

"No. I had a letter from Kita-san saying that I traveled on Lord Azuma's business." She paused, not knowing how to explain the rest. "I was sent because Rutledge-sama needs to return to Katayama right away. It was thought—it was hoped—that I could be your interpreter in Iwase."

She heard his quickly indrawn breath and was afraid that he would refuse immediately. "Where's Rutledge?" he asked abruptly.

"He has gone. You were sleeping soundly, and he didn't want to disturb you." She drew a deep breath. "I will really try my best to please you, Lord Alex."

"Will you indeed, madam?" He spoke bitterly, and she bit her lip. "Well, it seems as if I don't have a choice. There's no use returning to Katayama when Lord Azuma waits for me."

In spite of her relief that he was not going to refuse her as an interpreter, Zanna felt a small stir of anger. Did he think she wanted to be here? After those words they had exchanged before his departure, she'd sworn not to seek him out, think of him, see him as anything but her duty. But, alone with him, she felt her fine resolves crumbling against a surge of hurt at his indifference and anger at his cold lack of feeling.

"Are you hungry?" she asked coolly. "I have already eaten, but your meal is still hot. If you wish, I will serve it to you."

"Thank you. I'm perfectly capable of serving my own meal."

She was almost grateful for his curtness. It set the mood for their relationship over the next few days. "In that case, I will bring your meal here and leave you." Her voice was as cold as his, as she slid open the screen door of the adjoining room and went to carry in a tray of rice, fish, soup, oddly shaped shells that were heaped in a basket.

"What in God's name is that?" Alex wondered.

"Snails, my lord. It is a specialty of the inn," she told him stiffly, and stiffened further at his exclamation of disgust.

"Snails! Seaweed! Cold rice! By God, what I'd give for a decent meal in a decent country!"

Her gray eyes flashed as she faced him. "I wish the same," she said evenly. "However, it's not possible. You are here, Lord Alex. Getting angry can't change things or—or make me disappear." In spite of her resolve, there was a tremble in her words as she

127

added, "I will do my duty, as I have said. I am sorry about Rutledge-sama, but I had nothing to do with that."

"If you cry, I will send you packing immediately." Alex could not believe that he had said those words, and in such a cold, harsh tone. He felt at sea, adrift, his emotions hopelessly warring between rage that she was there and a desire to crush her in his arms. Damn Rutledge!

"I have no intention of crying," she said, though her eyes were suspiciously bright. "I think you are—I think I dislike you very much, Lord Alex. And if it wasn't for my duty to Rutledge-sama, you could go alone to Iwase!"

She turned and walked from the room, shut the screen doors behind her and stood staring blindly into the darkness. She knew she should regret the things she had said, for they were unforgivable. Perhaps it was this that caused her chest to hurt when she breathed. She felt as if she wanted to cry, but there were no tears in her. All she could feel was a heaviness that invaded her breast whenever she thought of the harshness of his voice and her own angry response. *But,* she thought with a flare of that same anger, *I meant it! He need not have been so hateful.*

She could hear him moving in the other room. Eating, she supposed bitterly. Men could eat and sleep and fight and conduct business at times when a woman could only weep inwardly. Well, she would not become a helpless ninny because of him! She would conduct her business so well and so exactly that he would respect her for it. And she would do her duty to Rutledge-sama and follow all his instructions.

She could hear one of the inn maids next door removing Alex's meal, bringing down the sleeping quilts. The girl was giggling and flirting, and Zanna knew why. She'd heard about Alex's exploits with the sumo wrestler. The fact that she had worried about him at all made her grit her teeth now, and she loathed herself for being concerned for his possible hurts.

His hurts! Zanna drew breath in sudden consternation. She had promised Rutledge-sama—but surely, after what Alex had said, she wasn't bound to that promise? Surely, surely not! She couldn't be expected to go into his room now and offer to massage away his hurts?

The maid left Alex's room with another soft giggle. She could hear him moving around, and then the light in his room went out. Zanna wrestled with her conscience and with herself. Duty was duty, and a promise to Rutledge-sama was binding. And he had been especially insistent on this: "He must be in fine physical condition when he reaches Iwase. Think how Lord Azuma would despise an envoy from England who was so sore he couldn't bow correctly!"

Slowly, Zanna rose to her feet and crossed the few feet to the sliding door. She knelt down and drew a long breath, as if this would give her courage. Then she said, "Forgive this intrusion, Lord Alex."

He did not answer at once, and hope leaped in her that he was asleep. If he were asleep, she needn't follow through on that promise to Rutledge-sama! But then he said, "Come in, Zanna."

She slid open the door and blinked in the uncertain half-light of his room that poured in from the doors that opened into the garden. She realized that there must be a small fountain in the garden, for she could hear the nearby splashing of water against stone and smell the cool scent of wet earth.

"I'm sorry to disturb you," she forced herself to say. "I heard—Rutledge-sama told me—about your wrestling bout with Dai-suké. He told me to make sure your muscles were not aching."

"And if they were aching, then what would you do?" He was lying on his quilts, his *yukata* white against the darkness. Propped up on one elbow, he watched her as she swallowed.

"In Isudai, when my uncle was tired from his work at the forge, I massaged his shoulders and back. I did it for Obasan, the old housekeeper who took care of his house."

"And now you will do the same for me." There was rueful admiration in his voice. "In spite of my bad temper and bad manners a while ago?"

The change in his voice frightened her, and

she tried to gather her dignity and her distance around her. "None of that matters, Lord Alex. I was just instructed to make sure you come before Lord Azuma in good physical condition." He seemed to be considering this, so she added, "It was Rutledge-sama's special command to me. May I begin?"

For answer, he turned onto his stomach. "Begin, Zanna," he agreed, and she bowed a little and came to kneel beside him, placing her hands on the small of his back and feeling through the soft cloth the tight, lean strength of muscle and bone. She could sense his tension against her hands and pressed down.

"Does it hurt, my lord?"

He made a noise that could have been a grunt or a laugh. "It is—uncomfortable, Zanna." She pressed again, her fingers sure and skillful, and he said, "You're very strong for a woman."

"I was taught to massage by an old blind masseur who lived in Isudai." Talking helped to quell the effects of his nearness on her, the sensations caused by contact with his body. "The old man was called to ease the aches of mighty daimio and rich merchants, and sometimes I went along to show him the way." She smiled suddenly, remembering. "He explained to me all the important nerves of the body." She hesitated, then added, "If you would remove your *yukata* from your shoulders, Lord Alex, it would be easier."

Wordlessly, he slipped his arms from the loose garment. "Is this better, Snowflower?"

She wished that he had not called her this. A knot of confused warmth and fear had lodged in her throat, but she forced her hands to remain firm as they pressed down over his shoulders. She felt the smooth strength of the shoulder muscles, then registered their bunching as he shifted.

"Your bout with Dai-suké must have strained these muscles," she murmured, kneading and pressing with her fingers and the heel of her hands. "If left alone, they would hurt you tomorrow, but I am going to soothe out the stiffness. Do you feel the difference?"

He said nothing, and she slid her hands down across the hardened musculature of his back. The skin felt smooth and cool to her touch—a smoothness she remembered vividly. Drawing another breath to try to banish such thoughts from her mind, she drew the palms of her hand up his sides, into the socket of arm and shoulder. "Tell me if I hurt, my lord," she murmured.

Suddenly, the passage of her hands was stilled as he turned on his elbow, half sitting up to face her. "The hurt has nothing to do with my battle with Dai-suké, Zanna," he said quietly. "Surely you know what your touch is doing to me?"

Her eyes had become accustomed to the gloom, and she could see the shimmer of his intent blue eyes. His fair hair glistened pale against the rocklike planes of his face. His mouth was unsmiling, tense. She tried to speak, could not. "I only . . . ," she finally managed to get out.

"I know. You only follow your father's instructions. Does he think you so undesirable, so. . . ." Alex shook his head to stop himself, and added, "You had better go, Zanna."

She wanted to go. More than anything, she wanted to leap to her feet and run away from the room and the half-naked man on the quilts. But he held her with his eyes and she could not move. What he had said, what she had answered—none of it mattered. What mattered was the shape of his face, and the curve of his mouth, and the hard, unyielding strength of his body. *It is not only you who hurts*, she wanted to cry at him.

"Aren't you going away, Snowflower?"

That name again, the one only he used, the foolish name that filled her heart with such a rush of feeling that she could not breathe. Without conscious thought, she reached out and touched the warmth of his mouth, and was surprised when he turned his head and kissed the palm, his mouth a strange warmth in her hand. Then, without speaking, he drew her down to him, against him.

She opened her mouth to his as his lips took hers. His breath was her breath, the sensuous battle of their tongues an almost painful ecstasy. He took his mouth away to whisper her name, and to stroke back her hair from her face, stroking downward, pushing aside the collar of the *yukata* she, too, wore. His lips followed his hand, moving to circle her breasts before suckling deep on the upthrust, rosy nipples. Then, shifting his weight, he straddled her, untying her simple sash and drawing aside the edges of her cotton robe, removing the delicate cloth that shielded her loins.

His robe had fallen from him, and in the gloom she saw the perfection of maleness, the broad shoulders, the depths of chest covered with fine gold fur, the narrow, flat abdomen and muscled thighs. And he wanted her. She sensed it as much in his tension as in his fully aroused manhood. And yet, for all his impatience, he held back, still following the line of his touch with cool, sure lips, trailing fire from her nipples downward, kissing with openmouthed kisses her delicate ribs, the curve of her waist, the gentle hollow of her navel.

"Alex, please. . . ." She did not know she breathed this consciously until she saw him tilt his head to look at her.

"Please what, Snowflower? Do this—and this?"

She gasped with pleasure as he cradled her buttocks in his hands, lifting her to him. But instead of the hard press of his man's desire, she felt warm kisses teasing the delicate skin of her inner thighs, moving upward until her body seemed alive with fire. She felt her hips begin to move, undulate to the liquid current generated by his lips and tongue, and the strength of her response made her cry aloud. He held her still, arousing her until she was fully open to him, yearning for more closeness, for the full weight of his body pressing against her, pressing into her.

"Alex, please!" This time, he could make no mistake of her desire. She reached down, twining her fingers in his gilt hair and tugging gently, drawing him closer. He came to her at once, and she could feel his maleness against her, instead of the warm mouth that had teased her so wonderfully.

She did not know that she tensed, but Alex felt it. *Don't think!* something within him cried. *She's here in your arms and she wants you as much as you want her, have always wanted her! Even this first time, she'll enjoy your lovemaking.*

Yet he hesitated, and she felt this hesitation just as he had sensed her uneasiness. "Alex?" she whispered. "What is wrong?"

He kissed her fiercely, wanting to shake his uneasiness. Wrong? But all this was right! Sweet mouth eager for his, warm breasts pressed against his chest, thighs parted for him. Damn it! It was the custom here to take a companion. Rutledge himself had said. . . .

Rutledge—the name beat like a fist against his passion. Rutledge, who took a woman for a companion and then discarded her, took another, slept with roadside wenches without thought to consequence. Was he going to end up acting like *Rutledge*?

"Oh, Snowflower," he groaned, and felt her tremble.

"Alex, I am not made of snow!"

With an effort that left him shaken, he pulled away from her welcoming body. "Neither am I." She stared at the change in his voice, and she spoke his name questioningly as he told her, "We cannot do this, Zanna!"

He drew the widespread edges of her *yukata* together, quickly covering the body still warm from the imprint of his own. He tried to find words that would make sense to both of them. "We are. . . ." In spite of his efforts, he stumbled, started again. "This is an important journey we are on, Zanna. We cannot jeopardize it in any way. You are my interpreter, I am my uncle's envoy here. We must— maintain that relationship."

She sat up slowly and faced him, forcing her eyes not to roam over the body she had seen such countless times in her dreams. Broad shoulders, furred chest and belly, man's desire—she closed her eyes and opened them again to look directly into his eyes.

"If that is what you wish," she said, and was surprised at the softness of her voice. He nodded. "I will get back to my room, then. We must start early tomorrow if we're to cross the river by nightfall. It's said to be wide and deep and very rough."

He bowed his head, unable to trust himself to speak. Desire raged through him still, and he had to clench his fists tight as she got up and slipped soundlessly through the flimsy wood-and-paper door. It would be no barrier to him, and she would welcome him no matter what he had said. He knew that! He held his suddenly aching head, wondering how long his noble decision to stay away from Zanna would last *this* time. Again, he damned Rutledge to the blackest pit of hell. Didn't the man *realize* his own daughter ran the risk of becoming Alex Curtis's "companion"?

Chapter Ten

ZANNA POINTED DOWN THE ROAD. "LOOK, Lord Alex! A procession!"

Her voice had an almost childlike eagerness, and she attempted to twist in the saddle so that she could see better. Alex found it hard to turn his eyes from her to watch the progress of the procession.

It was early morning, and mist, as ragged as white spider webs, clung to the trees by the side of the road. A mountain loomed in the distance, its top half sheathed in the mist. A shrine at its foot, whose red, curved roof was barely visible, seemed to offer benediction. Somehow, all this reminded Zanna of her home in Isudai, and she felt easier, even happier.

Alex misread the shine in her eyes. The poor girl had seldom had a chance to see anything like a procession, cooped up in a mountain

village and then in Katayama! Her eager gray
eyes made him grateful that he'd put a stop to
their lovemaking in time. "Can you see if it's
some lord's triumphant progress?" he quer-
ied, and she shook her head.

"No, not from this distance. But they are
coming toward us, and we will see them well
enough." She added, after a moment, "This
time, my lord, we'll have to get to the side of
the road or into the drainage ditch. It is a very
big procession."

When in Rome . . . Rutledge's words
breathed past Alex's ears, and he scowled.
She looked anxiously at him, so he nodded to
counteract the frown. "I'll be guided by you,
Zanna. You are in charge of my safety and
well-being."

Gravely, she questioned him with her eyes.
Was he joking again? But perhaps she would
never understand him or men from his country. She had been so afraid to face him this
morning, so unsure whether she would find
coldness or rejection. Instead, he had been
the first Alex Curtis she knew—friendly but
without deeper emotion. It was as if last night
had never been.

But it had! Zanna spurred her horse suddenly and rode forward to distance herself
from Alex and the memories of last night.
Confused impressions of hands and lips and
strong arms, and then the thought: *He was
right. If we had become lovers, it would have
done his important mission harm!*

"Are you riding to catch up to the procession?" Alex asked, and she saw he had spurred his roan stallion to catch up with her. "You fill me with admiration. I didn't know riding was one of your talents."

She was wearing dark trousers over her kimono for easier riding, and her head was shielded by a wide, sloping sun hat. It was easy to see the village girl in her as she said, "There was an old, *old* horse in Isudai, and I rode him sometimes. That was how I learned, my lord. Later, I began to be brave enough to ride his son, a fine stallion. My uncle was shocked." She dimpled suddenly at the memory. "He said that girls didn't do things like that."

"What else could he expect from the best mountain climber in Isudai?" Her laughter was clear and unexpected, and he said, "Where were all the youths of Isudai while you bested them? I imagine they were all half in love with you."

He had said it to make her laugh again, but she sobered quickly and shook her head. "No one fell in love with me. They thought my eyes were an ugly color." She glanced up at him, and saw the tightening of his lips. "Of course, they are wrong," she said hastily, afraid that she had offended him. "Gray is beautiful for *English* people."

For you, too, Zanna. He did not say it aloud, but he felt it so strongly that he was sure she must hear the unspoken thought. Yet what she had said made him even more relieved

140

that he hadn't lost his head last night. Zanna had suffered enough as it was.

The procession had by now swung into full view, and Alex and Zanna guided their horses to the safety of the side of the road. They dismounted, and to Alex's amazement the two apprentices with them fell flat on their faces, bowing into the dust. "It's the custom, my lord," Zanna said, but when she would have followed suit, he caught her by the arm and kept her on her feet.

"In England, it's the custom just to bow. Since you are in my employ, you must do as I do."

"But. . . ." She looked uneasy, but curiosity made her crane her neck to see the procession approach. "It must be some sort of deputation, my lord. See? There are the banner-men."

At least twenty men passed by, all holding gorgeous cloth flags and streamers that fluttered and flapped in the wind. After them came warriors, proudly holding bows and arrows and spears. The fighting men were in turn followed by several palanquins carried by sweating bearers. One of them was made of gold leaf, and obviously carried an important person.

"The head delegate," Zanna whispered, her voice awed. She moved closer to Alex as another contingent of mounted knights swept by, most of them staring with curiosity at Alex's stature and gilt hair. These knights were followed by the obvious rear guard: sweating bearers who carried monstrous baggage on their backs or urged pack animals on. "I'm afraid that's the end of it," Zanna sighed.

Alex was curious. "Couldn't all that baggage have been better drawn by horses and carts?" he asked.

"No carts are permitted on the great roads." Carefully, Zanna led her horse back onto the road and waited for Alex to help her mount. "The great roads are made for men and horses only. The shogun feels that heavy traffic will damage the highway."

She tried to continue talking normally, but the pressure of Alex's hands on her waist as he lifted her into the saddle awakened feelings she could not forget. To subdue the rush of emotion she pointed down the road. "Look, my lord. We have company! So many people take the great road each day that it's said one is never lonely on a journey."

Alex was careful not to look at her as he agreed. He had felt her tremble as he helped her mount her horse, and it had answered a deep, continuing hunger within him. "Our traveling companions are certainly a motley crew," he said.

They passed families traveling to Iwakuni, beggars, medicine men, cheerful pilgrims en route to the nearest temple or shrine. Many of these people stopped with them when they rested at a spotless wayside station that noon. Here, while horses were fed and watered and the apprentices gorged themselves on huge bowls of noodles and soup, everyone gathered about to gawk at the golden-haired foreigner. Finally, Zanna felt that enough was enough.

"Countrymen," she said, decidedly, "the English man I am with is a kind person, but he has a harsh temper when provoked. I've known him to work foreign magic when his privacy was threatened!"

The warning was enough to clear the immediate area, except for a thoroughly persistent seller of charms. He had made his rounds of the crowd and had sold very little; now he approached Zanna gingerly. "Missy, since you're traveling with that foreigner there, maybe you need an amulet against the evil eye," he suggested.

"Have you seen *her* eyes?" someone whispered, and the amulet seller looked nervous but soon rallied.

"A charm against the river near Iwakuni, then," he suggested. "It's said that the waters are unusually rough because it's rained all week."

Zanna hesitated. She did not care for rivers or water, and she reminded herself that she could not even swim. But before she could make a decision, Alex asked what was the matter. Zanna explained. "He wants to sell me a charm against the river," she said, and was a little indignant when Alex laughed.

"Don't worry about the river, Zanna. The apprentices and I will take care to see you come to no harm."

Zanna frowned. Alex could seem so superior when he wanted to be! "Don't English people use charms?" she asked.

"Many do. I've never seen the sense of it." He got up good-humoredly and came closer, not realizing that the amulet seller had begun to quake at his approach. "Now, if you wanted something pretty for yourself—like this, for instance—I could understand."

He had picked up a tiny pink shell on a slender golden chain. It was meant to be worn around the wrist, and as Alex held it, it reflected the noonday sun.

The amulet seller was breathless with apprehension at Alex's nearness. "It's a love charm, missy. He gives it to you—he falls in love with you. Never fails!"

Zanna caught her breath, then shook her head almost violently, handed it back to the peddler. "I don't need it. . . ."

Before she could finish, the charm was whisked from the man's brown hand and placed in her palm. "It's a pretty thing," Alex was saying good-humoredly. "I would like to buy it for you, Zanna."

"No, my lord!" she protested, but he was already paying the bowing charm seller who, having made his sale, hurried out of the reach of these foreign devils. *Alex, you don't know what this is for,* she thought, looking at the shell on its slender golden chain. *You would not have bought it for me had you known.* But—there was no way she could give it back.

Carefully, she placed the amulet around her

wrist. "We must make haste to get to the river," she said. "If the seller of charms is right, it will be hard to cross it."

Perhaps the charm seller affected luck adversely, for one of the apprentices' stout horses threw a shoe soon after they left the way station. There was a long search for a blacksmith who could reshoe the beast. They reached the banks of the Nishiki River after sunset. Zanna's heart sank. The river was broader than she had expected, and the current looked fierce. There was no bridge.

"There is a barge that crosses in the daylight," Zanna said.

Alex could see the weariness on Zanna's face and wanted to put his arms around her in comfort. "We'll find a place to stay," he told her bracingly. "I'll go and inquire at the inn."

He broke off then, as he realized several men had come out of a hut built on the river bank. They wore nothing but loincloths and their skin was covered with huge blue tattooing.

"They're river coolies," Zanna explained to Alex, who had a hand on the pommel of his sword. "They carry people across the river on their shoulders."

The largest of the tattooed men had sauntered closer, and he tugged at the ragged edges of his loincloth. "The foreign one is big," he commented, sucking on his teeth. "It'll cost you double for him, missy."

Zanna, about to refuse their offer, felt

Alex's hand on her arm. "Can they really carry us across?" he demanded.

Zanna's nod was reluctant. "He says he can. He says that he and his comrades sometimes have to form a human chain across the river to stop the mighty current from upsetting the barge. He says he and his mates know all the shallows where a crossing might be attempted." She paused and added, "Don't you think, my lord, we should wait for the barge?"

He was frowning. "At any other time, I would agree. But my mission is of great importance and I'd like to travel on some more today." He looked down at her, his frown deepening. "But I will not cross if you do not wish it. This must be your decision, too, Snow-flower."

He had called her by his name for her! Unconsciously, she touched the smooth face of the shell she wore on her wrist. *I must not delay him with my foolish fears,* she told herself. "It will be all right," she said, and with great resolution began to bargain with the river coolies.

In the end the coolies consented to take them across for half their original demand. A price was soon set. Zanna and Alex were each lifted onto the shoulders of their coolies.

"Are you all right, Zanna?" Alex asked.

"Of course, my lord. We're going to start now. The coolie who is carrying you asks that you stay very still, because sometimes a current is very swift and can knock a man's feet from under him if he's not sure of what he's doing."

She wished she was as sure as her voice, for she trembled as her bearer strode into the water. It swished and bubbled beneath her, rising higher and higher—up to the coolie's thighs, over his scanty loincloth and his buttocks, over his waist. Now, she could feel the cool of the dark water coming nearer. With an effort she wrenched her eyes away from the swirling pools and looked for the others.

"Stay still, missy," the river coolie warned. "You wouldn't like to be dumped in this. Rain water's made it mad as a unpaid whore." His slurred words added to her fear.

The other side was nearer. If only the man who carried her could hold up a little longer. She prayed under her breath, keeping her eyes fixed on the stolid, even progress of Alex ahead of her. Suddenly, her bearer gave a little grunt and stumbled. She screamed once, heard the river coolie curse, and fell forward into the water.

The water closed about her, cold and black and *fast!* A current swirled about her legs, pulling her downstream, tugging at the heavy sleeves and skirt of her kimono. She broke the surface once, screaming Alex's name. In a moment she would be dashed against rocks, or carried downstream until she was flung, a drowned corpse, on some sandbank.

But then something caught her, some

147

strength as strong as the current that tried to pull her under. And she felt her face turned upward to the surface of the cold black water.

"Don't . . . fight me!" Alex gasped.

Alex had found her. But he must not stay! The current would get him, too, and they would drown together. "No," she cried, but he held her around the shoulders, dragging her back and away from the terrible sucking current. She heard a babble of voices around her and saw the bobbing fire of lanterns on the shore. She would not drown. Through a roaring in her ears she heard herself whispering his name. "Alex. Alex!"

"It's all right. I saw you go over. Your man misjudged his footing and was caught in a fierce current." He was holding her against him as she clung, coughing and gasping. She was so cold! Every part of her dripped with the icy river. "Are you hurt?" Alex was asking.

She shook her head, and her throat felt raw as she said, "You could have drowned, too." His arms tightened around her. "I'm going to get you to the inn and into a hot bath," he said grimly.

He did not need to speak the language to make his purpose clear. The nearest inn had heard of the near drowning, and concerned maids hastened to lead them to rooms, ushering the way to a great tub. When the maids had left, Alex stripped the sodden riding trousers and kimono from her.

"I can do it myself," she protested through chattering teeth, but her hands shook so much she could not use them. Ignoring her, he stripped the last garment from her and lifted her into the tub. She cried out in pain as the heat of the water tore into her cold skin, but he held her where she was.

"Easy. The water was cold but not cold enough to freeze you. It's shock you're feeling now—the shock of nearly drowning."

"I am afraid of water. I can't swim," she confessed, and then she felt him kneading the back of her neck, her shoulders, laving them with hot water. "Oh," she whispered, "it feels so good!"

Suddenly she was acutely conscious of her nakedness and his nearness. The memory of last night was strong, very strong, and she felt torn between a desire to escape those stroking hands and to take them in hers and draw them over her breasts.

"I'm better, my lord," she said carefully. "I—I think I had better sit here a little longer. But what of you? You're all wet, too."

He seemed to notice it for the first time. "So I am." Before she realized what he was doing, he was removing his own soaking clothes. "Luckily, the bath is big enough to fit two people."

She could not restrain a gasp, but he paid no attention, methodically stripping off shirt and breeches and throwing them on the latticed floor of the bathing room. For a moment, the muscular, rock-hard male body filled her eyes and mind, and then she turned quickly away as he stepped into the tub beside her.

"After all," he was saying, "it was you who told me men and women in this country bathe together."

"Yes, but. . . ." But that was different. She was intensely aware of him beside her, but she was also aware of how cold he must be, how wet. She said, carefully, "I am thankful to you for my life, my lord. You could have drowned with me."

"The coolie who carried you was drunk." His voice was suddenly grim. "If I hadn't been in a hurry to get you warm, I would have beaten him for risking your life."

Suddenly, she laughed, a breathless gasp of merriment. "We should have listened to that charm seller!" she exclaimed. "I knew it! Perhaps he foresaw my dip in the Nishiki!"

He laughed with her, his deep tone mingling with her light one, and she felt some of the uneasiness in her fall away. She realized that he wasn't going to try to touch her, but she was too conscious of his lean hardness beside her, the strong musculature of bone and muscle and sinew that her hands had traced in the dark last night.

Perhaps he felt it, too. "Are you warmed?" he asked, and there was a slight change in his voice.

Zanna did not look up to meet his eyes. "Yes," she said, and thought, *How I am warmed in your presence.* Carefully, she added, "I'm going to find us some dry clothes to wear. You sit here a little longer."

"Are you sure you're strong enough to do anything at all?" He did not try to stop her, though her newly warmed body glowed like the iridescent shell on her wrist. He watched as she rose from the water, which dewed her arms and shoulders and the pale, rose-tipped breasts he longed to kiss. Though the urge to cradle the rounded hips and draw her astride his knees was strong, he did not move. His desire for her was no longer a rage to possess, but a strange mingling of gratitude and fear. Thank God he had reached her before the strong current caught her billowing robes and whirled her away. If it had . . . !

The thought made him sound gruff. "You're just warmed. You should go to sleep at once, Zanna."

The smile she turned to him was as dazzling as always. "I will. I'm very tired, but I'm hungry, too." She paused and added, uncertainly, "It's strange. I don't hurt anywhere or feel anything or even remember too much about—about the river. I just feel sleepy."

Later, after they had eaten and the thick, soft sleeping quilts had been put down in the adjoining rooms and the lights put out, the horror of what had almost happened hit her like a physical blow.

She was suddenly wide awake, all her senses recalling the black water reaching out to her, the current grasping her hair and robes and dragging her down—pulling her down to

151

the slime and cold of the river bed, strangling the breath from her, filling her lungs with filthy, mucky water.

"Zanna—Zanna, it's Alex. I'm here, sweeting." Where had he come from? she wondered. What was he doing here? She had curled herself into a fetal position and was shivering so hard that he had to use effort to break her hold on the nightmare. He drew her close, her back pressed against his chest, tucking his legs under hers as he wrapped both arms around her. "It's all right," he whispered.

He could feel the rapid beat of her heart above his hand, the shaking of her slender body. "You're on dry land now, and safe. I'm holding you safe," he crooned, rocking her against him. "Nothing can harm you, Snow-flower."

She felt her shivering relax against the warmth of him. "It was horrible. . . ." But not so horrible now, not with him here. "You came again," she murmured, made drowsy by the hard welcome warmth against her back and legs. "You came when I needed you."

Though her breathing told him that she slept, she remained as close to him as she could. Though he still felt deeply protective, the warmth of her supple body and the softness of her breasts against his arm stirred him passionately. Yet, it felt different from the overwhelming desire that had swept through him before.

It was too difficult to think this new feeling

through, so he let it go. He shifted, drawing her into the circle of his arms so that her cheek rested against his shoulder, the still-damp silk of her hair brushed against his mouth.

"You came when I needed you," she had said. With his last waking thought Alex found himself wishing that he could always be there when she was in danger and needed him.

Chapter Eleven

THEY REACHED IWASE BEFORE NOON. A QUIET-
er, more countrified roadway led to Lord
Azuma's castle. As they trotted their horses
down this road, people gawked at them and
more than one child ran after them shouting,
"Red hair! Red hair!"

"It seems that they're not used to barbarians from the west, either," Alex commented.

Zanna was embarrassed. "You must excuse
them," she said. All morning she had felt
confused when talking to Alex. Had he really
held her through the night and kept her safe
and warm? She had slept deeply and without
fear. She had awakened to a feeling of trust
and a soul-stopping joy.

"We're almost at journey's end," Alex continued. "I want you to be well when we reach
Iwase, Zanna, and face the daimio." Well,
there was the reason for all his solicitude!

Hadn't he told her how important this mission was?

Alex began to question her about their journey. Zanna had made inquiries at the inn and was able to answer that Lord Azuma's principal fief was famous for cloth dyeing. "Iwase dyers work with cotton and silk, crepe or wool," she explained.

"No doubt this enriches Lord Azuma." Alex was thoughtful. "Is that why he stays in Iwase? Why not visit his other fiefs, at least?"

Zanna leaned closer. "It's said that the shogun is wary of Lord Azuma's power. He makes sure that the lord stays here in Iwase."

"Of course. A daimio like Azuma could raise men and armies." Alex grinned, wryly. "It all comes down to power and wealth, Zanna—and opportunity, of course."

They had come to the end of the humble country road, and now they stopped their horses to admire the sight before them. Iwase Castle, the focal point amid miles of flat parkland and fields, stood proudly against a clear blue sky. Used to the European idea of a castle, Alex was surprised to see that its Japanese counterpart was a many-storied building, each tier narrower than the rest, so that the entire structure seemed to taper like a pyramid into the sky. It was built for defense. From the top of the building a lookout could see for miles around, and the huge, rugged stone wall and wide moat that circled the castle could withstand a siege.

They first found an inn, where they bathed

and changed from their travel clothes, and then approached the castle on foot. Zanna wore her silver and blue kimono, for it was the best she had, and she knew that appearances meant a great deal to nobles like Lord Azuma. Nervously, she inspected the neatly clad apprentices who walked behind them holding the gifts Alex had brought for the daimio.

"I hope that the great lord will see us today," she told him, "but there's no guarantee. We can only state our business and hope."

He smiled down at her concerned face. "I can be a patient man when needs be, my Lady Winter Blossom."

He looked, Zanna thought, like a great lord himself. His court clothes were of brocade: a full-sleeved doublet with slashes showing a taffeta underlining of sky blue. The lace of his white shirt intensified his tanned features and fair hair, and the brocaded breeches and calf-length boots fitted and followed the powerful contours of his big frame. He had wished to wear the Isudai sword, but she had dissuaded him. It was not, she said, the custom of anyone but samurai and nobility to wear swords to a lord's castle.

They were stopped at the drawbridge and questioned. The summons from Lord Azuma was scrutinized. Then they were led over the drawbridge by a deputation of guards who wore the crest of Lord Azuma on the backs of their surcoats, and taken to a gateway in the great stone wall, where their papers were examined again. Alex, watching, marveled at

Zanna's poise. One would think that she did this sort of thing every day, that she was a fine lady bred at court. Not by word or gesture did she show impatience, not even when they were told that the apprentices must wait at this point.

"We will need to carry our own gifts," she said, apologizing to Alex, and he nodded agreement. "They are *very* careful of whom they allow into the castle."

So much was evident! A new troop of guards led them through the stone gateway and up a flight of stone stairs to another checkpoint, still far below the swoop of the castle, and finally to another gate, made of wood so thick that Alex was sure it could withstand cannon. Here, the longest and most detailed cross-examination took place, with the samurai in charge demanding why Rutledge, the director general, himself had not come with the English lord.

It took some time for Zanna to explain this to the man, and Alex saw the samurai looking from her to the foreign barbarian, his insolent, narrow black eyes measuring him as a man. He smiled back, thinking, *If you and I were alone, I would teach you more respect, my lad*. His desire to get the samurai alone flamed to white heat when he saw a fiery blush stain Zanna's cheeks, even though her answers remained cool and remote.

Only the knowledge that he must not jeopardize his mission kept him silent, but as they passed through the wooden gates into a magnificent garden beyond, he turned to her. "What did that man say to you?" he demanded, and saw her blush again.

"It was nothing," she said hastily. "He merely wanted to know if I was your interpreter."

The man had actually demanded whether Zanna was companion to a barbarian. It had not been the insolence that had made her blush, however, but her own tangled emotions. To pull her thoughts away from this she continued to talk. "We are now in the castle gardens. I'm told that the Lady Yoné, Lord Azuma's wife, is an avid gardener."

They crossed the garden and entered the castle itself, where silent samurai formed an escort up narrow stairs and down a dark corridor. Passing huge windows slatted by wood against times of siege, they were ushered into a large apartment, where many people were sitting on the golden tatami. Alex commented on their silence and patience, and Zanna whispered that she was sure many of them had been waiting for hours. "This may be our fate, as I have told you, my lord," she added.

"But at least we're here! And due to you," he added, seeing her quick smile come and go. "Not even Rutledge could have managed all those guards and samurai so skillfully and with such grace."

"You're kind, my lord, but I don't think it had anything to do with me. If Lord Azuma hadn't wanted to see you, no one could have gotten you inside Iwase Castle."

Alex was looking around him. "Where are we, exactly?" he asked, and Zanna explained that they were in an anteroom. "This daimio knows how to live," Alex commented appreciatively. The ceiling was painted red gold, and huge scroll paintings covered the walls. It was bold, impressive, and it smelled of wealth.

As he finished speaking, the folding screen doors to the anteroom sighed open, and a gentleman in ceremonial robes called a name. At once, a group of people rose and, bowing deeply, followed him from the room. The screen doors closed again. "At least," Zanna said hopefully, "he is seeing people. We may be next, my lord."

They waited an hour; two. Outside the waiting room they heard voices and footsteps, and from the garden below came the soft trills of a flute. Zanna leaned close to Alex. "I think that may be one of Lord Azuma's consorts, my lord." She saw the question in his eyes. "One of his lesser wives," she amended. "He has one chief wife, and then consorts. They all have their apartments somewhere in the castle."

Alex shook his head. "And they live in harmony?" he asked, doubtfully.

"I don't know if the women enjoy sharing their lord, but what can they do?" Zanna's voice was practical. "This is the way it is."

"But you don't think it's fair?"

159

She hesitated, shook her head. "No, my lord, but there are many unfair things in a life. I am sure Lord Azuma's ladies know this and are making the best of things."

Before Alex could remember Rutledge's words about compliant women, the sliding doors once more opened. The lord of Azuma would now graciously see the Englishman Alex Curtis and his interpreter.

Merciful Buddha, Zanna thought, *let me do my duty well! Don't let Lord Alex be ashamed of me!* Alex grabbed her hand and held it tightly. She could see the excitement in his eyes. "He's glad to be here and he has confidence in me," Zanna thought, and felt her spirits soar.

The gentleman who had called their names stopped them before another door. "You will approach the lord Azuma on your knees," he instructed. "You will remain kneeling until he so signals. If he motions to you, you may then address him."

Zanna explained protocol to Alex. Together they went down on their knees as the doors slid open. Zanna, head down upon her joined hands, did not venture to look up but heard Lord Azuma's voice telling them to approach.

The lord was sitting on a golden dais on a jade green cushion. He was a small man, but he wore his kimono of gold cloth and stiff ceremonial trousers like a king. The dazzle of his robes kept Zanna from realizing at first that the room was lined on both sides with samurai and courtiers, who knelt on their cushions and awaited the daimio's orders. They watched cautiously as Alex and Zanna approached the dais of their lord.

Several yards from the dais, they were told to halt. Bowing again, Zanna began to translate Alex's compliments and greetings. Lord Azuma listened, his head a little to one side like a golden bird. Then, he replied.

"He is taller than the director, Rutledge. He has the look of a lord, and I understand his uncle is a very powerful man in his own country. I am glad to welcome him to Iwase, and would talk more with him. Ask him his reason for coming to Japan."

Alex now launched into the purpose of his trip to Katayama and Iwase. Zanna translated quietly, expressing Alex's desire for more trade, for a cooperation between the two islands. When he came to this, Lord Azuma stopped him.

"He's talking about the Hollanders, of course. I suppose he wants me to have them crucified, or at least expelled from the country." When this remark was translated, Alex shook his head. The Dutch were rivals in trade, he answered. As rivals, there would be disagreements, naturally.

"But all I ask for the London Company is that we are allowed an expansion of our present trading rights here in Japan. I ask for a chance to prove ourselves equal or better than the Dutch East India Company. In the end, this chance would benefit both England and Japan."

Zanna translated carefully and was relieved by Lord Azuma's nod. "He says you speak well," she told Alex. "He says that most Europeans are a bloodthirsty lot and that this tires him." Then, as Lord Azuma waved a hand, she instructed Alex to bow deeply. "This audience is over."

"But I haven't said half of what I need to say!" Alex objected.

"You will have a chance—later. Lord Alex, you have made a wonderful impression on the daimio! He has asked us to remain in the castle and join him at his evening meal." She allowed herself a satisfied sigh.

Zanna and Alex did not long wait until the hour of Lord Azuma's feast. This time, their samurai escorts were courteous and even respectful when they were summoned. No doubt, news had circulated that the tall foreigner and his translator were in favor. "The lord and his ladies are in the moon-viewing pavilion," a samurai explained, as they led the way through the many corridors of the castle. "It is Lord Azuma's custom to spend some time there before going in to eat."

When this was translated to Alex, he could only shrug. "Now I am completely lost. And you, Snowflower?" Zanna nodded, unhappily. "No matter. Remember that the two of us together are a match for a hundred moon-viewing pavilions!"

He had hardly spoken when they came to a large apartment with screen doors opening into the garden. Flaring torches and round paper lanterns decorated the entrance to the apartment and lit a white stone pathway that led away into a clearing. Here stood a simple thatch-roofed, open building. Though this was in darkness, they could see the glitter of robes worn by Lord Azuma and his court.

Following the samurai's lead, Alex and Zanna walked to this building and bowed deeply. "Come up, come up!" Lord Azuma directed. "You are just in time for the viewing." He motioned them to take their places on silken floor cushions, then asked, "Has Lord Alex any knowledge of moon viewing?"

Zanna shook her head, and the daimio pointed to the silvery glow that just burnished the trees and bushes that grew about the thatched building. "In a few minutes, the moon in its beauty will rise above the trees. It is our custom to watch it from this pavilion and write a poem which is inspired by its splendor." Glittering dark eyes moved from Zanna to Alex. "I would invite the Englishman to participate in this ceremony."

Zanna knew that this was not some idle game Lord Azuma was playing. Why? she asked herself, and knew the answer. Lord Azuma wanted to see what Alex would do, how he would react to the unexpected. Keeping her voice quiet, she translated the lord's remark to Alex, adding, "Be careful, my lord. I think it's some kind of test."

Alex was silent for a moment, and then he bowed. Zanna could see the gilt of his hair in the growing light of the moon. "Tell Lord Azuma that I'm honored at his invitation and hope to prove myself a fair poet," Alex said.

This answer seemed to please the daimio. He ordered that paper, ink and a fine Japanese brush be brought for the English guest. As Alex took the brush and dipped it in ink, he smiled into Zanna's worried eyes.

"Do you know that moonlight turns your eyes to silver? Now *that* would be a better subject for a poem. 'Silver in my lady's eyes. . . .'"

"Please don't joke!" Zanna said uncomfortably. "Lord Azuma is a clever and guileful man. He's watching every move you make."

Alex was aware of the daimio's scrutiny. Was Lord Azuma simply testing his wits and his reaction to an unfamiliar situation? he wondered.

The ladies seated next to their lord now murmured in pleasure. Alex himself was momentarily diverted by the splendor of the moon. It rose over the tops of the trees and bathed the occupants of the pavilion in translucent silver light. Beside him, he heard Zanna's whisper: "How lovely!"

It's the same moon I've seen in England, Alex thought, and suddenly he knew what Azuma wanted. Carefully, he picked up the brush and dipped its point in ink. When he had done writing, he heard Lord Azuma give a crisp command.

"He wants to hear your poem," Zanna whispered. "If you will give it to me, I'll translate as best I can."

The pavilion suddenly seemed to have fallen quiet. Zanna's voice was determinedly calm and clear as she read a translation of Alex's verse. "East moon or west—silver, it falls everywhere."

Alex looked at the daimio. The man's face showed no emotion, and he was suddenly afraid that he had not read the man right after all. But then, the daimio began to clap. Soon, the entire crowd in the pavilion applauded.

Zanna leaned close, her voice weak with relief. "He says that he is pleased that you are a man of wit, as well as diplomacy. He says that he esteems a man who does not laugh at the customs of another country and can think of the harmony that could come between Japan and England." As the daimio rose to his feet, she added breathlessly, "He is ready to go into dinner now, but he has told me he wants to speak to you again."

Chapter Twelve

"I HADN'T THOUGHT YOU COULD BE SO CLEVer!" Zanna breathed.

They were walking homeward after the long, ceremonious dinner had come to an end. It had been a successful evening. Lord Azuma at table was a jovial, almost thoughtful host, and they had been plied with sake, excellent food and entertainment. Lord Azuma had questioned Alex about England and the London Company, but had steered clear of any business talk, instead expressing a desire to see Alex again in a day's time. Acceptance, hospitality and a private audience, all in one glorious, heady day!

"It's more than I ever expected," Alex admitted, and laughed out loud as Zanna actually gave a little skip beside him. She looked about twelve years old, and her eyes were sparkling in the uncertain light of lanterns held by the two sleepy apprentices. "What was that for, Madam Snowflower?"

"I am glad for you," she said frankly. "I am also glad that I was able to help. I've been so afraid. . . ."

Suddenly, she stopped talking as Alex gripped her shoulder. "Hush," he said softly. "Stop walking."

"What is it?" She strained her hearing but could make out nothing but the sigh of a warm night wind that had blown out of the great parks surrounding the castle. "It is dark," she went on nervously. "I think we'd better get back to the inn, my lord. There may be thieves about."

He nodded, and they began to walk again, but quicker, and without any of their earlier pleasure. Zanna could read tension in Alex's movements, and her every sense was pitched to catch the slightest change in sound or sight around them. "Alex," she whispered worriedly, "there is nothing!"

And then she heard the soft slap-slap of straw sandals on the road behind them. "Someone's following us, has been since we left the castle." Alex's voice was quietly grim. "Zanna, we aren't far from the inn. You and these two hurry ahead. I'll come after you."

"No!" she protested. "What can you do? You don't even have your sword—I made you leave it at the inn!"

The apprentices had heard the footsteps too, and were already ready for flight. Zanna spoke to them softly, sharply, and they pulled

167

themselves together, moving closer to Alex and holding their lanterns high to try to pierce the darkness all around. Suddenly, one of them let out a scream and pointed.

"Here they come!"

Zanna saw them at the same moment— dark shadows running toward them swiftly, sandals slapping the dirt road as they came. "They're all around us!" she screamed.

One of the apprentices turned and fled toward the inn, shouting for help, but the other began to flail his lantern as a weapon, shouting defiance of the faceless shadows. Then into the bobbing ring of light sprang a huge mountain of a man with flat, brutish features and cruel little eyes. In his hands he carried a huge wooden staff, and Zanna realized he was dressed as a traveling monk.

"Get behind me," Alex shouted at her. At the same time, he lunged at one of the shadowy attackers, and she heard the sound of tearing fabric, a blow. The next moment, Alex had seized the man's weapon, a stout stick, and was using it to disarm another of the attackers who had hurtled down at them. As the man shrieked in pain, his weapon clattered to the ground. Zanna seized it, almost without thinking, and realized she held a stout bamboo pole in her hands.

Several attackers charged toward her and she struck out, protecting Alex's back as they came with weapons upraised. One of them had a sword. She saw the glint of the blade in the moonlight and struck out with all her

168

strength, deflecting the wicked point. She gasped as something thick and hurtful caught her shoulder and arm, and dropped her bamboo staff. She went down on her knees at the same time as Alex turned, drawn by her outcry, and caught the full strength of the raised swordblade on his stick. Zanna heard the weapon clatter to the ground. When Alex straightened, the sword glinted in his hand.

"Now," he said softly, and his voice held that deadly gentleness Zanna remembered. "Now, it's more even."

The second apprentice had succeeded in fending off his own attackers, and bent over Zanna. "Miss—are you all right?"

Alex hoarsely called out, "Zanna, are you hurt?"

Her shoulder was on fire, and her arm numb. "I'm well. Don't worry about me. Alex —look out!" she screamed, for the huge manmountain was now plunging at Alex and brandishing his staff.

Alex fought off the blow with his sword, which shattered. Zanna saw the huge fellow raise his club again and she stumbled to her feet. Hardly realizing what she did, she snatched the lantern from the apprentice and flung it full into the man-mountain's face.

He roared and went backward, and then Alex threw himself on top of the struggling giant. As they rolled on the ground, Zanna heard shouting in the distance. Help was coming!

Alex had succeeded in pinioning his massive attacker's arms. "Are you all right, Zanna?" he shouted, and she told him she was. "You saved my life," he added. "Without you protecting my back, I'd have been a dead man!"

She knew she should reply but could not. She was suddenly breathless and dizzy, and images flashed in and out of the dark before her. She sank down on the road, thankful only that Alex had survived this attack. In a moment, she felt arms around her, lifting her. Then, Alex had scooped her up and was carrying her toward the inn.

"I can walk . . . ," she murmured, but he did not even listen to her.

"Just rest," he told her. "The townspeople will make sure that big lout doesn't escape until the daimio's samurai get here. It's Daisuké, the wrestler fellow I bested in the sumo ring. I suppose he had a grudge against me for making him lose face among his admirers."

Her reply was a murmur. His arms were welcome, but the pressure of his chest against her aching arm and shoulder was so painful that she could hardly keep from crying out. "I can walk," she tried again. "I was just a little faint. Truly."

He did not set her down until he had carried her into the inn and reached her room. Then, he frowned down at her white face. "You *are* hurt," he said grimly. "Where?"

He would not listen to her protests and, noticing her wince as he unwittingly touched her arm, pushed up the flowing sleeve and stared at the huge, raised welt on the white flesh. "It's nothing," she said, for his eyes had gone to hard blue stone and there was a whiteness around his mouth. "But you, my lord! You're bleeding!"

"A scratch. What else did they do to you?" He inspected her equally bruised shoulder and turned toward the doorway of the room with murder in his eyes. She caught his hand with both of hers, demanding to know where he was going. "To find them," he replied tersely. "Azuma's samurai should be out looking for them by now. I'll help them."

"No, please. No more—." The violence, her fear for Alex's life, the tensions of the day, all churned up within her in one unbearable surge. She could not keep the tears back. As she wept, he turned back to her and whispered her name as he drew her to him, cradling her face against his chest.

"I can't bear to see you hurt," he said, and for the first time since she had known him, she heard the tremor in his deep voice. "I *will* not have anyone hurt you."

Not even myself. He knew he should let go of her, should go to his own rooms or at the very least call in one of the inn maids to minister to her hurts, but he could not. It was as if she were a part of him, the softness of her an extension of his own hard body. *I* must *not do anything to hurt her,* he thought, and as he did, she spoke.

171

"Back there, I prayed—that if anything were to happen to you, it would happen to me, too."

She tipped back her head to look into his eyes, saw the intensity there and knew his thought. She trembled but would not move from the circle of his arms, and raised her face for his kiss. But instead of the passionate pressure of his lips, his mouth was soft, barely brushing hers. "Snowflower," he said, unsteadily, "if you'd been hurt, I doubt if I could have borne it."

With a surprise that jolted him to the core, he knew he meant it—had never meant anything more. "I love you," he said in wonder. "I think I love you more than my own life."

She could think of nothing to say but his name, and then there was no need for words. His lips pressed hers, the texture of his mouth so sweetly familiar now, the shape and taste of his kisses so much a part of her they were like the beat of her pulse. He kissed her slowly and passionately, tongue and teeth and breath all joined in gentle torture as her longing for him rose higher, still higher, till she was dizzy again.

"Do you love me, Zanna?" he asked, and she thought, *Do you need to ask me, my lord? Haven't you known all this a long time?* She wanted to tell him, show him in a hundred ways how much she loved him, but voice and touch failed her. She could only whisper back his name, kissing him with small, passionate kisses as her lips remembered the taste of his eyelids, the contour of his bold nose, his jaw, his mouth.

As in a dream she helped him remove the ornate sash from her waist, and let the silver blue kimono crumple to the floor. She pressed against him, feeling the fine golden fur of his now-bare chest and belly chafe sensuously against the thin material of the chemise that covered her breasts.

She would have pulled it off, but he stopped her, holding her hands, running his tongue and warm, open mouth over her barely clothed nipples, teasing gently until she could not bear the sweet torment longer. Then swiftly, impatiently, he bared her breasts and stripped away the gaudy underpetticoat, so that she stood before him clothed only in the shadowy clouds of her dark hair and the white fold of cotton about her hips.

His clothes were easier to remove, and she murmured his name again, her eyes wide and silver in the light of the dim lamp as he stood before her in the full power of his passion for her. He would have pulled her to him, but she held him off, her gaze holding his as she traced the contours of his body. Broad chest, furred belly, rock-strong thighs. Her slender hands stroked his manhood.

He groaned against her lips, his body tense with desire for her, but he held himself in check as he lowered her gently onto her quilts. She raised her hips to help him as he slid away the cloth about her hips, and then raised her arms to draw him down to her.

She had thought they would come together swiftly, with a passion equal to the drumbeat in her blood. But there was no hurry in his kisses, and he let his mouth and hands love her as if this was all he wanted and all time was before them. As she returned his kisses, she felt as if she were drunk.

"What is it, Snowflower?" he asked her tenderly, and she smiled tremulously up at him.

"I think I feel a little drunk. A little dizzy."

He chuckled softly, touching lips and chin and curve of throat with his mouth. "And I. I don't think I can get enough of this kind of sake, Zanna. Even though I doubt it'll go to my head. . . ."

She giggled, and the tenderness of this shared humor lightened their passion, made her pleasure even more intimate, sweeter. She held his golden head close to her breasts as he took his pleasure from the rosy, tautened nipples, but when his lips roved lower, she shook her head.

"Not now, not now my Alex. I—I think I will die if you do not come to me now. I want you so much!"

Wordlessly, he drew her beneath him and took her mouth in one long, mind-drugging kiss. She felt the weight of him, the insistent hardness between her thighs, and instinctively lifted herself to meet his desire with her own. She tensed a little at his first thrust, and he stopped, caressing her breasts and her

174

inner thighs and whispering her name between kisses.

"Snowflower, I love you," he murmured,
and began to move within her carefully, gently. She knew he was afraid of hurting her,
that he loved her enough to curb and rein his
own desperate need of her, and she felt a rush
of fierce joy in her own womanhood.

With a gasp of mingled pain and pleasure,
she pressed herself against him, taking him
deep within herself. Ecstasy mingled with her
joy, and she felt the pounding of his heart
against her breast as he moved with her,
within her, as he cried her name.

"I love you," she whispered, then. "I love
you, my Alex, now and for always."

There was no need for more words. Only the
ancient rhythm of their bodies and the ecstasy
that caught them both and whirled them
away.

Later, they lay close, arms entwined,
breathing softly. Zanna moved her head
against Alex's chest and wondered at the days
of confusion, the misunderstandings, the
questions to which there had seemed to be no
answers. Why? she wondered, and realized
that she had spoken aloud when Alex's lips
brushed her cheek.

"Why what?" he asked, lazily.

She turned her cheek to kiss his chest, and
rubbed her lips against the soft golden down
that covered the great muscles. She felt

weightless, as if she had been taken out of her old body and set free to experience, with all her senses, the rapture of being alive. It was as if Alex's love had brought her into flower after a long time of frost.

"Why what?" he repeated again, and she sighed as she tried to put her thoughts together. It was so hard to think at a time like this, easier to feel. She wanted to sink back into the world of senses, hear the sound of summer insects in the summer night outside, listen to his breathing, smell the distinctive, clean male smell of him mingling with the scent of pine and spruce and the warm grass scent of the tatami mats.

"I was thinking it has been such a waste," she said, and could not go further; but he seemed to understand.

"I know. I, too. I've wanted you ever since we first met on the pier at Katayama, I think, but what I didn't know was in what way I wanted you." She looked puzzled, and he stroked the silky hair from her face. "There are many ways of wanting a woman, Madam Winter Blossom. I have wanted you as a mistress. . . ."

"A companion," she said, nodding. "I understand how it is," she added quickly, as he winced, "and it does not matter." She wanted to tell him that she did not care how he wanted her, that she had nearly broken her heart thinking that he did not care at all, but he stopped her.

"There are other ways to want, Zanna. I

want you to be mine and stay with me always."

She smiled at his words and his earnestness, but something in his speech made her sad. Had Rutledge-sama ever said these words to Oyuri? *Mother,* she thought, *I hope he did!*

"It's all right," she said softly. "I will be with you as long as you want me, my love."

He hushed her by kissing her, his teeth nibbling lightly against her full lower lip, swollen soft with after-passion. "I want you forever," he said quietly. "Zanna, I don't want you as a companion. I want you to marry me."

It took her a full moment to take in what he was saying. Then, she pulled a little away, shaking her head. Seeing this gesture, he hesitated. "Don't you *want* to marry me, Snowflower?"

"Alex, it's not necessary! I love you," she went on simply. "There's no need to offer me marriage." He started to speak, but it was she who hushed him now. "I know you come from a great English family, and I am only Zanna. I have no dowry. I can give you nothing at all. Alex, what would your family and Lord Jasper say if you brought home such as myself as wife?"

The thought sobered him, angered him because she spoke more truth than he liked. But he brushed it aside. "My family would love you. How could they not? Why do you speak like this, Zanna?"

Her lip quivered, but there was a curious

dignity in her as she half sat up on the quilts and looked down at him. "I don't want promises," she said softly, "only your love for a little while. I can give you nothing but myself, and so I only want a little of yourself in return."

He spoke more surely, smiling into her grave gray eyes. "You won't get a little, girl; you have the lot! And someday, God willing, children of our own." He touched her lips, silencing her. "I love you, and if we have till the end of our days to show each other how much, it will be too little. I want you for my wife, Zanna."

He drew her down to him, and she came and lay against him, her face hidden in his neck. He held her close and stroked her long, dark hair, marveling at the complexity of his love for her. He wanted to hold and protect her forever, and yet he knew from his newly awakened blood that he could never slake his passion for her.

A little movement against him proved that Zanna shared his feelings completely. "You're very tired," she murmured, and he detected a mischievous note in her soft voice. "You've done a lot of things today. Perhaps you should rest now?"

He grinned in reply and began to kiss her softly, knowing now how her body responded, how it moved, what evoked the soft moans of desire that fanned his need for her to a fine white heat. "Perhaps we both should rest, madam. After all, we have to see Lord Azuma again tomorrow. But we have unfinished business, you and I. You haven't said you'll marry me."

She tried to squirm out of his arms, but he held her close, his lips teasing, tantalizing every inch of her body. "Alex, no," she told him. "You must not. We must talk about this. I cannot let you do something that you will regret. Really, my love, you mustn't. . . ."

She gasped, then sighed as his lips caressed her nipples, bent lower. "No need to talk, Snowflower," he said huskily. "Just say, 'Yes, Alex.' "

"But I cannot. You are—oh, my love, please. I can't think."

"Will you marry me?" he asked, and she sighed deeply. "Does that mean yes, Zanna? Or must I convince you more?"

She gave a laugh that was half sob. "I wish you will convince me more, Lord Alex. I think I will need a great deal of convincing."

He paused in his caresses, leaned over her and whispered, "Say it, Snowflower. Say. . . ."

"Yes, Alex. Oh, yes. Only love me again."

Chapter Thirteen

LORD AZUMA WAS QUICKLY INFORMED OF THE attack. The next morning at dawn a contingent of samurai wearing his crest arrived at the inn and informed Alex and Zanna that they were there to escort them to the castle later in the day. They would be at their disposal for the remainder of their stay in Iwase.

"Though that great fellow, Dai-suké, is in prison, my lord is going to take no chances that you may be attacked again," the samurai leader explained. "Dai-suké is being questioned now. That huge tub of fat will soon tell us all he knows."

But apparently Dai-suké wasn't one to talk easily. When Alex and Zanna faced the lord of Iwase early that afternoon, they were told that nothing about their attack had been learned. "No one likes trouble on his land, and this attack on a foreign visitor is inexcusable," Lord Azuma said angrily. "I will have your assailants, you may be sure of that! I have put a careful watch on every checkpoint up and down the great road, and some of my men are waiting by the river near Iwakuni. They won't escape me!"

Though grateful for his concern, Zanna could not help but recoil from the cruel glint of Azuma's eyes, the angry flush along his narrow cheekbones. Had those men not threatened her Alex's life, she could have felt sorry for them.

Her Alex. She looked at him quickly—a fleeting look as loving as a touch of her hand— and he turned to her so that their eyes met. Last night had really happened, with its coming together, the spoken endearments, the promise of love. And this morning—Zanna felt her cheeks warm as she recalled the leisurely awakening and the long, sweet loving. So strong was that memory that she could almost feel the touch of his lips on hers.

"Ah." The daimio's murmur diverted her from her dreams and she glanced at him, embarrassed. To her surprise he was smiling. "Let us continue on to more pleasant topics," he said. "Youth and beauty can't concern themselves with death. We will talk about these trade concessions *your* Englishman wants."

Zanna blushed at Azuma's shrewd emphasis. But though she was embarrassed at having been so transparent, she was delighted at what the daimio was saying. He would, he told her, be willing to expand the London Company's trade agreements in Katayama to include his fiefs near Fukuza and here in Iwase. This meant that new branches of the London Company could be set up in these places, and the volume of trade between Englishmen and Japanese increased.

"I can't grant England a monopoly, however," Lord Azuma continued. "There are some in my country who feel that monopolies, given to one great trading power, are the answer. Others feel that all foreign traders should be expelled from Japan. I myself stand in the middle of these two arguments. I feel that trade with many countries is in the best interests of this country."

Listening to Zanna's soft translation, Alex found himself agreeing with the daimio. When he had finished, Alex bowed his agreement. "That's all I hoped for—a chance to expand, an opportunity to show what the London Company can accomplish. Perhaps in a few years Lord Azuma will see how profitable our association can be and allow more expansion in his fiefdom."

The daimio listened, nodded, then clapped his hands and called out an order. Almost instantly, a pretty young woman in court attire came gracefully into the room, carrying something in both hands. Alex glanced at Zanna questioningly, and she explained that these were gifts from Lord Azuma. "Probably for your uncle, my Alex. You must prostrate yourself with exclamations of thanks before you take the gifts."

But, to Zanna's surprise, the gifts weren't all for Lord Jasper. Though the very valuable gold pipe and lacquered box were placed in front of Alex, a larger gift, wrapped delicately in rice paper and banded in silver, was carefully put before Zanna. Lord Azuma laughed aloud at her amazement.

"Well," he said indulgently, "you have done your task well. I have learned that you're the natural daughter of the director general in Katayama and have lived in the country all these years. I always admire intelligence and loyalty, and reward it when I can." He made a motion with a thin hand. "Open it."

Inside the delicate paper was a kimono of Iwase dye, a garment that caused Zanna to gasp in astonishment. The silk pongee material was chastely white, and over it had been drawn or stenciled designs in blues, mauves, lilacs and rich purple interlaced with silver and gold thread. It was a garment fit for a princess, and within the neck folds nestled a square of paper with Lord Azuma's crest on it.

"My lord, I can't accept—it's much too fine—I don't know what to say," Zanna stammered, but Azuma had lost interest in this feminine reaction and was talking again of Dai-suké and the other criminals.

"I imagine that your plans are to return to Katayama within a day or so. I will send my samurai with you until Iwakuni, at least." He shook his head, and a deep frown made his eyes cold and rather cruel again as he added, "I can't understand why they would attack strangers on my land." He tapped sharply with his closed fan to signify that the audience was at an end, but then seemed to have an afterthought. "Tell your man to watch his back," he said briefly. "He may have enemies who hire other men to do their work."

Zanna translated the daimio's warning to Alex, but she herself heeded it most. Alex was too pleased with the success of his mission to be worried about some footpads who had attacked them in the night. And, he reasoned with her, Azuma's men were to travel with them as far as the river. "Are you afraid I can't protect you the rest of the way?" he added. "I promise to hold you close to me all during the night and never let you out of my sight during the day."

As if she were afraid for herself! Zanna's early training kept her from blurting out that he was being foolhardy. But you did not speak thus to a man, especially not the lord to whom you had become companion. For no matter what Alex said, she knew it was true. The talk of marriage was poetic, beautiful, and perhaps he even believed it. But—! Zanna sighed and counseled herself to be realistic. Even if Alex was serious about this madness, she could not let him go through with it. What would his uncle in London do? And Rutledge-sama?

She said nothing to Alex about her

thoughts, and when she lay in his arms at night, she blocked her own misgivings with passionate loving. She let Alex talk of their future plans, the possibility of his staying on in Japan and heading one of the new branches of the London Company in Iwase or near Fukuza. She thought she was pretending very well, until one night on the way back to Katayama he accused her of dissembling.

They had traveled all day with their samurai escort, bidding them good-bye at the river. Because Zanna could not face crossing in darkness again, they had settled into an inn to await the barge at dawn. They had bathed together, eaten together, and now lay together on soft futon listening to the sound of summer cicadas dreaming outside in a dark that was heavy with the scent of flowers. Zanna was weary, half-asleep, but Alex insisted on talking to her.

Drowsily, Zanna heard him making plans for their return to Katayama. "I will tell your father at once, of course," he was saying. "I want to marry you as soon as possible. As soon as the arrangements can be made."

If she had not been so tired, Zanna might have been able to keep up pretenses. But she could not help a small gesture of doubt, an ever-so-slight drawing away from Alex's cradling hardness. But the tiny movement was enough. "Why not, my love?" he asked her. "Is there some custom I'm not aware of?"

Customs were a tender joke between them, but tonight she found she could not laugh even for Alex. "There will be astrologers to consult," she said in a low voice. "Nothing in Japan is ever done without consulting the stars. Our horoscopes will have to be cast to see if we will be good for each other."

Alex was interested. "I know many in England who put faith in signs and portents even though the church frowns on such superstition," he said. "Suppose the stars say that we will make each other miserable, Zanna? What then? Which astrologer need we bribe, and what temple do we make some pilgrimage to?" Even now she could not laugh, could not turn to him. The small tension she had always carried within herself was as tight as a fist. She wanted to cry. *Alex, she wanted to weep, let's stop these games! I can never be your wife and you know it.*

"You don't believe in any of this, do you?" Alex said.

The change in his voice caught her by surprise, sloughed her weariness from her. She felt him draw away from her and sit up on their quilts. She half turned to protest his taking away his warmth, and saw in the dim light of the room that his face was hard. "Why haven't you kept faith with me?" he demanded grimly.

"Of course I have kept faith with you!" she cried, indignantly.

"Then why don't you believe what I say to you?" he wanted to know. "Maybe you don't like the idea and are too damned polite to say so! Don't you want to marry me, Zanna?"

She sat up in her turn and faced him squarely. "I love you with my whole heart," she told him. "Isn't that enough?" He shook his head, and she cried despairingly, "Why don't you see that this must be enough for us?"

"If it is enough to play the whore, I have misread you, madam," he said coldly. She began to speak, but he silenced her. "We've been over this before. I know that you have no dowry, that you're not legitimate. It doesn't matter!" Suddenly, unable to bear her bleak expression, he took her bare shoulders in his hands and shook her gently. "Zanna, I want only you, dammit. Not a dowry, not connections by marriage!"

Her head drooped and she whispered, "Alex, I—cannot marry whom I like. Surely this is the same in your country? Rutledge-sama sent me as your interpreter, your servant. How could he consent to allowing you to take a servant for your wife?"

He began to laugh. "Rutledge will dance with joy at being allied to my uncle's family. Now, listen, sweeting, and let's have done. I know you for the daughter of a companion." He felt her quiver, forced himself to continue. "What I feel for you is nothing—do you hear me, Zanna?—nothing like what Rutledge felt for your mother. I love you. I need you."

"Alex," she breathed, and closed her eyes. Could she believe? The voice of her reason spoke shrilly to her, but she only burrowed deeper into the arms that now were around her. *I* will *believe*, she thought. *I* will. Even so, she couldn't help adding, "Even if Rutledge-sama is—will consent, he won't give you a single yen for dowry. A wife should bring her husband wealth."

"But you do." He was smiling, she could tell, from the sound of his voice. "A skin like finest ivory and pearl, eyes fairer than silver, a soft ruby mouth."

She giggled suddenly. "You're talking foolishness, my lord."

"Am I, my lady? But at this very moment I need your breasts with their coral rosebuds, and the smooth, white silk of your thighs. You'll be my mistress, wife, mother of my children." He paused. "Still unconvinced? Should I show you what I mean?"

"Alex," she said low, "I love you so much that I'm afraid."

"When I hold you, you have nothing to be afraid of." He held her closer and started to kiss her, and drew her down to the quilts, their mouths playing variations of the now-familiar game, touching, teasing, drawing apart, joining breath as they shared the same lungs and heart. But when he began to caress her, she drew a little away.

"Alex," she murmured, and he could sense a hint of mischief in her voice, "I protest. You are a great lord and have been a traveler of the world, while I'm an ignorant woman. I think I have to make things right."

He joined her teasing, glad she had put

aside her earlier mood. "How would you remedy matters, Madam Winter Blossom?"

"By being a map maker," she said, and shifted out of his arms so that she was kneeling above him. "Since you are my world, your body is my world. I must make my own map of you."

He kissed her, wondering what she would do, wanting her desperately but eager for the light, warm trail of kisses she drew from the corner of his lips to each shoulder. "This the way my first voyage starts," she whispered. "And here—for here is your heart, Alex."

The crisp gold hairs of his chest tickled her lips, and she sneezed and chuckled and kissed him, moving quickly away when he would have drawn her astride him. "No, you must wait for the entire journey," she chided, and he lay still, caressing her satin-smooth back and smooth, rounded buttocks as she traced the pattern of his muscular frame with butterfly soft kisses.

Her hands were busy, too, tracing patterns over him, her touch now soft and tantalizing, now full of her own desire, so that he groaned with the restraint of keeping from taking her. Lower her lips moved, over his belly, her tongue flicking against his navel.

As her openmouthed kisses on his thighs moved upward, he could not help reaching down and running his hair in the silky tumble of her black hair. Her mouth and tongue brought the swell of his love for her almost to

189

pain of desire for her. He spoke roughly from his need. "That's enough of that journey, Snowflower. I would go on another journey and take you with me."

She came to him gladly, eagerly, and he drew her beneath him, running hard, yearning hands over her firm breasts as she opened to him. "I am here, Alex," she whispered, and cried out his name again as she felt the deep, slow thrust of his love. They were both home, she thought, home from a long voyage, safe in each other's love.

They reached Katayama without incident, arriving back at the Great House at sunset. Old Kenjuro spotted them first and roused the household, so that when their horses trotted up to the great gate, everyone was there to welcome Lord Alex and his party, even Rutledge and Kita.

"Welcome home!" Rutledge was the first to boom. "You've returned quickly from Iwase. From what I'd heard of Lord Azuma, I'd have thought you to be still cooling your heels waiting for his nibs to deign to see you."

Alex was determined not to let Rutledge's heartiness irritate him, but the man's manner grated on him after the long leg of their trip across North Kyushu. "It was Zanna's doing that we came so quickly and with so much done," he replied pleasantly.

Zanna looked at Alex anxiously. Her heart was beating quickly, and she felt a little breathless. She knew Alex enough to realize that he was going to speak to Rutledge tonight after discussion of business affairs. In spite of his reassurances, she felt worried. Suppose Rutledge refused? By the laws of Japanese loyalty, she was bound to obey his commands. And yet, she could not live without Alex.

Sensing her anxiety, Alex turned to her and smiled, his eyes both tender and purposeful. "Rest and refresh yourself," he said gently. "Later, your father and I will need to speak with you, Zanna." Suddenly, she felt very tired and was grateful for Kenjuro's assistance in dismounting from her horse.

"Are you all right, honored miss?" he asked her worriedly. "You look very tired and pale. Perhaps you should take a bath and lie down before you eat."

But Zanna had no chance to do more than bathe hastily and change from her travel-stained clothes, for Rutledge required her presence at the evening meal. They dined in the formal atmosphere of the Chrysanthemum Room. Zanna poured sake and pretended to eat as Alex spoke of the gains made in Iwase. When he came to the new branches of the London Company, Rutledge slapped his thigh in disbelief.

"The lord of Iwase must have taken a fancy to you indeed!" he exclaimed. "It's something I've dreamed of for years, negotiated for years, and it falls into your lap like a ripe apple." He shook his head. "This indeed is news to cause celebration!"

"If you're in the mood to celebrate, there's

more." Nothing could have been easier than the tone of Alex's voice, but Zanna felt herself turn to stone. Even her heart beat slowly, weakly, as he went on. "I've got news for you, Rutledge. Since you abandoned me on the trip, I've gotten to know Zanna better. The result is that we wish to marry."

"Marry!" The incredulity in Rutledge's voice made Zanna turn hot, not cold. *He will refuse*, she thought. *Oh, Buddha, he will refuse*. Desperately, rebelliously, she found herself vowing to follow Alex anywhere.

But Rutledge was still talking. "Marry! My God, Alex, *why*? This is Japan. . . . There's no need to marry!"

"You're talking about your daughter becoming my companion?" The silk in Alex's voice was so obvious that even Rutledge broke off. "I wish to make Zanna my wife. Unless you have an objection?"

Even if you have an objection, his tone implied. Zanna noted the hardness around Alex's mouth. He was furious with the director general.

"Of course I have no objection!" Rutledge was shaking his head. Now, he held out a hand and shook Alex's heartily. "I was surprised, that's all. An alliance with your family!"

Zanna was dazed with relief as Alex reached out to take her hand in his. The warmth of his clasp was tender and reassuring. "I'd like the marriage to take place as soon as possible," he was saying.

Rutledge smiled. "Of course we will have the marriage soon! But we must take all the correct steps. I will first need to legitimize Zanna—." She started, and he nodded at her. "Now that you are marrying Lord Jasper's nephew, that must be seen to without delay. Then, there is need of a great feast to which the local merchants must be invited. At the feast we will celebrate both your betrothal and our decision to expand the London Company to Fukuza and Iwase. Eh, Kita?"

Up till now Zanna had paid no attention to the manager. Now, she saw that he was watching her through shuttered, opaque eyes. There was no joy in his voice, no pleasure as he spoke in badly accented English. "Yes, yes. I congratulate you, Lord Alex. You and—the honored miss."

And as he bowed to them, Zanna had the uncomfortable feeling that Kita was not pleased at this latest development. Not pleased at all!

Chapter Fourteen

"Is the water hot enough, honored miss?"

There was no hint of sarcasm today in Mit-suko's tones, but Zanna could hear sullen envy rising to the surface of the forced polite-ness. "If it's not satisfactory," Mitsuko added, "I'll see to it at once."

"No, it's perfectly fine," Zanna said. She could well imagine the consternation that had shaken the servants' quarters at the an-nouncement of her betrothal to the English lord. Excitement, envy, perhaps spite. Old Kenjuro was the only one who wholeheartedly rejoiced in her change of status from Isudai waif to a daughter of the house.

Zanna closed her eyes and let herself relax in the hot water for a moment longer. She knew she would have to step out and dry herself and then be helped into the magnificent kimono Lord Azuma had given her, but she wanted just a moment longer in which to dream. It was so hard to believe that all this was happening. *I am being readied for my betrothal feast,* she thought. *I am soon to become my Alex's wife.*

Alex. Her body felt the familiar ache that it experienced whenever she thought of him. In the bath water her coral-tipped nipples tautened, and a slow, delicious liquid warmth filled her loins. It hadn't been easy, these last few days, to be away from each other, but they had agreed that they could not share a room together while they lived in the Great House.

"Nor must gossiping servants see me slipping from your chamber to mine," Alex added. Since Rutledge had decided that he would change her legal status by adopting her as his legitimate offspring, her reputation had to be carefully guarded. "We must cherish your good name as I cherish your body."

"Honored miss!" Mitsuko's tart voice pushed its way into Zanna's daydreams. "If you sit in there for much longer, you'll look like a red pickled plum."

Zanna obediently stepped from the bath and dried herself, while Mitsuko carefully removed the cloth hood that had shielded her hair. Today, Zanna's hair had been elaborately coiffured, stiffened with camellia oil and arranged in the great, puffed loops that were the height of Japanese fashion. Mitsuko clicked her tongue as she followed Zanna from the bathing rooms to her new and more elaborate chambers, where the Iwase kimono glimmered on a bamboo rack.

"You should have some combs or hair ornaments, mistress," she said, sounding pleased to have something to criticize. "I suppose nobody thought of buying you any, though."

"The kimono will be fine enough," Zanna said, peaceably. "No one will look at my hair, anyway."

"You'd be surprised what these merchants' wives and daughters will see," Mitsuko said. Spite rose again in her voice as she added, "Some of them knew Oyuri, you know."

Zanna thought of her mother, who had been so young herself when she fell in love with Rutledge. Oyuri had been very close to her thoughts all day, and Mitsuko's sharp remark hurt. She had already considered the merchants' ladies. People of that class had sharp eyes and noses and narrow ideas about morality. *I don't care what they think, it's what Alex feels that's important,* Zanna told herself.

But Mitsuko wasn't done. Carefully dusting Zanna's rosy body with rice powder, she mused. "I imagine those busybodies will want to know why you're marrying a foreigner, mistress." She ventured a chuckle. "Of course, it may be different for *you.* . . ."

"Yes, it is different." This time there was enough steel in Zanna's voice to discourage further talk. In silence, Mitsuko helped to fasten the soft cotton garment around Zanna's hips and add the other immaculate undergarments. She could not restrain a gasp of grudging admiration, however, when she draped the glittering kimono over Zanna's shoulders.

"Now, this is a kimono worth something!" she mumbled. Zanna smiled. The wretched woman was probably wondering what she had done to cause this generosity from the great lord of Iwase.

She said nothing, however, as Mitsuko wound the six yards of stiff brocade around her waist and arranged it into the flat knot at the back. This done, she was about to dismiss the maid when Kenjuro called softly at the door.

"What's he doing here?" Mitsuko said, bristling, but Zanna bade him enter; and the old man's mouth hung open in almost toothless wonder at her appearance.

"Child—I mean, honored miss! How beautiful you look! I would never have recognized you." Water spurted into his eyes and he shook his head. "Your mother would have wept with pride to see you today."

Zanna felt a lump rise in her own throat and was almost grateful when Mitsuko demanded what he was doing there. "I have something for honored miss from Lord Alex," Kenjuro said with great dignity. He spoiled the effect by staring inquisitively as Zanna took a carefully wrapped package from his hand and a folded letter. "Open it, mistress!" Kenjuro demanded.

Zanna tucked the letter into her sash and opened the parcel. Inside was the small silver plum-blossom box she had returned to Alex, and within that box a pair of jeweled combs. Mitsuko sucked in her breath with admiration. "Now, how did he know you needed these?" she demanded.

Kenjuro stuck out his skinny chest. "Of course he knew! They're getting married, aren't they? They're in love!"

Zanna paid no attention to the quibbling servants as she opened the letter and read Alex's firm, sure script. "My Snowflower," it began, "wear these together with my heart."

She refolded the note and placed it inside the folds of her kimono next to her skin. Then, she carefully slid the lovely combs into her dark hair. The unease she'd felt about meeting the merchants' ladies disappeared in the warmth of Alex's love.

But Zanna's courage wavered when, followed by Mitsuko, she arrived at the entrance of the Chrysanthemum Room. Today there was the sound of laughter and talking from within, and as Zanna hesitated, Mitsuko made a little grimace. "There are a lot of guests waiting to see you," she said.

I know! Zanna wanted to snap. Mitsuko knelt to open the door and she stepped inside, her head down like a dutiful, shy maiden. Rutledge signaled her to approach, and she did so, sinking down onto the mats to bow deeply to him and to Alex, who sat beside him.

Alex had initially objected to the seating

arrangements, which would banish Zanna to a woman's table on the other side of the room, but he had been powerless against custom. Today the guests in the Chrysanthemum Room were seated at long, U-shaped tables before the honored *tokonoma*. Rutledge and Alex sat at the table's head, flanked by Umezono and the cadaverous Yamaguchi. Kita sat close by, as black as a crow in his formal silk kimono and stiff outer trousers. The faces of other guests swam before Zanna's eyes as she carefully straightened from her ceremonial bow.

"Zanna." Rutledge's voice was booming, benevolent. "Gentlemen, you know my daughter." A low murmur of curiosity and greeting dinned at Zanna's ears, ebbed away. "Now, go and sit with the women, child," Rutledge continued. "Enjoy yourself."

Zanna caught Alex's rueful, commiserating eye for a second before she bowed again and went across to a table on the other side of the room. As she walked, she unconsciously touched the combs in her hair, proof of Alex's love and regard, and pretended not to see the way some of the women hushed their talk and leaned forward to catch a better look at her. Some whispered together as she approached. Ignoring this rudeness, Zanna bowed deeply.

"Welcome to this house. Your presence gives us all great honor," she murmured.

The women simply sat and stared, their faces blurring before her eyes. *I wish I could run away*, Zanna thought, desperately. If only there were a mountain as there was in Isudai—how quickly she'd take to her heels and climb it to get away from these staring women!

Still, nobody spoke. She took some steps toward the ladies' table. "May I sit among you?" she asked in a bright tone born of despair.

"Of course, child! It's your betrothal party, isn't it?" The crisp, matter-of-fact voice belonged to homely Mrs. Yamaguchi, and Zanna could have hugged the older woman. "Come and sit here next to me, and we'll get you some sake. I know that brides-to-be have to look pale and pensive, but I think you're overdoing it. You look scared to death."

She gestured to a servant, who came and filled the cups of all the ladies. "We'll toast the bride-to-be," Mrs. Yamaguchi commanded.

Cups were raised and a polite murmur ran around the table. Zanna remembered that this kind woman had been the only one who had befriended Oyuri, and was even more grateful to her. If nobody else talked to her, she'd at least have one friendly body nearby! But as the thought crossed her mind, one of the other merchant ladies leaned closer.

"I've been trying to be polite, but I can't keep quiet any longer. Is it *true*?"

"Is what true?" Zanna asked, bewildered, and Mrs. Yamaguchi clicked her tongue impatiently.

"Really, Kazuko-san! Can't you let the poor

girl relax a while before you shower her with questions? I'm not sure that your questions are in good taste, anyway."

The other woman wasn't deterred. "I've heard," she whispered, "that western bar—that people from the west like to press mouths together while making love. Has your husband-to-be done that to you? Has he sucked the breath out of you?"

Perhaps it was the sake she had drunk, but something daring and impish woke in Zanna. The question was so insulting, so lacking in delicacy as to be almost funny. "Oh, yes," she said, seriously. "It is only too true!"

There was a deep gasp from around the table. Now, she could see Mrs. Umezono. The fat merchant's eyes were as round as coins. "Oh, merciful Buddha! You mean, you poor girl, that he's tried this, I mean, er . . . ?"

Zanna dropped her eyes lest the dancing in their silvery depths give her away. "We are taught to cooperate with our husbands-to-be—to a point," she added, and everyone nodded vigorously. "But I can't explain. That would be unmaidenly."

Mrs. Yamaguchi nodded. "You're quite correct, of course. We can't ask any more questions about such an—such an aberration!" She sighed morosely, then brightened up. "When you're a married woman, though, we must know all about it! Out of earshot from these silly girls, of course."

"Oh, mother!" One of her daughters made a

saucy face and giggled. "Anyway, Zanna-san, your Englishman has a beautiful body, no matter what else he does."

"What do you know about men's bodies, I'd like to know!" Zanna laughed with the others, feeling not the hostility she had feared but a camaraderie, an acceptance. More sake was poured for the ladies, but before they could drink from the thimble-sized cups, the door of the Chrysanthemum Room slid open and a late-coming guest was announced. Zanna looked up quickly and was astonished to see that the man was a European—and familiar. *Why*, she thought, *it's the Hollander we met that day Alex chased off the* ronin!

As the thought crossed her mind, the Hollander bowed low to Alex and his host, then came across the tatami to bow before her.

"My dear lady," he murmured in bad Japanese, "my felicitations on this happy day of your life." In equally guttural English he added, "How fortunate that you arrived home safely from Iwase. I hear that there are brigands everywhere along the road!"

Automatically, Zanna stood to return his bows and compliments. Her mind was moving swiftly. It wasn't surprising that van Feinstra knew of their journey or of the attack on them. News traveled fast in Katayama and its environs. But why should he choose to congratulate her and at the same time refer to past dangers? Straightening from her bow, she looked at the Hollander carefully and saw that Alex had also risen to his feet. There was a cold, assessing look of hostility in Alex's eyes.

Van Feinstra seemed ignorant of Alex's feelings. He smiled as he took Zanna's hand in the European way and kissed it. "You will make a beautiful wife," he told her. "I hope that you will safeguard yourself and those closest to you. It would be so tragic if one so lovely should be made a widow."

"I don't like the man or his arrogance," Alex snapped. He paced the length of the director general's rooms, came to a halt and added, "Zanna, you should have told me earlier what van Feinstra said."

"How could she tell you? *What* should she have told you?" Rutledge demanded. "Van Feinstra was there because I invited him. I told you about him, Alex. . . ."

"I know you've had some idea of using the man for working against the Dutch East India Company. I think you're being foolish." Alex's raised hand stopped Rutledge's angry protest. "Think a moment, James! You yourself intimated that that attack on us at Iwase could have been bought and paid for by the Dutch."

"It's *possible*, but so are a lot of things! However, I can't believe van Feinstra was behind that attack. The man hates the Dutch East India Company! Why should he hire men to kill you and thus profit them?"

Alex was not put off. "I think he's working neither for the Dutch nor for us. He's strictly for himself. Perhaps he wants to start his own concern and would like to be rid of Lord Jasper's nephew and the London Company, as well."

Zanna nodded, quickly. "I had that same feeling, Rutledge-sama." She had been so quiet till now that both men looked at her in surprise. "There was something very strange about him today. As if he were daring Alex to start something."

"I think it's time to talk with our Hollander," Alex said, abruptly. "I'd like to ask him some questions."

Rutledge held out a restraining hand. "Easy, Alex. I still think we can use the Dutchman. However, I'm not going to take chances. You're too valuable to the London Company, and there is Zanna to be considered, too. Perhaps you are right and van Feinstra is playing both sides against the middle. If so, my spies will soon find him out. Meanwhile, I want you and Zanna to go to Isudai."

Zanna felt Alex's sudden tension. "Make sense," he said curtly. "This problem is more mine than yours. As my uncle's representative it will little become me to hide in Isudai."

"You wouldn't even go for Zanna's safety?" Rutledge asked, craftily. As Alex frowned, he pressed on. "Remember what van Feinstra said to her! *If* the man is playing us false, those words were a warning."

"He would not dare to harm her," Alex snapped, but Zanna saw the sudden worry in his eyes.

"You mustn't be concerned about me!" she

said quickly. "You must stay here, of course, as you plan. If necessary I will go back to Isudai."

Alex still looked worried, and Rutledge continued quickly, "I'm not thinking solely of keeping out of the Dutch East India Company's or van Feinstra's way, Alex. An English ship is due in Katayama within the week, and I am short a valuable shipment of Isudai swords that are being made for me by Zanna's uncle. I need to have them by the time *My Lady Fair* is ready to load." He paused. "Would it be so bad if you were to travel to Isudai, stay there some days and bring the swords back to Katayama? It would give you a chance to meet Zanna's uncle, eh?"

"Would you like that?" Alex asked Zanna. She could see that he was still tense, and fear for him clutched her heart. She would never ask for herself, but his safety was another matter. If she left him here in Katayama and went to safety herself, how would she bear to hear news that harm had come to him?

In Isudai we would be safe, she thought, as she remembered the great, friendly mountains and her uncle's house. "Oh, yes, Alex," she said eagerly. "Let us go as quickly as we can!"

Chapter Fifteen

"*KATANA,*" OLD YASUTOMO WAS SAYING.

"*Katana,*" Alex agreed. Reverently, he picked up the blade of the untempered steel that the swordsmith was readying for the fire.

It was only his second day in Isudai, but already he had absorbed a great deal of Yasutomo's terms. A *katana* was a slender, flexible samurai sword.

Where *was* Zanna? As interesting as the old swordsmith's craft was, Alex's mind dwelt on Zanna. He could hear her laughing some distance away, evidently helping the old cook and housekeeper, Obasan, with the housework. She laughed easily here in her uncle's home and moved with an unconscious lilting swing that spoke of great happiness.

This was another side of Zanna, and it pleased him to see her so full of carefree joy.

Alex realized he was smiling and that the swordsmith was saying something to him. Zanna had begun to teach him to speak Japanese and he could pick out some key words in conversation, but he hadn't as yet advanced enough to understand Yasutomo. However, from the way the old man was looking at him, he understood he was talking about Zanna. Relying on his tone of voice and expression to convey his meaning, Alex grasped the old fellow by the shoulder.

"Don't worry. I love your niece. I will make sure that Zanna is happy when she's my wife."

"What are you talking about?" Zanna had come up behind him and put her arms around his waist, looking around him to smile up into his face. "You look very serious, my Alex. Is my uncle boring you with his swordcraft?"

He looked down at her and couldn't help grinning as he thought of their first meeting. There was nothing of the snow cool lady now. Her dark hair had been caught at the nape of her neck in graceful carelessness, and her blue cotton work kimono had been tucked up so that the hem came to midcalf above her small, straw-sandaled feet. Her sleeves had been tucked up above her elbow, too, and there was a whisk of soot on her nose.

"What have you been up to?" he asked. "You look like an imp who's just invented mischief."

Like a child, she recounted her morning's

activities. "I've helped Obasan wash clothes by the river, and I heard all the gossip. Who is to marry whom, who *should* marry whom, and so on. Then, I gathered sticks for your bath this evening, my most adored lord. And all this time you've been standing here doing nothing but look beautiful."

He bent to kiss her, and she leaned up to meet the kiss, unconscious of anything but her radiant love for him. From the stooped old uncle came a few growling words. "What did he say?" Alex asked.

Zanna spoke in Japanese before translating. "He says that I should act like a decorous young maiden and not some impudent city hoyden. I have reminded him what he was like as a youth, and added that he is growing old."

She smiled at the old man, who shook his head tolerantly.

"If you are truly happy," he said, "I am content. If this foreigner has made you smile like that, I am prepared to like him. He's not so bad as foreign barbarians go! But bid him attend me, for I am about to start tempering the blade."

Zanna explained, and stepped a little away from Alex so that he could give Yasutomo his undivided attention. With great concentration the swordsmith tested the fire by throwing a palmful of water into its heart. Then, with a grunt, he plunged the blade into the flames.

"How long will he keep it there? How will

he tell when the heat is right?" Alex wanted to know.

"He just knows. The fact that he's showing you how this works is a great compliment, my love." Zanna touched Alex's arm fleetingly, unwilling to be parted from him even at this small distance. "He rarely shows anyone how he tempers a blade."

Alex bent down to whisper, "The heat of his flame is no greater than my own. I've missed you."

"And I, you!" she said softly. "But you must now attend! My uncle always says that this is the hardest part of all. The color of the heated blade tells him when the sword must be pulled from the flames. If he misjudges this, the blade is ruined! Uncle says that the color of the metal must be the same red as that of a sunset sky."

They waited silently, intent. Then Yasu-tomo ordered, "The bucket, Zanna!"

Quickly, Zanna pulled over a heavy iron bucket and positioned it by her uncle's foot. The old man grasped the handle of his sword and pulled it from the flame. Alex noted that the blade did glow a fiery crimson. When the blade was plunged into the bucket of water, clouds of steam filled the air.

Zanna realized that she had been holding her breath. No matter how often she saw this tempering process, it was always exciting, a sort of magic. She was glad to see the awe in Alex's eyes. "I've seen something of swordsmithing," he told her, "but nothing this elaborate! The Isudai swords are the work of a master."

Zanna slid her arm through his and drew him some distance away. "I think that my uncle would like us to go away so that he can work in peace," she said. "He always says that he must have a quiet space of time with a newly tempered blade so that he can examine his soul and its spirit." She paused. "If you like, we can go on a walk up my mountain."

"I will go anywhere where we can be together," he said, and drew her closer to him even though he saw Isudai villagers pointing and whispering. He had caused a great stir with his fair hair and blue eyes, and there had been even more fuss when Zanna's engagement had become known. "I have a plan, Snowflower," he added, as they walked through the village and up a pathway that led away into the hills beyond. "When I return to England, I'd like to see whether my brother, Griff, would be interested in this process of sword making. The Japanese blades are as fine or finer than anything I've seen in Europe. The venture could be a profitable one."

"It is a good plan," she said.

But he had somehow read her thought. "Are you disturbed when I talk about England, Zanna?" he asked, gently. "We have to talk about it sometime. Since England is my home, it would be my wish to take you there. You needn't live there if you don't like it—but there are many places in the English country-side that would remind you of Isudai. Though I'm a younger son, I have enough capital to settle us comfortably. I can see you there now. . . ."

"Tell me what you imagine," Zanna said with a smile.

Alex began to describe his vision. He spoke of the house that they would have. "I can picture you standing near the roses. Your dark hair would be arranged in the latest fashion and the bodice of your gown would be cut low, edged with lace of a whiteness to almost compare with your skin."

"Do you mean women bare their necks and shoulders?" she asked, shocked. "Don't English people have any modesty?"

He grinned and swung her around until he held her in his arms. "Not in dress, I fear! The décolletage is very low, nearly down to the nipples." He traced the line of the imagined garment on her breast, and she pressed closer for an instant to his leaping desire. "Except that I, as your husband, won't permit such a public display of charms meant only for me!"

They kissed, but when his hands would have begun to push aside her kimono, she caught them. "Alex, there is more to our walk," she said breathlessly. "We must walk a little further to reach my favorite glen. It's my secret, and today I want to share it with you."

They had climbed to a place that was bathed in wildflowers. A songbird trilled its heart out in the trees nearby, and the air was drowsy with lazy sunlight and the heavy scent of wild grass. Zanna stepped aside from the narrow path and drew Alex with her up the steeper side of a hill, cutting through tangles of brier, a grove thick with saplings. When he protested, she shook her head at him. "Really! And I thought Englishmen made good mountain climbers!"

"Mountain climbers are one thing, goats another! What use would a mountain goat be to you, Snowflower?" But he let her lead him up another steep mountain and down into an unexpected gully bristling with tall pines. "Enough, Zanna! Where is this retreat of yours?"

"On the other side of the pines." Letting go of his hand, she ran ahead, pushing through the tall, concealing pines. Alex protested laughingly, but his laughter stopped as he, too, broke through the barrier of trees into what seemed to be another world. Sheltered by the pines was a small grassy glade surrounded by azaleas and wild roses. A noisy little brook meandered through, and its bank was thick with dandelions, clover, and huge, shaggy scarlet flowers that bent as if to kiss the water.

"Do you like it?" Zanna asked shyly. "I used to come here often—to play my flute or dream. I don't think anyone else knows of its existence."

He put his arms around her and drew her

212

close, not in passion but with an echo of her own happiness. "It seems indeed like Eden before the Fall," he said, and, when she did not understand, told her the story of Genesis. She nodded thoughtfully when he had finished.

"Perhaps when Eden was destroyed they forgot to take this away," she said softly. "But I have never thought of it as paradise before. Perhaps that was because you were not with me."

He kissed her then, desire filling them so strongly that there was no room for speech. She helped him loosen her simple sash, and the rough work kimono slipped from white shoulders that caught the light of the sun. He placed their clothes on the ground, forming a soft bed over the clover and sweet grass and the warm, sun-scented earth. His passion for her grew as they knelt on this bed, kissing, touching. But when he would have begun love-play, she shook her head, her forehead creased a little in the concentration of her desire.

"I want you to come to me now," she whispered. "I think I am in danger of dying for want of you."

He had meant to take her gently and lovingly, pleasing her and himself in a thousand different ways before losing himself in the undulating warmth of her body. But at her voice his control snapped and, groaning her name, he drew her beneath him. She received

213

his weight, welcoming him deep within her with a passion equal to his, straining against him as she whispered his name.

"Alex, this is enough—all I want," she gasped, drawing him deeper still, kissing and touching and nipping with her teeth, then cresting the wave of passion as she heard his own shuddering cry. Then, she held him close, glorying in the sweet weight of him, running her fingers through his thick hair and drawing in the clean, male scent of him along with the mingling fragrance of flowers and sunlight.

He kissed her lips and chin and throat, then, still holding her, rolled sideways so that they were facing one another. "I dreamt of this a hundred times at least," he said huskily. "I nearly went to you a dozen times in Rutledge's house. And last night it was in my mind to steal into your room and kidnap you as you slept beside that old woman." She giggled at the thought, and he ran a hand down her silken back and sweet curve of buttock and thigh. "But now I am glad we waited. It was right to find Eden together."

He began to caress her breasts again, taking his time now, his fingers sensitive as they traced the contours of the rosy nipples and then lingered on the taut peaks. When he took them in his mouth, she moved against the pull of his mouth and tongue, feeling his desire harden in her again. They loved a long time, prolonging each moment, spinning out the golden threads of their passion by kiss and touch, love talk and shared laughter. And when they could no longer wait, it seemed to Zanna as if she were being whirled time out of mind, soul out of body. It was as if, in one moment of life-stopping wonder, she were free of everything except her very spirit, and that this spirit was no longer only hers but Alex's as well. Of all the times they had made love, trying to become closer and share more of pleasure and joy, she knew that this time had brought them farthest. No matter what happened, she now had a part of his soul and he had all of hers.

She tried to explain that to Alex later as they lay together, loving and drowsing and talking. She was half-afraid that he would laugh at her, but it seemed that in this still place they had come closer than lovers ever had before.

"You're right," he told her. "Loving you—." He tried to find the words to explain that possessing her lovely body was only an expression of his love. He didn't get very far, but she kissed him, satisfied, and rose from his side to walk to the spring to drink. She looked so natural and beautiful that he sat up to watch, and when she brought him cool mountain water in her cupped hands, he licked her fingers dry and kissed them and tried to explain once again. "When I say I love you, Snowflower, it seems different. I've said the words before, but it's never been this way. Perhaps nobody but you and I have said these words before and meant what we do to each other. Perhaps you and I have discovered them together."

She knelt a little distance from him, her dark silk hair ruffling in the gentle summer breeze, sunlight glinting from the silk of her skin and the roses of her breasts. "You wanted to discover more than love when you came to this country," she reminded him, seriously. "You told me that money and power were the only things that mattered. Do you still believe that?"

After a moment, he nodded. "I think they *matter,* but not in the way I did back then. I want those things for you, for us. I would like to see you the proud wife of a rich man, a woman without a care or a want in the world."

She brushed aside her rippling hair and he saw the gentle movement of her breasts, the slim, rose-silk loveliness of her thighs. He reached out to draw her to him, but she was not thinking of lovemaking. "Alex," she said seriously, "suppose I tell you that I want none of those things? I have never been wealthy or powerful. I have been happier here as a poor girl in Isudai than a rich one in Katayama."

He started to tell her that what he was offering her was not the same, but something stopped him. Looking into the deep, silvery gray of her eyes, he spoke words he had never thought to use. "I would do whatever you wanted to be happy. We would live here in Isudai forging swords, if you like. Or on my father's estate—or in that country house I spoke of in England! It would not matter to me where we were as long as you were with me."

Her smile lit up her face, dazzling him as always with its beauty. "And I feel the same," she said, and drew a deep sigh.

She took his hands and kissed them, then held them tight against her breasts in a gesture that was both passionate and tender. "It's that way for me, too, Zanna. Everything that is mine is yours—My heart to love you and honor you, and my body to protect you as long as we live."

Softly in the distance, a deep, gonging sound broke the silence. Alex looked up, startled, but Zanna's clear laughter proclaimed her delight. "Do you know what you've just done?" she cried. "You've sworn to love me just as the temple bells began to ring. That means you must keep your solemn vow to cherish me even if you get tired of me!"

Catching her lighter mood, he leaned out and drew her to him. "I'll never get tired of you, Snowflower, as long as your kisses give me so much pleasure!"

They came down from the mountain at twilight, hand in hand. They made no secret of their joy in each other, and though they did not touch each other when in the village, their love was clear. Even the old Obasan, surveying them with Yasutomo at her side, could sense the current of fire that seemed to flow between them.

"Look at the lovers," she said, and shook

her head half in amusement, half in pleasure. The old swordsmith clicked his tongue.

"I see them," he said. "I have never seen Zanna so happy. She reminds me of Oyuri long ago when she first met *her* Englishman. I hope that my niece will be luckier than her mother, Obasan."

Chapter Sixteen

"MAKE SURE THAT HE TAKES DOWN MY AC-
tions word for word," Yasutomo told Zanna, as
Alex sat by him scribbling. "If indeed he's
serious about introducing my method of
swordsmithing in his far-off country." The old
man handed Alex a gift of carefully crafted
chisels. "I have made every one of these tools
myself," he explained through Zanna. "Nothing else comes near the delicate instruments
needed to carve the handles of fine swords. If
he had more time, I would teach this man of
yours how to execute designs on scabbards.
He has a good eye and a steady hand."

Zanna blossomed under this praise for Alex.
She thought him very wise, not realizing the
knowledge she, too, was acquiring. Under
Alex's tutelage she was learning to write simple phrases in English, and now when they
climbed the mountain to savor the private

paradise of their glen, they spent as much time in work as in lovemaking. One afternoon, beside their brook, she shyly handed him her first love letter. It read: "Alex, I loved you before Isudai, but not as much."

Praising her careful letters, he agreed with the message. He had thought he loved her as much as a man could love a woman before their arrival in this quiet mountain village, but time spent here had proved him wrong. Before, he had wanted to protect and possess her, keep her close and safe. Now he realized that he loved Zanna not only for her beauty and her brave loyalty, but for her quick intellect that was every bit as exciting as her body.

"Your father was wise to send us here," he told her as he put away her letter and drew her close. "It's not a chance given to many to *know* one's beloved before marriage."

She leaned happily into the circle of his arms. "We are lucky," she agreed. Then, her mood changed and she shivered violently. She had remembered that the gods in their paradise do not care for mortals who are too happy.

Alex had no such thought, however. His lips roved against her silky neck and throat, teasing with small kisses. "When we get back to Katayama I'll insist on marrying at once—the astrologers be damned." He raised his head as solemn temple bells began to fill the air. "The temple bells bless us, and that's surely enough to give us happiness."

With a sigh, she pulled away from his arms. "We must go down now, Alex. Obasan keeps giving me knowing little looks if we stay out on the mountain too late." Her smile was a little sad as she added, "I know we have to return to Katayama soon."

He nodded. "As soon as the swords are finished. Your uncle thinks that will be in a day or so."

Zanna said nothing, but as they began to leave the glade she looked back over her shoulder with another little sigh. "I am sure that we will be happy in Katayama, too. I will be happy wherever you are, my lord. But it won't be the same as it was here, will it?"

For answer, he put his arm around her and kissed her, picking a wildflower for her hair and tickling her with it first until she laughed. She insisted on picking flowers also until he was garlanded with clover blossoms. They were both in good spirits as they came down the mountain path, and Alex was trying to teach Zanna an English song when they heard a piercing bird cry nearby.

"What in God's name is that?" Alex demanded.

All happiness had been erased from her face. "A bird in a trap," she replied briefly. "Nothing else sounds like that in the mountains."

Just then, a group of boys came through the woods and onto the path. One of them held a net carelessly slung over his shoulder while dangling a large wicker cage. In the cage was a small white bird with black markings. It fluttered its wings despairingly against the bars of the cage and uttered another shrill cry.

"Oh, the poor bird!" Zanna's eyes went wide as she remembered another wild bird she had trapped years ago. She motioned to the boy with net and cage. "Is that your bird?"

The boy hesitated, then nodded. "I caught it on the mountain," he said. "It should sing, but it doesn't. It just makes those awful noises."

"Will you sell it to me?" Again, the boy hesitated, and she added, "With the money, you can buy a tame bird that can sing beautiful songs. This wild creature cannot sing because it is in a cage. It won't sing again until it's released."

Alex, who had followed the gist of the talk, had already taken money from his pocket and was holding it out. Sunlight glinted on the coins and made them irresistible. The boy seized them and shoved the cage into Zanna's hands. With many backward stares at Alex's fair hair and tall frame, he and his mates hurried away.

Zanna quickly opened the crude door of the cage. "Come, bird," she coaxed. "Go free!"

The bird screeched and plastered itself to the wall of the cage. "It's too scared to move," Alex said. He began to tap gently on the bars of the cage, and the bird fluttered about in the small space, squawking in terror. Zanna was distressed.

"What shall we do? If we leave it like this, the boys may come back and decide to keep it.

But I don't want to hurt it by forcing it from the cage."

Alex took hold of the bars of the cage and pulled the whole structure apart. For a second, the bird did not seem to know what was happening. Then, with a woosh of wings, it soared away, screeching loudly. Alex grinned. "Those sounds are more like curses than thanks."

"Our thanks will come when it has found its voice again and can sing to us when we visit our glade." Zanna tucked her arm through Alex's in deep satisfaction. "Thank you, my love." She would have added more but at that moment she saw someone laboring up the path. "Alex, it's Obasan!" she exclaimed. "She's too old to climb the mountain. Something must have happened!"

The old lady was out of breath and could not speak at once. Only when Zanna had insisted she sit down and rest could she form the words. "Kenjuro came from Katayama," she panted. "He has word for you from Rutledge-sama. Word that can't wait!"

Zanna's eyes met Alex's. "About van Feinstra?" Alex asked, and Zanna's heart sank to see by the alert glint in his eyes that the glorious days of love and learning were over.

But Obasan did not know what news Kenjuro brought, and so they restrained their impatience while they helped her down the mountainside and through the village to Yasutomo's small house. Zanna immediately knew that something was wrong, for the old swordsmith was not working but instead sat with Kenjuro and argued with the servant in an agitated way.

"Why does Rutledge-sama require my niece to come all the way back to Katayama to nurse him?" he was demanding. "Doesn't the Great House have enough maids to wait on their master?"

"Is Rutledge-sama ill?" Zanna asked, and old Kenjuro nodded unhappily. He had obviously been traveling for a long time, for his travel clothes were splashed with mud and covered with dust.

"Yes, honored miss. It began with a bad cold, and the director general didn't take care of it. It's gone to the lungs now, and the doctors say he must take care of himself. But he's a very bad patient, Zanna-san. He won't listen to Mitsuko or any of the maids!"

"And so you need me to come back to Katayama and nurse him?" Zanna tried not to feel a twinge of rebellion. It was her duty, she remembered, to take care of her father always! "I'll get ready at once," she told Kenjuro.

As she turned to go into the house, Alex stopped her. He looked stern. "I've been trying to follow what you two said, and I take it Rutledge is ill." She nodded, and he continued, "You're no servant of his. Others can help him."

His words sounded cold, even to him, and he knew he had made a mistake. Zanna's rounded chin rose in quick denial. "I owe my father loyalty, Alex," she explained quietly. "It is a bond I cannot break."

"And what I feel or say doesn't carry any weight?"

She was disturbed by his terseness and looked up at him worriedly. "When you are my husband, you may forbid me to do anything," she said. "But even if you forbade it, I would have to go, I know. Rutledge-sama needs me."

"That selfish old bastard can take care of himself a great deal better than you can care for yourself," Alex growled. He looked to Yasutomo for help and saw that the old swordsmith was glowering and grumbling too. Of course the old man would dislike Zanna dancing attendance on Rutledge. "What does your uncle say?"

Zanna's eyes were suddenly bright with tears. "He feels the way you do, but he's Japanese. He won't keep me from doing my duty." She added, imploringly, "Please, my love, I must go with Kenjuro. We'll start in the morning."

Alex knew it would be impossible to ask her to wait another day until the swords were ready so that they could travel together. He felt mean and despicable as he played his last card. "It's hard to imagine walking the mountain without you," he said.

The tears in her eyes threatened to fall, but she kept them resolutely at bay. "Don't you think I know that? I'm ashamed of myself because right now I'm thinking more about missing you than I am of poor Rutledge-sama!" She began to go into the house, looking so forlorn that Alex could not bear it. He strode after her swiftly, and caught her by the shoulders.

"I'm as selfish a swine as he is," he told her, roughly. "Go, Zanna. We'll be together soon in Katayama. I'll make sure that Yasutomo and I rush to ready those swords."

She nodded, but did not seem cheered by his words. "Perhaps," she sighed, "we were too happy after all. I was afraid, don't you remember, my love? Afraid of too much happiness."

Chapter Seventeen

It was not a pleasant leave-taking the next morning. Obasan wept; old Yasutomo scolded and swore to avoid the tears that were crowding his own eyes. Alex rode with them to the banks of a shallow river several miles from Isudai and there said his farewells.

"Don't let Rutledge talk you into spending long hours caring for him," he told her, and she nodded, wishing that he were coming with them. "I won't have you tiring yourself out, Zanna." His voice softened then as he added, "You belong to me, and I love you, Snowflower."

She held his love as tight to her as Kenjuro clutched the coins Alex gave him for emergencies during the journey. The coins came to a generous amount—far more generous than the sum Kita had grudgingly doled out for the journey. When they had forded the little river,

Kenjuro turned to his mistress and shook his head.

"Sā, sā," he said, "it's possible that your lord is right in this. You're not a servant girl, honored miss. You shouldn't be summoned back to Katayama like this."

He said it so sincerely that she felt a rush of affection for the old servant. She said firmly, however, "It's my place to be there. Is he very ill?"

Kenjuro shrugged. "He's had a fever, Zanna-san, but I don't think it's a matter of life and death." After a small pause he blurted, "The fact is that Rutledge-sama is a selfish man! He treated your mother badly and you, too. I know I should not criticize my employer, but the truth is the truth."

Zanna was astonished. She started to admonish Kenjuro, but found that deep down she was agreeing with him. *That comes of being with Alex*, she thought. *This is English, not Japanese thinking!* She suddenly felt a wave of such intense need of Alex that she wondered if he could feel it. What was he doing now? she asked herself, silently. *Is he missing me as I miss him?*

"Poor Oyuri." Kenjuro was shaking his head sadly. "She loved Rutledge-sama too much. If she hadn't, maybe she would not have lost him."

Zanna was shocked. "What do you mean?"

Kenjuro scratched his head. "Your mother adored your father, Zanna-san. She put her heart, her spirit and her body into his keeping.

She did everything for him. She learned English, dressed to please him, ignored everything in the world but him. She made herself so completely his that he grew tired of her. If he'd loved her as she loved him, he wouldn't have cast her aside, of course, but Rutledge-sama was always self-centered. If Oyuri had been a clever, cooler woman, she might have made him marry her."

"You're right, Kenjuro, you mustn't say such things about the master." Zanna felt a small stir of fear at his words. Kenjuro had described how she loved Alex. For him she was willing to give up her country, her language, her people. She would even give up Buddha if he asked her, and worship this Christ he told her of. *Suppose I go to England with him and he tires of me, as Rutledge sama tired of mother?* she wondered.

She tried to put the thought away quickly, but it still haunted her when they rode into Katayama many weary hours later.

Tired as she was, Zanna immediately asked to see Rutledge. Mitsuko pursed her lips. "He's sleeping—now," she said, implying that Rutledge was a difficult patient, indeed. "He seems better, honored miss. He has had a high fever, but it's come down a little; and today he even ate a big breakfast." She added, "A while ago, Kita-san came to see him with ledgers from the company."

Zanna smiled her relief. If Rutledge was able to think of business, he was definitely on the mend. "I'm glad," she said. "I'll just stop and tell him I'm back from Isudai. Then I would like to have a bath, Mitsuko, please."

Still dressed in her dusty travel clothes, Zanna walked down the cool polished wooden hallway to Rutledge's rooms. She called softly for admittance, but there was no answer. She slid open the screen door. The director general lay in bed, a huge mound under heavy quilts, and a snore told her he slept. A fat ledger that had been under his arm had slipped and fallen to the floor.

Zanna walked into the room and picked up the ledger. As she did so, she dislodged a piece of paper that had been inserted in the ledger pages. Almost automatically, remembering the lessons in Isudai, she began to make out the words: "As we have discussed, I am willing to agree to terms." Wouldn't Rutledge-sama be impressed at her reading ability? "When the Englishman is in Isudai, I will come to finalize our agreement. Be sure that the Dutch East India Company will pay well for your cooperation. You will not be the loser by allowing us to uproot the London Company. . . ."

What *was* this? Zanna stared at the paper. What had begun so harmlessly now frightened her. She let her eyes skim the rest of the letter and then went to the signature at the end of the page. The letter was from van Feinstra!

"The Dutch East India Company will pay you well"—for what? "When the Englishman

is in Isudai I will come"—to finalize what
agreement? There were no answers in the
letter, and she opened the ledger she had
retrieved from the floor. These figures and
entries were in both Japanese and English,
and she could make no mistake. The knowledge they gave was chilling. The ledgers said
that Rutledge had realized a huge sum of
money—greater than any that could be
earned by mere trade. And beside this sum of
money was van Feinstra's name and the in-
itials "D.E.I. Co." The Dutch East India
Company had indeed paid Rutledge for his
cooperation. The director general of the London Company had sold his services to Hollanders!

Zanna realized that her hands were shaking. They were trembling so hard that the
ledger threatened to slide out of her hands
again. *It can't be true!* she thought. There
had to be some explanation.

Rutledge moved on his bed, muttering
something in his sleep. As if this sound and
movement had forced her into action, Zanna
backed out of the sick man's rooms. She still
clutched ledger and letter against her. When
she found herself alone in the narrow, cool
corridor, her only thought was to get somewhere where she could be alone and read the
letter and ledger entry again. "I am sure that
it's a mistake," she told herself, firmly.
"Rutledge-sama would never do such a thing.
He's often talked of using van Feinstra-san for
the company. Maybe all this is a ruse."

She carried the ledger and letter to her own chamber. In her absence, the paper-and-wood doors leading to the garden had been closed and shuttered, and the room was stifling hot. She threw open the shutters and, still unable to breathe, went outside to sit on the stone step that separated her room from the garden beyond. She spread out the letter again, re-reading slowly, mouthing and translating each word and hoping for a mistake. On second reading, the letter was as damning as it had been at first.

Next, she examined the ledger. This was, she realized, not a company ledger but a personal one bearing the *han*, or seal, of Kita and Rutledge. As she went through the pages, she could see *why* it was private! Several huge sums of money leaped out at her—money that had all been paid to "J. Rutledge" from "van Feinstra" of the "D.E.I. Company."

"Zanna! I had heard you were here."

The sound of Kita's voice immediately behind her made Zanna gasp out loud. She made a swift, involuntary movement, and ledger and letter tumbled from her lap into the garden sand.

"I'm sorry I startled you." Kita looked like an unfriendly crow in his black kimono. "I want you to know it wasn't my idea to send for you. Rutledge-sama fancied that he might be dying and wanted to see you." There was scarcely concealed scorn in his voice. "You've seen him?"

"He was asleep." Zanna moved so that her travel kimono and riding trousers would conceal the ledger and letter, but Kita had already seen them.

"I see. Is that why you are going over things that belong to him?" he demanded in a stern voice.

Those tones might have quelled Zanna just a month ago. Now, she faced him and asked a question of her own: "*Do* they belong to him, Kita-san? Oh, yes, and to you, too? I think that their proper owner is Lord Jasper's nephew!"

There was a silence. For the space of two breaths Zanna could hear the summer cicadas in the pines, laughter from the servants' quarters, silvery wind chimes overhead.

"It seems that I've underestimated you, girl." To her surprise, Kita's voice was calm, almost friendly. "I hadn't realized you could read English quite so well. But you could be mistaken."

"I don't think so." She picked up the ledger and the letter and held them tightly. "Why did the Dutch East India Company pay you?" Kita moved as if to come to her, and she added sharply, "If you so much as come near me, I'll shout for Kenjuro and the servants. I'll have them run for Lord Azuma's samurai." From Kita's wince she knew he was not willing to take that risk.

"How proud you've grown," he muttered. "I knew it was a mistake allowing you to become legitimate, allowing this ridiculous betrothal.

And now you think you're so good that you'd betray your own father. Where's your sense of duty and loyalty—honored miss?"

"Where was yours to the London Company?"

The obsidian black eyes narrowed. "I have no loyalty to a pack of western barbarians! I am loyal to gold, as is your father." Almost affectionately, he patted the tatami beside him. "Come sit down and learn the whole story, since you know as much. No? Well, stand and listen. The trade wars have gone on for a long time, Zanna, and now the Hollanders weary of the struggle. They've successfully contained the Portuguese trade, and now they want to be rid of England and the London Company. So they approached your father with an offer."

"Not to trade for the London Company," she said, woodenly. Her mind was flying to Isudai, to Alex. When he found all this out. . . .

"To trade very *little*," Kita was correcting. "To do nothing would have aroused suspicion. But if things went badly in Katayama, the English merchants behind the company would recall Rutledge-sama and the Dutch would be trade lords in Japan."

Her voice was tight. "When Lord Alex finds out, it won't end the way you've planned."

He began to laugh. "Lord Alex! Lord Jasper's golden-haired nephew! Don't you realize you'll never tell him about any of this? Apart from the fact that he'll undoubtedly loathe you for being daughter to such a traitor, he won't live long to use his knowledge. Van Feinstra bungled his last two attempts to have your Alex killed, but I will succeed should you tell him anything."

The last two attempts on Alex's life! The attack in Iwase, and the wrestling match itself had been van Feinstra's doing, she realized. Zanna felt such a rush of anger that she could not speak for a moment, and during this silence Mitsuko came to the open door. Rutledge-sama, she said, was awake and would like to see honored miss.

Kita took charge. "We'll both go," he said, glancing a warning at Zanna. "Zanna-san has naturally been worried about her father."

She followed him in silence and could not even make herself bow respectfully as they entered the sickroom. She clutched the ledger tightly as the sick man, flushed but smiling, rose on an elbow. "Zanna!" he called. "So you're back! It might be I've snatched you back from Tsudai for nothing. You see I've recovered. . . ."

"It wasn't for nothing, Rutledge-sama." She held out the letter and ledger, but he did not seem to understand. "You see, I found these."

Kita clicked his tongue. "She read the letter you so stupidly had about you when you fell asleep, director general."

Surprisingly, Rutledge looked more sheepish than upset. "Those can be explained, Zanna," he said.

"How?" Zanna asked, and Kita told Rutledge not to be a fool.

"She knows about van Feinstra. Better tell her the rest," he said.

The rest? Zanna's mind was sluggish. What more could there be? she wondered, as her father gave her an almost pleading look.

"No one meant any harm to you, Zanna. It was just that you were perfect for the part. You could speak English and you're lovely. We felt—well, that you'd distract Alex Curtis from looking too carefully into the London Company's affairs."

Kita added, "We knew when we heard that he was coming that we'd need to do something to keep him from ferreting too deeply into the books and ledgers. We could have found him a dozen interpreters, but we chose you for your looks and brains and history. The daughter of a companion—what better lure to offer a man? If he sported with you, he'd not care so much about his precious uncle's business."

She knew what he was saying but she would not believe it. "You brought me here to seduce him? To play the whore for Alex?" Her voice rose. "I was just your tool?"

With a wince, Rutledge fell back against his pillows. "My head aches," he moaned. "Zanna, listen to me! Alex wouldn't have understood how it was. I was an exile from my own country eking out an existence while fat merchants and rich lords took the profits. Van Feinstra offered me wealth."

Her hands were clenched tight. "You kept throwing me together with him! You sent me to Hamabashi and after him to Fukuza and to

236

Isudai!" She added, "I can't believe that any human being could be as vile as you, Rutledge-sama!"

"He asked you to marry him, didn't he?" Rutledge fairly bellowed. "Zanna, if you keep quiet and be a good girl, everything will work out well. After all, I'll be kin to the great Lord Jasper, and your husband won't speak up against his own father-in-law!" He paused, and then added, "But if you foolishly speak about what you've learned, I'll be imprisoned, ruined, perhaps even hanged."

"Besides," Kita was murmuring, "do you honestly think your Englishman will believe you acted in total ignorance of all this? He will believe that you knew our aims from the very first and, as you say, played the whore very nicely."

Zanna could stand no more. She turned and pushed past Kita and out the door. Once in the corridor, she stood and stared about her blindly. A single thought throbbed in her mind: she must get away.

She began to run down the corridor, almost colliding with Kenjuro. He caught her by the arms to steady her. "Mistress, what's wrong? The director general's worse?"

She shook her head so violently that some of her long dark hair escaped its combs and fell about her pale cheeks. "Oh, Kenjuro! I wish I were dead!"

For a second the old servant stared. Then, he began to drag her down the corridor to his small room in the servants' quarters. He drew her inside, sat her down by a low, modest table, and poured hot tea for her. "Drink this down slowly," he instructed her. "When you can, tell me!"

She could not touch the tea. "Kenjuro, I have to leave this house," she said, brokenly. "Please don't ask me what has happened, but help me to get away!"

The old man stared at her in shocked surprise. Just yesterday she had been so happy! "Where would you go, child?" he protested.

"I don't know. Perhaps you know of someone who will take me in." She covered her mouth with both hands to press back a sob, and then continued, "It must be some place where neither Rutledge-sama nor—nor Alex can find me."

Kenjuro exclaimed out loud. "You sound like your mother," he said sadly. "Thirteen years ago Oyuri sat where you're sitting down and cried. She asked me to help her get back to Isudai because the director general had found a new companion and didn't want her any more." He paused, waiting for Zanna to tell him why *she* wanted to get away, but she said nothing. "There's an old lady—Oshin—who lives in Hamabashi. She's a good old body and won't gossip or ask questions. But you can't stay there forever, child."

Zanna unconsciously drew herself erect. The turbulence inside was tearing her apart, but she showed no sign of this in her face. It was almost as if a frozen mask had etched her features in stone. Her voice was cool and remote—the careful, controlled voice she had first used when Rutledge's bidding brought her to Katayama.

"I won't impose on her long. Uncle Yasutomo has kin on Shikoku Island. As soon as I can contact them, I'll go there. I can't go back to Isudai—they'll all look for me there." She added, "I have some money, and there are the combs. I could sell them."

The combs her English lover gave her! "There's no need of that; I have money," Kenjuro quavered. "Stay here and rest, child. I will go at once and arrange for you to stay at Oshin-san's home."

Zanna nodded her thanks. But as the old man was slipping off, she called him back. "Kenjuro, do you have brush and paper? I must write a letter."

Once alone, she sat for a long time staring at the white paper and the black ink ready for her brush. *How can I do this?* she asked herself, and a stab of pain shivered through her as if her spirit were being shredded by what she was about to do.

Dipping the tip of her brush in the ink, she began to write: "Dear Alex. . . ."

Chapter Eighteen

SHE KNELT IN THE SMALL DARK ROOM AND waited for the old lady to return. She was very still and held her hands loosely on her lap. Her head was bent. She hardly seemed to breathe. She was trying to meditate, trying to pray, trying to subdue her thoughts of Alex. But in spite of everything, she still thought of him. He wouldn't have returned to Katayama yet, she was thinking. He would still be in Isudai.

When he came back and found her letter, she knew, he would be angry and hurt. She hoped that his anger would be greatest, because then he'd forget her more quickly. Eventually he would hardly think of her at all or, if he did, he might remember her as his companion for a few weeks.

Kenjuro had brought her to Oshin-san's house last night, brought her through a side

gate of the Great House and on foot to Hamabashi's poorer section, where the old woman
lived alone. The old lady had been very kind
to her, letting her share the small room where
she lived and slept, insisting that Zanna eat
something before she retired for the night.

"You'll be safe here, child," she had said.
"No matter who looks for you, he won't find
you here."

Now, Oshin-san had gone to the market to
buy fish and some millet for their meal. "I'm
sorry it's not white rice," she had apologized.
"You stay in the house, child, and keep the
door closed and the shutters, too. No one will
bother you till I return," the old woman had
continued.

Zanna had agreed listlessly.

There was a faint sound from the entrance
of the small house, and Zanna sighed. Old
Oshin had returned. She knew that she
should go and help the kind old lady, but
before she could get to her feet, the door to the
room was almost torn open, and Alex stood
framed in the empty doorframe glaring down
at her.

She had thought of him so much that she
could only stare at him foolishly, as if she had
conjured him up just by wanting him. But
that he was the man before her was clearly no
part of her imagination. His boots were caked
with mud, and his clothes dusty from the
road. His face was harder and angrier than
she'd ever seen it. She started to her feet,
shaking her head wildly. No!

241

"Yes," he said harshly. "I'm here, Zanna. Did you think you could disappear so easily?"

"You returned so early—." Her voice was a gasp. *Oh, Alex,* she mourned, *why did you come? I have already said good-bye to you in my heart. I cannot tear myself away from you again!*

"I wanted to be with you, so Yasutomo-san hurried as much as he could. We started out yesterday and I arrived today. That was when I found your letter." Again, she shook her head in denial, and he strode booted onto the tatami, seizing her arm and pulling her around to face him. "The letter told me that you no longer felt that a marriage between us was possible. You said that you didn't want to see me any more. Did you write all that?"

"Yes." To her surprise, she spoke quite calmly.

"Did Kita or Rutledge make you write that letter?" She now realized that his anger was directed toward them, not toward herself. "If they did, that's the last filthy trick they play on you—London Company or no!"

Alex, if you knew! His concern and love for her dug claws inside her, lacerating what remained of her heart. Every instinct in her wanted his arms around her, the feel of his lips. She had only to tell him! And then she remembered Kita's quiet threat: *"I will not fail."*

"Zanna?" He tried to draw her to him, but she pulled back. "What is it, sweeting? Why have you run away here?"

242

Her lips carefully mouthed the words: "Did you ask—them? Rutledge-sama? Kita-san?"

"No. The sight of them would have made me itch to strangle them. I looked only to find you, and that was difficult enough. Kenjuro would not tell me anything, but that maid told me, finally—Mitsuko."

How had Mitsuko found out? No matter, Zanna thought miserably. "I'm sorry that you came," she said, after a moment. "I had wanted to—to spare us both this meeting."

"Wh-a-t?" He thought she was joking, playing some game, and though he laughed he frowned. "Snowflower, don't tease," he said. "I've worried about you, and I'm still worried. What have that precious pair done to you?"

"They've done nothing to me, my lord." Her voice was cold and wooden. "Whatever happened was my idea. Nobody forced me to write that letter, either. I thought it best I tell you that way. I did not want to hear you rage and storm."

He did not take his arms away from her, but the blue of his eyes hardened. "Explain. I'm not proving quick at understanding today, it seems."

Buddha, give me strength! she thought. "I want to terminate our relationship," she told him.

"Termi—Zanna, what is the matter with you?" He shook her a little, staring down into her face. His eyes seemed to be penetrating hers, looking into her heart. She knew that in another moment her control would break and that if it did, she would tell him. *If I tell him, Kita-san will not let him live,* she told herself. Kita-san was no bumbling Hollander. He was sly! He would hire an assassin who could slip through the shadows and plunge a knife into Alex's broad back. . . .

"Don't you understand clear speaking, my lord?" With a gesture of supreme contempt, Zanna shrugged away from Alex's grip. "I don't want to marry you anymore. You see, my fortunes have changed in the world."

He said nothing, but his eyes glittered like hard blue stones. She forced herself to meet them as she continued, "Since you—ah— offered to marry me and my father decided to legitimize me, my position in the marriage market has altered. I wasn't aware how much until just recently. With the director general as my father, I became quite desirable." She paused to let this sink in. "One of the merchants has made me an offer of marriage."

He did not touch her, but she felt his concentrated attention. "An advantageous offer, no doubt." His voice sounded dangerously gentle.

"Of course, my lord! This is why Rutledge-sama used his health as an excuse to get me home from Isudai. He could hardly send me the message by Kenjuro, could he?" She forced a hard little laugh. "We discussed the match, and I agreed to the marriage."

"You agreed! Zanna, look at me!"

He spoke so quietly that she could not help the gasp that came to her lips. To cover it she said, "I want this marriage, my lord. It would mean that my place in Katayama society is assured. And, most important, our children will be Japanese and not—and not the children of a barbarian."

"This is truly what you wish? You're not doing this to fulfill some twisted idea of loyalty to Rutledge?" he demanded roughly.

For a long second she drank in the sight of him, the shape of his face, details of eye, nose, chin, well-loved mouth. Then, she nodded. "I'm doing this because I want it." She was beginning to feel the same numbness she had felt when her mother had died. "I would like you to leave me alone, now."

"And what we shared at Isudai—that was make-believe?"

"It was a dream." Unconsciously, her voice changed, trembled with memory. "A beautiful dream. Forest glades and mountain streams are lovely but—but one has to live in the real world. You are from another country. I don't want to leave Japan for you. I'll stay on here in Katayama and—and help my new husband's family grow in wealth and influence."

From the look on his face she knew he believed her now. "The lure of power and wealth," he said, and that silky tone she so dreaded was back in his voice again. "Now I believe you. I told you that it was the only thing worth taking in life!" He laughed suddenly—an ugly bark of sound. "Why weren't you frank with me from the first, madam? I could have understood your motives better than I understood all this trumped-up talk about loyalty and duty! And why run away? It would have been kinder to tell me to my face and not write a letter."

Please go away! she wanted to shout at him. She clenched her small hands within her wide sleeves. "My father was sure it would be for the best. Men from other countries sometimes are irrational in times of anger. He was afraid of what you'd do if I told you to your face. When your anger had cooled, we were sure you would be able to accept what had been decided."

"Were you, by God?" Suddenly, he reached for her and caught her by the arms, and she gave a small, shocked cry of pain and fear at the expression in his face. "What do you think now, my lady? Do I look more *reasonable* now?"

"Please let me go!" she cried.

He ignored her. "I think you've used me somewhat unfairly, Snowflower. To hear you tell it, you achieved your status as legitimate daughter of Rutledge only because of *my* offer of marriage. That means I'm responsible for your advantageous match, too. It's not just that some merchant with fat, slobbering lips and pudgy hands takes his delight of you while I get—nothing!"

"Please!" But he had pulled her hard against him, his lips bruising hers. There was no love in his kiss, no tenderness at all, only a mindless, grinding fury that demanded her absolute submission. She whimpered as his teeth nipped down on her lower lip.

"Alex, please! Don't do this!" He held her with one arm and with the other hand methodically began to strip away her clothing. He would not free her to protest, but punished her mouth again, and she heard the feral sound he made deep in his throat. Somehow, he had managed to twist loose the knot of her sash, and the stiff, formal length of cloth slid to the floor. With a powerful, ripping motion he now tore open the folds of her kimono and plunged his hands beneath her thin undergarments to grasp her body.

He hated her. It was hate that made him pull her to the mats and grope for her breasts. It was someone who hated her—not her Alex! Terrified, she tried to double up her knees and roll away from him, but the movement only made it easier for him to strip away her undergarments. Now, he was undressing himself, divesting himself of doublet, shirt, breeches.

She fought him until she knew she had no fight left in her. Then, when his mouth left hers for a moment, she pleaded. "Alex, Please!"

"Would you have me play the courtly, considerate lover?" He mocked her. "Considering that this is our farewell encounter, why not accommodate me? You did well on the road from Iwase."

Memory of those nights of love and the realization of why she had been sent to Iwase made her sob out loud. In the dusky half-light of the small room, he knelt above her, broad shoulders set and hard, the rock-hard body and the passion manifest in that body menacing and somehow twisted, evil. *Don't let this be the way we say good-bye,* she wanted to weep, but his lips were on hers again, and now he was spreading her thighs to meet him. "A dream was it, in Isudai?" he muttered, savagely. "This is another sort of dream, madam. Remember it when you lie with your 'advantageous' mate!"

The cruelty of his voice made her cry out, and yet he stirred her. His touch was magic. The feel of his furred chest against hers, the way his powerful thighs gripped hers, the scent of him and taste of him all coalesced into a desire that was part pain. Involuntarily, she felt her breasts thrust against his rough hands, her mouth become yielding under his.

She could feel his body change. The painful, bruising kisses changed to a remembered warmth and tenderness. Mindlessly, she felt the lessening of his tension as his fingers gentled against the taut peaks of her nipples, and she welcomed him, arching her body to seek his. But he did not take her, instead smoothing his hands over the curve of her waist, the smooth, flat abdomen, the swell of her hips.

"Oh, Alex—." The words were dragged from her, drawn from beyond any conscious desire or wish. *Take me now,* she whispered silently. *I need you, my love!*

She felt him pull away. The tension in his

body was back, but this was different, directed against himself and not at her. She opened her eyes and saw him staring down at her with a bitter, closed expression in his eyes.

"You want me to, don't you?" he asked her, tersely. "You want me to perform like a rutting beast for your pleasure." His eyes raked her angrily. "Would that prove you're desirable to me even after what you've done to me? You'd better be careful, madam. If your future husband learns of your—ah—appetites, wealth and power might avoid you even now!"

He got to his feet and started to draw on his clothes. She sat up, fumbled for hers. "Cover yourself up," he said harshly. "For God's sake, save yourself for this marvelous merchant, this advantageous mate! I want no more of you."

She wasn't fooled. Desire was still shaking him as it had caught and held her. His back was held ramrod-straight with effort. She had felt his love for her even through his anger. If she held out her hands to him now, told him everything, he would understand and forgive her. Love her!

For one moment she let herself think of possibilities. Couldn't they run away to Isudai? Perhaps they could go to England together on that English ship that had just reached Katayama inlet, the *My Lady Fair*. But she knew that these were just dreams. Alex would confront Kita and Rutledge, and the result would be his death.

And even if it doesn't mean death for Alex, Zanna, she told herself despairingly, *can you turn against your own father? What would Alex think of you then?*

"This will not happen again," he was saying. The quietness of his voice told her that he meant his words. "You can go back to your father's house, Zanna," he said. "I wish you joy on the path you've chosen for yourself."

She heard him stride away through the little house and close the outer door. Slowly, she gathered her kimono about her, adjusted the sash with numbed fingers. It was not until the last of his footsteps had sighed away that she made a sound, and then just to repeat his name, over and over. "Alex, Alex. Alex!"

Chapter Nineteen

Alex rode out of Hamabashi like a man possessed. He urged his horse into a lather and nearly mowed down several fishermen near the bamboo glade where once the *ronin* had done their damage. He didn't even see the scrambling men; his mind was still on the look Zanna had given him when she spoke about her new and advantageous marriage. The gray eyes he had loved were like frozen, shadowed snow. And when he had kissed her, her lips had been like ice.

And yet, when he tried to use her as brutally as she had used him, she had responded to him. The thought of that response twisted deep in his soul like a savage knife. He had meant to insult and hurt her, and he hadn't been able to do it. He had felt only the slender, cool body against his, and all his old love had come flooding back.

"God help me," he muttered. "I love her still!"

He had come to the outskirts of Katayama now, and was passing through the mournful place of execution. Some newly executed criminals were hanging from their crosses, and he looked at them and gritted his teeth. These poor fools had it easier, he thought. They were dead and couldn't feel. *He* would remember Zanna all his life, and even if he held another woman in his arms, had his way with a hundred willing wenches, he would think of Zanna and want her. To want her all his life and not have her—it was easier to be condemned to the cross.

Only one thought stirred to comfort him: Rutledge's greed was at the bottom of Zanna's decision! No matter what she said, he still had the feeling that she'd never have turned to a better match had it not been for Rutledge's spurring her on. If he could get the director general to admit what he'd done, perhaps there was still a chance for Zanna and for himself! She had been cool as ice, yes, but there had been a moment when she had wanted him. He could not have mistaken that surge of desire that matched his own!

He came into Katayama at a gallop, and nearly upended a servant as he cantered through the great gates and threw the reins to a groom. As he did so, he caught sight of Kenjuro. The old man was peering at him in an agitated way that made him resemble a frightened ape. When Alex called to him, he scuttled away. No doubt, Alex thought grimly, the old villain was deep in this plot. Rutledge had probably sent him to Isudai so that he could explain the "advantageous match" to Zanna on their way to Katayama. He'd always seemed to hang about Zanna. . . .

About to kick off his boots and stride into the Great House demanding Rutledge, Alex checked himself. *I have to compose myself,* he thought. *It won't do any good if Rutledge thinks he's dealing with a maniac!* He would walk in the gardens for a while, finding not only control but the right way in which to approach the director general.

As he bypassed the doorway of the Great House and stepped into the Japanese gardens, Alex realized that he was not the only one to walk the gardens. Carried on the warm breeze came two male voices speaking Japanese. One was Kita's voice, the other familiar even at this distance. Alex consciously softened his footfall as he drew nearer, swore softly as he recognized the other speaker as van Feinstra. The Hollander here? Cautiously, Alex edged closer and positioned himself behind a large pine that almost overlooked the place where the two men stood. As he took his stand he heard Kita speak Zanna's name.

Alex frowned in concentration, trying to follow the quick flow of Japanese. Zanna's tutelage had provided him with some key words, but he could only grasp a bare gist of what was being said. Kita spoke Zanna's name again and then spoke the word for silence. His gesture of fingers against thin lips only emphasized this. Then he spoke the word that stood for gold or money.

Van Feinstra didn't like what was being said. He protested, then shrugged. Then, to Alex's intense surprise, the man dug in his pockets and hauled out a sack, which he put in Kita's outstretched hands. Kita was being paid off! For what? Alex watched as the bag disappeared into Kita's kimono sleeve, and it was all he could do to hold himself back.

But he watched the drama unfold, stood still as the Hollander spoke his farewells and then was let out by a side gate in the garden. Then, while Kita stood by and drew out his sack, Alex stepped forward. The manager was smiling at the sack, hefting it, when Alex put a hand on his shoulder.

"Good afternoon, Kita-san," he said pleasantly. "And how do you find yourself today?"

The flash of consternation that came and went from those narrow eyes spoke of guilt. Then Kita smiled and his eyes went opaque. "Nice you home," he murmured. "Not know you came."

. "I'm sure you didn't. Tell me, Kita-san, what kind of business has just concluded between you and van Feinstra?" Alex's voice was still pleasant, but Kita looked wary and shook his head.

"Wakaranai!" he muttered.

"Oh, yes you understand very well. Tell me, why did the Hollander pay you?" As Kita started to dart away, Alex's arm shot out and plucked the bag from his fingers. He tore open the bag and upended it, and Kita let out a hoarse cry as golden coins fell in a singing stream to the sand. "It seems a great deal of profit," Alex said, gently. "I want to know why he paid you—and why you used Zanna's name."

"What in hell is going on? Oh, it's you, Alex!"

Rutledge had emerged from the house, and was staring at Alex and at the spilled gold coins.

Alex kicked at some of the coins that had rolled near his foot. "I think perhaps the explanations should come from you," he said. "I want to know two things. I need to know about Zanna—and I want to know what business you've been conducting with an employee of the Dutch East India Company."

"He's working for us—."

"And paying you for that privilege?" Alex noted that Rutledge's florid face had become pale. He looked haggard, suddenly. "I want some answers," he told the director general.

The heavy shoulders of the director slumped. "So Zanna did tell you," he muttered.

Kita instantly launched into sibilant Japanese, evidently warning Rutledge against talking. Alex stopped him by catching the folds of his kimono and pulling tight. "Kita-san, I warn you that I'm in no mood to be patient. Be quiet, or I will force you to be quiet," he said.

"No need for violence!" Rutledge almost squealed. "There's no use trying to hide matters if you've tracked Zanna down." He paused to see if Alex would disclose her whereabouts, then added, "The girl disappeared from the Great House yesterday. It was a bad plan to use her."

"To—what?" Alex released Kita so suddenly that the manager fell backward into the sand. "Explain yourself!" he snapped.

Rutledge bit his fleshy lip. "No doubt you've heard it all from her, anyway? It was Kita's idea to recall her from Isudai and make her your interpreter. We thought that if the two of you were thrown together—." He made a crude gesture with his hands and then swallowed at the murderous look in Alex's eyes. "What else could I do? When we learned that Lord Jasper was sending you, we knew we had to do something to distract you!"

"I should have guessed," Alex cried. "The low volume in trade, the lack of profit—even your involvement with van Feinstra. Was I slow-witted that I didn't see?"

"You didn't guess because part of your mind was always on Zanna." Even at such a time, Rutledge seemed smug. "The chit *is* a beautiful woman, much like her mother. That's why we relied on her to do the job."

The monstrous implications of what he was saying broke through at last. Zanna had been brought to Katayama to act as a decoy, and it had worked! From the very first moment he had seen her, he had wanted her; he had found her irresistible, just as these two had hoped!

And Zanna had gone along with them! That knowledge hurt worse than the coldness and the rejection with which she had met him earlier today. He had loved her with all his heart and soul, and she had been laughing at him all along. Even worse was the possibility that she'd been disgusted by the lovemaking and had submitted only because of her cursed 'duty' to her father. He remembered what she'd said about her children not being the offspring of a barbarian.

"There's plenty of gold." Kita's sibilant whisper penetrated his thoughts. "We can divide three ways, not two."

Hot, healing rage coursed through Alex. "Get out of my sight," he roared at the manager, who leaped up and hurried into the house. Now, he turned to Rutledge. "Well, director general," he sneered at him, "you've done well for yourself, haven't you? Your nest is feathered with Dutch guilders, but they'll serve you nothing now that your daughter isn't here to cover up your activities any longer. What do you plan to do now?"

Rutledge started to take Alex by the shoulder, thought better of it. "Don't be hasty," he implored. "Try to understand how it was. When I got here the Portuguese and the Hollanders had full sway. Van Feinstra's offer seemed a good one."

"It won't seem so good now. You'll get it both ways, won't you, my fat friend?" Alex vented his anger in a silkily smooth voice. "From the Hollanders who will feel you've betrayed them, and from the London Company. The penalty of such crimes could be death, Rutledge."

Rutledge paled. "There's Zanna to consider," he began heavily.

There was nothing silky in Alex's voice now. "Talk about her or try to use her to get me to change my mind, and I'll kill you myself," he said savagely.

Rutledge considered this and then sighed. "I realize that what I did was wrong, but Kita said that this was a sure and safe way to increase our profits. As to Zanna, you *did* fall in love with her." He held up a hand to check Alex's wrath. "If all this comes out, think of what will happen to her! Even if you don't want her any more, do you wish to see her life ruined? The daughter of a criminal— dishonored, penniless. Zanna's life will become a hell."

"What's that got to do with me?" But it had everything to do with him, and the crafty, selfish old bastard knew it well! Alex closed his eyes, trying to push away the image of how she had looked in that sun-dappled glen in Isudai, her dark hair swirling about her shoulders, the perfection of innocence and grace. He felt her take his hands and place them on her breasts. *Oh, God,* he thought, *I can't do it to her. I can't hurt her.*

Rutledge sensed his advantage and pressed on. "I swear that if you say nothing for the time being, I'll make it up to the company. I have contacts, Alex, and I can make the London Company pay! I will make those new offices in Iwase and Fukuza profitable! If you don't believe me, you stay in Japan and cut my throat the second you think I'm playing you false."

"It'd give me considerable pleasure to cut your throat right now." But if Rutledge meant what he said, things could possibly right themselves. After a decent time, he could have Lord Jasper send in a replacement for the director general. By then, Rutledge would have paid off some of what he'd bilked from the company. What use to have him caught and killed? Alex reasoned with himself. He'd be more use alive than dead.

"If you have me removed now," Rutledge was saying craftily, "the Hollanders will take over completely."

"I'm going to think it over, Rutledge, and I'll give you my answer later." But as the director general was retreating into the house, Alex called him back. "You say that you've used Zanna all along. Did you now arrange a marriage between her and some Japanese merchant?"

The man's surprise was so genuine that Alex's last hope sank. "If she's been casting around for a better marriage on the sly, I don't know of it," Rutledge said. His eyes narrowed. "What did I tell you about a woman recognizing her market value and improving her lot in life?"

All thought that Zanna had been forced to marry against her will was lost. It was *her* idea. She had only entertained him out of a sense of duty. She'd done her work well, and now she was making plans for the rest of her life.

"If she'd cared for me she'd never have sent me away as she did," he thought bitterly. He would have to accept that fact and live with it. Meanwhile, there was this difficult decision to make about Rutledge. The very thought of the big man made Alex feel ill.

He made his decision within the next few hours. Holding some sheets of paper in his hand, he summoned Rutledge and Kita.

"This," he said, "is an account of everything that's happened. It details your business dealings with van Feinstra and accounts for the monies he's paid you. The bribes must be all recorded and you will do so now."

The itemization took some time. When Kita and Rutledge had finished working on the list, Alex grimly demanded their signatures on the document.

"This will amount to a confession," he said. As Rutledge started he added, "I won't use it unless I have to. I am going to send it back to England when the *My Lady Fair* sails. It will be taken to my brother, Griff. If ever you play me false, if anything happens to me or you backslide in your agreement to pay back the company, this document will condemn you to the punishment you deserve."

"And that's all?" Rutledge was trying to still

his shaking hands, and Alex gazed at him in contempt. Even Kita was showing himself to have more courage.

"Hardly. I'm also going to write my uncle requesting that a new director general be appointed in Katayama. You will work under this man until all your just debts are paid. Kita will do the same."

"A replacement like yourself?" Kita sneered.

Alex did not look at him. "You have a choice. Sign—or I call the justice of Lord Azuma. From what I hear about Japanese prisons, I don't think either of you will like them."

Without further persuasion, Rutledge signed. Kita hesitated, then malevolently fixed his seal on the page and wrote his name in the flowing Japanese script. Alex found himself wishing automatically that Zanna were there to translate the written words, and this involuntary thought of her tightened something hard and heavy and burdensome in his chest.

"Advise van Feinstra of what has happened," he ordered the two men. "It must be done soon, for the matter has to be resolved before that ship leaves Katayama."

He gathered the sheets of the confession together and placed them in a hollow wooden tube. Then he looked thoughtfully at Kita's angry face.

The man had spoken the truth. If Lord Jasper were to replace Rutledge, what better

man to appoint as director general of Katayama, Iwase and Fukuza than Alex Curtis?
He was on good terms with many merchants
and was beginning to learn the language.
Much more important, he had the favor of the
dread lord of Iwase. *If I want the director-
generalship, I can have it,* Alex thought.

For just a moment he visualized how the
London Company could grow and prosper
under his guidance. It would rival the Dutch
East India Company, surpass it in time. And
power and wealth would be his!

That thought checked him. Not seven
weeks ago he'd arrived in Japan with dreams
of adventure and the end goals of wealth and
ambition dancing before his eyes. What supreme irony, Alex thought, that now that he
could have them, he cared for nothing except
a gray-eyed girl who had only pretended to
love him.

Chapter Twenty

KENJURO STEALTHILY CREPT TOWARD A SIDE gate. It was an hour or so before dawn and the household slept. He had just enough time to get himself and a bundle of Zanna's belongings to Hamabashi. He had meant to leave much earlier, but that spiteful wench Mitsuko had been up all night—kept on the run by Rutledge, who seemed to have had a relapse—and he hadn't wanted to take a chance of her spotting him.

That woman had made enough trouble already! Kenjuro fiddled with the latch of the side gate and frowned as he thought of Mitsuko's treachery. He'd been terrified when the Englishman found out where Zanna was—afraid that he'd force her to return or at least tell Rutledge where she was. He hadn't done either of those things, though, but had only shouted at Kita and Rutledge. Kenjuro smiled, suddenly. Those two deserved to be shouted at, he thought, piously. Buddha was just.

The bolt of the side gate clicked back, and Kenjuro was about to slip outside into the street when he heard heavy footfalls coming toward him. To his astonishment and alarm, they stopped just in front of the side gate. He drew back into the shadows, heart pounding, and as he did so someone came walking swiftly and silently from the shadowy garden and opened the gate.

"You are early, van Feinstra-san." It was Kita!

"I came as soon as I got your message." Kenjuro, cowering in the shadows, was sure that the two men could hear his heart beating like a huge drum. "I understood that the matter was urgent. I came early so no one would see me come."

Nodding, Kita let the Hollander through the garden toward the house. This was Kenjuro's chance to slip through the gate and speed toward Hamabashi, but his legs wouldn't move properly. As he strained to calm himself, he heard Kita say, "Of course the girl knows! There is the danger she will talk."

"It's a danger we must deal with," the Hollander replied grimly.

Kenjuro's legs suddenly regained their function. Those two were talking about Zanna! Clutching his bundle, he followed, and when Kita and the Hollander stepped onto the outer veranda and disappeared into the director general's suite of rooms, Kenjuro slipped up nimbly and pressed his ear against the sliding door.

He heard van Feinstra speak almost at once in his heavily accented Japanese. "So. The Englishman knows everything." There was an unintelligible mutter from Rutledge, and then the Dutchman added contemptuously, "And he's also made you sign a confession. Where is this document now?"

"In his room," Kita replied. "I know where he keeps it, but he won't let it out of his sight until the English ship sails. He's no fool."

"We must get the document away before the ship sails, even if we have to kill him." Kenjuro nearly fainted at this cold-blooded announcement. Perhaps Rutledge protested also, for van Feinstra added, "Or do you enjoy the idea of torture and death for what you've done?"

"I certainly don't want to be crucified," Kita broke in sharply. "We'll make sure of this Englishman. We will stab him while he sleeps."

"Now?" demanded the Hollander, and Kenjuro got ready to hurry out of sight in case they approached the door. But apparently Kita had an objection.

"It's too close to dawn. One of the servants might also have seen you, and that might be awkward." There was a pause, and then he said, decidedly, "No—tomorrow night after the house is still. That will give us time to plan for another disappearance."

"The girl's." Van Feinstra sounded matter of fact. "But you don't know where she is."

"My spies have traced her to an old woman's house in Matsubashi. It will be a simple thing to send a couple of hired men to do the job quietly."

There was a deep rumble of protest from the director general. *"Why?* What need? Zanna will keep her mouth shut. So far, she's done everything we wanted her to. No need to kill her, surely!"

Kita told him that it was no time to become tenderhearted. "You forget Zanna knows much too much," he reminded Rutledge.

Was there no end to evil in the world? Paralyzed with horror, Kenjuro kept his ear glued to the partition. "With a little effort we might even create a scenario that will explain their deaths," Kita was continuing. "After all, we must have a story of some kind to tell Azuma's samurai! Once they are both dead, we'll say that Alex Curtis discovered his betrothed with another man and killed her at the site of her tryst in Hamabashi. Then he returned to the Great House and, filled with remorse, took his own life." Kenjuro could almost see the grin on Kita's face. "The Japanese are used to double suicides, after all."

"No!" Rutledge exploded. "I won't be party to it!"

"The outraged father! Who acted as a pimp for your Zanna?" Van Feinstra demanded. "You made her into a harlot, didn't you, to suit your purposes?"

266

"That wasn't murder. I won't do it! I'd rather trust the Englishman. He's a man of his words, and—no, I won't murder Zanna!"

"And that's your last word?" Evidently, Rutledge signified that it was. "In that case. . . ."

There was the sound of a choked cry, a dreadful, gurgling gasp. Hardly aware of what he was doing, Kenjuro slid open the sliding doors and stared inside. The Hollander seemed to be embracing Rutledge, but as Kenjuro watched, the big director's knees buckled, and he slowly slumped toward the floor. Kita caught him, and now Kenjuro could see the dagger protruding from his chest.

"*Why?*" Even Kita looked horrified. "Now we are sure to be caught!"

"Not at all." Almost casually, the Hollander pulled loose his dagger and wiped it on a fold of Rutledge's doublet. "In fact, this makes a better story. The father objected at the last moment to his daughter's marriage. Furious, the Englishman killed him—and the girl avenged her father from a sense of duty, then took her own life." He paused. "We must hide him until nightfall, when the other two deaths can be arranged. Is there somewhere where we can hide the good director general?"

"In—in the storeroom. I have the only key. You are a clever man, Feinstra-san. Rutledge was weak, anyway. It will work!"

Kenjuro didn't wait to hear anymore. He tottered away on legs that threatened to collapse. "Are they monsters from hell?" he muttered. What further harm could they wish to do to Zanna?

For a second he stopped and considered going to the Englishman, but he soon put the thought aside. Lord Alex didn't understand Japanese; he wouldn't know what Kenjuro was saying. And for some inexplicable reason Zanna didn't want him to know where she was. "It's up to me to get her out of this safely," Kenjuro moaned. He felt very old and tired, and the road seemed even darker and longer than before. He positioned his bundle more comfortably and began to jog toward Hamabashi. With luck, he would reach Zanna shortly after dawn.

Zanna was helping the old lady wash the breakfast rice bowls when Kenjuro came panting into the entryway of the small house. He collapsed onto the tatami, and she ran to him with an exclamation of dismay.

"Kenjuro! Are you ill? What has happened?"

The old servant was so exhausted and upset that he could hardly talk, and Zanna ran for cold water. While he drank, she wrapped a square of cloth wrung out in cold water around his forehead. "What can be so terrible that you arrive here in this state?" she scolded him. As Kenjuro tried to speak, she shook her head. "You must not, Kenjuro. Rest a little first before giving us your news."

Kenjuro had been thinking, all this way, of

some easy way to tell her. Now, he opened his mouth and croaked, "Murder!"

Zanna's eyes went to pools of gray fear. "Not Alex?" she whispered.

Kenjuro shook his head. He would have to explain one thing at a time. "Kita and van Feinstra, the Dutch merchant, have killed Rutledge-sama."

Oshin covered her mouth with her hands and looked ready to faint. Zanna simply stared. "They *killed* him?" she asked, stupidly. Then, she seemed to gather herself together and before Kenjuro's eyes appeared to grow older, more remote, almost calm. "Tell me everything," she instructed.

As Kenjuro stumbled over what had happened, Zanna said nothing. This was so monstrous, so horrible. *I could start screaming and never stop,* she thought, *but that will not do any good. And if I panic, Alex will die. Somehow, I must save him!*

She stopped Kenjuro and made him repeat the terrible story once again: how Lord Alex had returned on a lathered horse; how he had nearly strangled Kita-san and poured a stream of gold onto the garden sand; how he had talked long and carefully with Kita-san and the director general and made them sign some paper. How, later, the Hollander had come. . . .

"How will they kill Lord Alex?" Zanna asked. Even to her, her voice sounded unnaturally firm and clear. No wonder Kenjuro looked at her so strangely as he explained. "So they won't move until tonight," Zanna murmured in that same clear, hard voice. "I do have some time, but not much."

"Child, what are you going to do?" Kenjuro asked, nervously. "Will you tell Lord Azuma's samurai?"

"They mightn't believe us. Besides, even if they do, they may not move swiftly enough—." Zanna touched icy fingers to her throbbing temples. She wished that her mind could focus on one thing at a time, that her thoughts wouldn't dart about like frightened fish. She thought of Alex and then she thought of her father protesting that he didn't want her killed. Tears rose to her eyes for a brief moment. No matter what else the man had done, he had cared for her just a little. It was the one comfort she could cling to just now.

Kenjuro was counseling urgently. "Zanna-san, you must get away to Isudai right now. Your uncle will hide you in the mountain till these murderers can be dealt with. I will go to Iwase myself and tell the whole story to Lord Azuma. He'll see justice is done!"

She nearly cried out at him. Run away and leave Alex here? But what Kenjuro had said about Lord Azuma was true enough. The lord of Iwase would mete out sure and terrible justice. If only Iwase wasn't so far away! Why, just one word from the daimio, she thought, and Alex would be safe!

Perhaps sensing what was in her mind, Kenjuro patted her hand. "Look, child, I brought you some of the things you'd left at the Great House. Here is the kimono that Lord Azuma gave you. He liked both you and the English lord, didn't he? Please send me to him. He's the one to help you!"

As he spoke, he untied the knots of the bundle and displayed the silken folds of the Iwase kimono. The memory of the only time she'd worn that kimono tore at Zanna's heart, and she started to push it away. As she did so, her fingers brushed something that crackled slightly. She frowned and drew a piece of paper from among the folds of the garment. It was a piece of paper with the seal of Lord Azuma.

She lifted it carefully, and suddenly her mind seemed clear, able to think again. *Of course*, she thought. *I'd forgotten about this. Lord Azuma tucked it into the kimono to give the gift greater merit, and perhaps he's given me the greatest gift of all.* She smiled. "After all," she murmured aloud, "Lord Azuma's word must always be obeyed!"

The old people looked at her as if she had lost her mind, and their bewilderment was so pitiful that she ached for them. Her tears were so near the surface, but they would spoil everything. She forced herself to square her shoulders as she asked Oshin for paper and ink and a brush. "I must write some important letters," she said.

She withdrew to a corner of the small room to write these, and the others left her alone.

That they were very concerned was obvious, for the moment she put down her brush Kenjuro said forcefully, "Zanna-san, now I must insist! You have to get on the way to Isudai. I'll take those letters wherever you want me to, but I'll only do it when you're safely on your way."

"But I'm not going to run away."

Both Kenjuro and Oshin burst into a volley of questions and remonstrance, but Zanna wasn't listening. "I am tall for a Japanese," she was murmuring to herself. "It will be dark. They will not notice and—at least, I hope not."

Without looking at the agitated old people, she went to a sliding closet in the wall of the room and removed her traveling clothes and the stiff riding trousers she had worn to Isudai. They were dark and would conceal her progress in the night.

"What are you *doing*?" Kenjuro was near tears.

Zanna came to him, knelt down and took both his hands in hers. "My dear old friend, I need your help—yours and Oshin-san's. Even if he's warned about tonight, Lord Alex will be in danger as long as he stays in Japan. Kita's spies and assassins will find and kill him. So he must get away from Japan. He must sail away on that English ship in Katayama harbor."

Kenjuro gaped at her. "But that ship isn't due to sail for at least a week! Besides—besides, it's impossible. Lord Alex would

272

never agree to run away from Kita and the Hollander!"

"I've thought of that." Carefully, Zanna gave her instructions. "This letter goes to the captain of the English ship. You must take it there at once."

Kenjuro took the paper and frowned at it. "What does it say?" he asked suspiciously.

"Nothing that need concern you. When you return from delivering the letter, I will tell you what more I need you to do for me."

Kenjuro stared at her in awe. Zanna was issuing orders like a shogun! How different she was from her mother, he thought, and he was suddenly afraid for this beautiful, brave girl. She seemed to read his mind, for she put her arms around him, pressing her smooth, fragrant young cheek to his old one.

"Do this because you have always been my beloved friend," she whispered.

Kenjuro wept openly as he hobbled out of the house clutching the letters.

A soft sound behind her reminded her that Oshin was still in the room. "You said you had something for me to do, also," she said.

"Yes. I am going to ask a great deal of you, Oshin-san, and—and there is no way I can repay you." Quickly, Zanna numbered the favors she needed. "First, you must sell this silver box and get what cash you can for it. It's old and very valuable, and perhaps you can find a pawnbroker who will not ask too many questions." The old woman nodded and Zanna went on, "When you have the money, there is still an important favor. Would you take a letter for me to the English lord who lives in the Great House?"

"May I ask what the message will say?"

Zanna looked away from the questioning old eyes. "Only that I want to meet and talk to him," she said evasively. She prayed that Alex would be curious enough to come in answer to her invitation. It was his only chance.

Chapter Twenty-one

WHY WOULD ZANNA WANT TO SEE ME? ALEX asked himself. He frowned down at the fragile piece of paper in his hands, going over the familiar, careful script for the hundredth time. Why a meeting now, and why on the pier of all places? If she wished to see him, why had she not arranged a rendezvous at the old woman's house in Hamabashi? And why at ten o'clock at night?

The old woman who had brought the letter provided no information, and when he had tried to question her, had seemed so genuinely terrified of him that he'd not had the heart to persist.

It was a trap, of course. That was his first thought and made the most sense. It was a trap set up by Rutledge and his foul manager, and Zanna was the bait. *I won't go*, Alex decided. But then, in an unguarded moment,

275

he held the paper closer and inhaled the faintest trace of the flower-and-spice fragrance Zanna wore.

"God damn them all," he swore angrily, and realized then that he could not stay away.

He stayed at the Katayama office until late, gulping a hasty meal at Rutledge's desk while he discovered even more evidence of how badly the London Company had been cheated. Though most of the books were in Japanese, those he could make out were damning. "If it hadn't been for you and your sickly director general, the London Company might have been even more successful than the Dutchmen," he told Kita toward nightfall.

Kita shrugged. "Hard to say, Lord Alex. Time to go, now? It late, and tomorrow Rutledge-sama will feel better and you can talk of many things."

Alex returned to the Great House and changed his clothes. "Time to go," he finally said to himself.

He thrust the Isudai sword through his belt hiding a poignard near to hand. He drew a dark doublet over his white shirt and covered his fair hair with a hat. *Now*, he thought grimly, *I will be hidden in the dark.* He took a single unlit lantern from his room, and let himself out of one of the Great House's side gates.

In the cool moonlight the Katayama road was silent and deserted. A warm summer wind rattled the bamboo in the garden, rustling their leaves and swishing through the bending tops of the great Japanese pines. The breeze carried a scent of flowers, a faint, faraway fragrance that reminded him of the Isudai hills. From faraway a dog barked, and the soft, sad sound of a flute trilled faint but clear. Gradually, the flute stopped, the breeze died, the scent of flowers disappeared. Alex felt as if he alone were awake in the world.

Making as little noise as possible, he began to walk down the road. He kept his pace even, his hand within easy reach of the pommel of his sword. He passed the town limits, made his way through the dismal execution grounds. As soon as he was clear of this place, he lit the lantern he had brought. Its fragile light seemed little use against the darkness.

He met no one and saw nothing, and he walked swiftly. It was not until he was almost at the pier that he realized that he was conscious of a difference, an uneasiness, an awareness that someone was following him. So it was to be a trap after all! Some last spark of hope of Zanna's love died as his mind and spirit rose to grapple with the struggle that must come. *When?* he asked himself, and gave the answer: *When we reach the pier. The water is a fine place to hide a corpse, even the overlarge corpse of a western barbarian!*

Outwardly he walked as easily as before, but now all his senses were honed and keen. He was alert to the sound of a twig snapping, to the flicker of darker shadow against dark night. Once, as if the action was a casual one, he paused and held his lantern high, scattering light about him. He was almost sure he'd seen shadows melt back out of the lamplight. How many? He didn't know, but he'd met heavy odds before. Back in Iwase, he and Zanna. . . .

"Christ!" he swore, "must I remember her always?" Almost savagely, he pushed the thought of her away. He needed his wits about him if he was going to get out of this one alive. But he would survive, he promised himself grimly. It was Rutledge and Kita who would be sorry this time. And if Zanna were affected by their punishment, it was her own fault.

He turned a corner and caught his first whiff of brine, the smell of drying fish and salt, tar and pitch. He loosened his poignard surreptitiously. He walked along, unmolested, until he could see in the distance the shimmer of moonlight playing on the inlet waters. And there, black-masted and at anchor, was the *My Lady Fair*. "Almost there," Alex told himself. "Be easy. Steady!"

He felt the wood-and-stone pier under his feet. Up ahead, toward the end of the pier, stood someone in a pale kimono, a hood over her head. "Zanna!" Alex exclaimed.

He'd been so sure that this was a trap, so intent on the following footsteps, that her presence completely confounded him. He could only stand and stare as the figure turned and glided toward him. His heart began to pound. His throat was dry, and a great, soaring gladness that he had never hoped to taste again roared through his senses and his heart. She *had* wanted to meet him. It had not been her father's or Kita's doing. She was here!

"Zanna! Snowflower. . . ." He took two great strides forward onto the pier before he realized his mistake. As he moved, so did several figures that seemed to ooze out of the darkness and surround him. He'd been followed after all—and this was worse. These men, whoever they were, could hurt Zanna! Alex knew that if he turned and faced them now he would stand a much stronger chance of besting them, but the thought of Zanna's danger made him throw logic to the winds. "Get behind me!" he cried, quickening his pace toward the pale, approaching figure. Now he was almost close enough to touch her, to grasp her and put her behind him. . . .

Alex swore. It was not Zanna's face that was turned up to meet his in the moonlight. Instead, he stared down at the wrinkled, terrified face of Kenjuro. "You! Where's Zanna?" Alex demanded.

As he spoke, the first attacker leaped upon him with a loud cry. Acting instinctively, Alex parried a blow from an upraised club. He caught the man by his shoulder and swung him out and over the pier. There was a shriek and the sound of a great splash while, as if this was some sort of signal, the others surged forward.

They were a motley crew—all sizes and shapes, all armed. Alex, seizing a staff from one of them, began to flail out, knocking many into the water. "Where's Zanna, God rot you?" he bellowed at Kenjuro. "Did she send you?"

He had no chance to even draw his sword, let alone use it—the swarm that closed in around him reminded him of games he had played with Griff and some of the stable lads on his father's estate. Only, this was no game! A whistling bamboo, sharp as a whip, slashed across his back, and a knotty club missed him by inches. "You will, will you?" Alex snarled.

Suddenly, it seemed as if the attackers had fallen back. They were regrouping, Alex thought. As he reached for his sword, he heard a new voice. To his infinite relief, it spoke in cheerful, Manchester-accented English: "Now, Mr. Curtis! What's all this, then?"

A little man in the uniform of a British merchant sea captain stood on the pier. He held a respectable pistol in his hand, and behind him stood several brawny members of his crew. Alex could have laughed aloud in his relief. "The captain of the *My Lady Fair*?" he inquired.

"Captain Ezra Dawes, sir, and at your service. Seems like there's been trouble." The little captain nodded to one of his brawnier seamen. "Let's get on with it, Reuben."

Alex slid his sword back into its sheath. "I am grateful to see you," he told the captain. "These fellows followed me from Katayama, I think. They—what in the name of hell are you doing?"

The large seaman, instead of dispersing the now grinning crowd of attackers, had come up behind Alex and placed a huge paw on his shoulder. "If you'll come with us, please, sir?" he growled.

"Are you mad?" Alex could only gape. Captain Dawes looked a little uncomfortable.

"I'm sorry about all this," he said, "but those were my orders—I hope you won't hold them against me, Mr. Curtis. At least, you don't look harmed. Are you?"

"Whose orders? What orders?" Alex tried to pull loose from the clasp on his shoulder, couldn't. "What in the devil are you talking about?"

For answer, Captain Dawes pulled out an official-looking sheet of paper. "See for yourself! It's in the heathen Jappo script, but I had it translated—sent it up to the representatives of his mucky-muck lordship, Azuma! It's an order, with Azuma's personal seal; that's what it is. It commands me to sail out of Katayama Point on the tide and to take you with me to England!"

"Azuma! But that's impossible. . . ." Alex was being impelled forward by the great hand on his shoulder. "Why?"

"Didn't say. Them great lords never do, do they? That much is the same in Japan as well as home!" Captain Dawes looked very embarrassed. "Please understand my position, Mr.

Curtis. What was I to do?" He added, as Alex was firmly escorted over the side of the pier and into a waiting longboat, "It was a bit of a shock to me, to say the least! What I'm going to tell the London Company when I dock back home I'll never know! I was going to bring home a cargo of lacquer and swords this time."

"May I ask you who brought Lord Azuma's letter to you?" Alex asked the captain. "One of his samurai, perhaps?"

"No. Odd that you ask. I thought it strange myself! It was a little old body—a servant of some sort. I thought it so peculiar I had the seal checked."

"Was it that man?" Alex pointed at Kenjuro, who suddenly ducked behind some of the watchers on the pier and started to run away. "Catch him!" Alex roared. "If you'd sailed tonight, it wouldn't have been at Lord Azuma's order! That man can explain it all!"

"Now, Mr. Curtis! We were told you would be difficult. If you'll just sit down, we'll make sure. . . . Mr. Curtis! Hello!" But Alex had thrown himself clear of the seaman's grasp and had leaped the distance from boat to pier. Wood planking echoed under his feet as he pursued the running Kenjuro.

There was no contest. Within a hundred yards or so, Kenjuro fell to his knees and sobbed for breath. Alex granted him no reprieve. He grabbed the old man by the shoulders, hauling him unceremoniously to his feet. "Zanna did this, didn't she?" he demanded, grimly. In fractured Japanese, he added, "Zanna? Where is Zanna?"

Kenjuro burst into tears. A flood of broken explanation poured from him, and he crumpled again to the ground, bowing into the dust and rocking back and forth in such total misery that Alex could only stare. "What's he saying?" he demanded, as a puffing Captain Dawes came up to him. "Can you speak the language?"

Captain Dawes looked uncertainly at Alex. As the tall fellow didn't seem ready to run again, he replied, "I can—after a fashion." He grinned. "A woman taught me. She was one of those com—."

"Translate," Alex snapped. He hauled Kenjuro to his feet again, holding him so that the old man's feet dangled inches off the ground. "Now, Kenjuro-san, speak. And slowly!"

As Kenjuro spoke, the captain's face was a study. Surprise, then disbelief, then anger and finally horror came and went. "My God, Mr. Curtis, but this is totally unbelievable!" he sputtered. "You were right! It wasn't Lord Azuma that ordered me to sail—it was some woman called Zanna! She apparently used Lord Azuma's seal without his authorization."

"What else? *Why* did she want me gone from Japan?" Alex demanded. Kenjuro's tears made him cold with some terrible presentiment of evil.

"That's the most unbelievable part! Apparently, her father's the director of the London

Company. He was murdered by a Dutchman named van Feinstra yesterday—."

Rutledge, dead! Alex grasped the captain's sleeve. "Go on. Hurry, man. What of Zanna? Where is she now?"

The captain gulped. From the look on the young man's face, he didn't really want to continue. "According to this old man, the man who murdered the director has more killing in mind. He and the Japanese manager of the London Company are plotting to—er—kill you in your sleep tonight."

Alex shook Kenjuro. "Zanna?" he shouted. "In the name of God, she hasn't gone to the Great House to try and stop them?"

The meaning, if not the words, was unmistakable. Kenjuro raised streaming, swollen eyes to meet Alex's. "She's not trying to *stop* them, my lord Englishman," he quavered. "When they go to murder you, they will find Zanna in your bed. Don't you understand? She's going to die in your stead!"

Chapter Twenty-two

It was very dark in the garden, for the moon was partially hidden behind the tall pines. When she turned her head, Zanna could see the dark outlines of the Great House limned in faint light against the sky. From the branches of the pine trees, a sleepy bird called once and was still.

Alex would have left for the pier by now. Zanna wished him Godspeed, using the quaint English word he had taught her. She tried to imagine him safe and free, pacing the deck of the English ship that would carry him to safety. She did not want to dwell on the fact that the men who were to ambush him and deliver him to the captain of the ship might hurt him. He would fight them all, her Alex, but in the end numbers would prevail. "I am sorry, my love," she murmured softly. "It was the only way I could think of. Had you known the truth, you wouldn't have left Katayama."

It was almost as if he were with her, could understand her. Zanna wished that she had written him a letter of explanation, but at the same time she was glad she had not. If he knew what she was doing, he would return even if he had to swim all the way—she knew her Alex. The knowledge gave her both pride and sorrow, and she prayed he would never find out. "And if you learn of this when you are back in England, my dear love, it will all be over," she said, gently as if to convince herself. "I have sent a humble letter to the Lord Azuma explaining what has happened. I have placed it with my own hands in the keeping of his representatives here in Katayama. Lord Azuma will punish Kita and van Feinstra and avenge my father—and me."

She drew further into the shadows of the garden as the old gateman, muttering a little about the late hour and his aching joints, made a last inspection before double-locking the gates and going to rest. As soon as he had gone, she would slip into the Great House. Kenjuro had left one of the folding doors leading to Alex's rooms unlocked.

Kenjuro—she smiled a little at what Alex must have thought and said when he discovered Kenjuro dressed as herself. How Kenjuro had protested! She had convinced him that this was necessary, however, and he did not know that she had done this to save his life. He guessed what she was about to do, and

Zanna knew the old servant would have gladly died defending her if left to his own devices. But now he was safely out of harm's way.

She began to move stealthily toward the house, and a small, green-glowing firefly floated in front of her and seemed to light the way. "Thanks, sister," Zanna smiled, and then remembered one night in Isudai when she and Alex had stood, hand in hand, outside her uncle's house and watched such fireflies dance in the velvet dark. Suddenly, she was achingly sad—not only for Alex, not only for the love she would never taste again, but for life itself. *I'll miss not being alive,* she thought. *I won't see the mountains again or hear the songbirds or visit my glade. Will anybody ever discover it again after me?* She remembered how happy she had been there, and felt, for an instant's instant, Alex's arms about her and the sweet weight of his body.

She gained the outer veranda and carefully tested the sliding doors until she found the one left open. She must not think of life, she told herself, sternly. Tonight she must renounce all earthly things and be calm, be ready for death as hundreds of men and women had been ready before her. She thought of them all—all loyal, devoted people who had given their lives willingly for their lords. There was a story Oyuri had told her once, a story of a woman who had taken her samurai lover's place after she'd learned of an assassination plot.

Had she been scared? Did her hands shake

and feel like ice? Zanna's hands did, and her breath came in great gasps as she closed the sliding door and crossed the short distance to the inner doors that led to Alex's rooms. Her legs felt stiff, but no one was about to see her as she reached these doors and carefully slid them open. For an instant, her heart beat fast. Suppose Kita and van Feinstra had already been there? But she had seen no one enter from the garden. She knew she was in time.

Now that her eyes had grown used to darkness, the room seemed almost too light. Moonlight filtered through the paper-and-wood screens and illuminated the thick quilts. *If the moonlight falls on my face they'll see I'm not Alex,* she thought, and began to turn the quilts around so that her pillow would lie in darkness. The pillow now pointed north, and she shuddered. In Japan, only corpses lay with their heads pointing to the north!

"Don't be foolish," she said to herself in English, but she was shaking again. She'd been so calm all day that it had almost frightened her. She'd written that "order" from Lord Azuma without a single mistake, written to Alex, written finally to tell Lord Azuma what was happening in his fief. All this she had accomplished in almost inhuman calm. And when old Oshin had brought the money from the silver plum box, she had just as serenely instructed Kenjuro to go to the eating rooms and tea establishments nearby and round up a dozen stout ruffians who wouldn't mind acquiring a few bruises in a night's work. "Only, they mustn't hurt Lord Alex. If they do, I'll make sure that Lord Azuma punishes them," she had threatened.

Calm as death she had been—but not now. The spell had worn off and with it the sense of unreality that had insulated her against shock. She had not realized that it would be this hard to wait to die. Worse still, suppose she disgraced herself and involuntarily screamed when the moment came? If she did that, she'd let the murderers know they'd killed the wrong person, and Alex might not have time to sail away on the tide.

She lay down on the quilts and covered herself, pulling the top quilt over her head. *They must not know*, she told herself. *They must not realize until they go to the small house in Hamabashi and find me gone.* She thought gratefully of Oshin-san, now safely hidden away at a friend's, and of all her help. True, the murderers would probably make a shambles of that small house, but she'd already paid Oshin-san to find another small place elsewhere. . . .

In the middle of her thought, Zanna tensed. Had that been a footfall? She listened, frozen with fear, but there was nothing. The gardens were quiet except for a breeze that rustled like moving fingers sliding over the door. *Think of Alex*, Zanna told herself. *Think of him safe in England, safe. Think of his happiness.*

Step . . . step! There was no mistaking those sounds now. Zanna burrowed her face deep into the hard Japanese pillow. Her hands clenched tight and one fist pressed into her mouth to stifle any sounds. Step—creak—step! Someone was standing on the outer veranda. She began to pray quietly, her terrified mind stumbling over the words. Then, the words of prayer were stilled as she realized that she was quieting, that her muscles were relaxing. It was as if these quilts of Alex held a remembered scent of him—the clean, male, beloved scent that enfolded her like a lover's arms. She breathed deeply and felt the terrible tension within her die. She was still afraid, but now it would not overwhelm her. The love she felt for Alex was stronger and closer and the only thing that mattered.

Softly, sighing ever so slightly, the screen door of the room opened. A shaft of moonlight fell across the quilts and, peeping out of the bedclothes, she saw the silhouetted figure of a tall man in the doorway. Van Feinstra. For a second, he simply stood there, then he advanced into the room. Moonlight glinted against the dagger he was holding.

Zanna felt her moment of calm ebb away in renewed terror. Closing her eyes tightly, she prayed again. *Blessed Buddha, don't let me fail. Let me be brave for Alex—Alex!*

There was a sound beside her. Zanna's eyes flew open. Moonlight now spilled on the Hollander as he raised his dagger high. Now! she thought, and almost felt relief. But the blow didn't fall, and there was a hiss in Kita's voice from the outer veranda: "Someone's coming!"

Van Feinstra hesitated. Then, he backed up against the wall of the room, melding himself against the shadows there. "Who?" Zanna heard him whisper.

At that moment there was a loud pounding on the gates. "Open!" Alex's voice thundered. "Open, damn you!"

Van Feinstra cursed. He kicked aside the quilts and stared down at Zanna. "You!" He might have stabbed her there and then, but before he could move a flood of torches blazed into the garden and Zanna could hear Kenjuro shrieking her name.

"Honored miss! We are coming, honored miss! Are you alive? Are you still alive?"

"Here!" she tried to scream, but her voice was like a hoarse croak. Van Feinstra glared at her and then swung into the garden at a run, followed by another shadow that must have been Kita. Someone must have spotted them, for she heard a chorus of shouts.

"There they are! There are the murderers! Don't let them get over the wall!"

Zanna tried to get to her feet but couldn't. She felt dazed with shock. Alex was here. She was alive. And Kita and the Dutch trader were running away. She couldn't take it all in. Outside, there was a howling that indicated one of the two had been apprehended. She crawled, on hands and knees, out of the rooms and onto the outer veranda. The first thing she saw was Kita, all trussed up. But where was Alex and van Feinstra?

291

"Zanna-san! *Child!*" Kenjuro was hurrying toward her, still wearing his absurd kimono and tripping on the hem. He was weeping and laughing at the same time. "I was so afraid we would be too late!" he shouted.

Zanna clung to the old man. "Alex?" she whispered, but her teeth were chattering and she was shaking so hard she could not stop. "Kenjuro, Lord Alex! Is he safe?"

"Don't you worry about him, Zanna-san. He's out there trying to find that Hollander that killed the director general." Kenjuro's voice swelled in a strange kind of pride. "He's quite a man, your Englishman. He discovered about your plans and fought off all those sea rats. What's one van Feinstra to such a man?"

Just then, Zanna saw van Feinstra dart out from behind the servants' quarters and hurry toward the wall that surrounded the garden. He was halfway up it when Alex shouted his name.

"Van Feinstra! Are you thinking of running away and letting your partner take all the blame?"

Hands reached up to grasp the Hollander's boots, and he was hauled off the wall. He regained his balance, however, and drew his sword, keeping would-be attackers away. "So, Englishman," he sneered. "You got your wench to take your place under the knife. Is there nothing the poxy English will not do to save their skins?"

Zanna saw Alex emerge from the shadows

WINTER BLOSSOM

and face van Feinstra. She drank in the sight
of him, loving him more than she had ever
done before. She knew that the Hollander was
trying to bait Alex, to get him to lose his
temper. She wanted to warn him but again
could not find her voice.

"You talk big, Dutch merchant." Alex's
voice was gentle. "But you're a bungler. You
couldn't keep your thieving arrangements
safe, and you couldn't even plan my murder
properly."

Moonlight caught the blade of the Isudai
sword as Alex drew it. Zanna clung more
tightly to Kenjuro. "Can you fight as well as
stab helpless women?" Alex asked.

"It was all Kita's fault." The Dutchman
seemed to have gone limp. He cowered, even
whimpered. "He made me do all this. Question him, Curtis. Look, I put down my sword.
We're both Europeans, both men of the
world. . . ."

As he lowered the tip of his sword, Zanna
saw the moonlight flash on the dagger in his
other hand. "Alex, look *out!*" she screamed.

Van Feinstra lunged, slashing viciously at
Alex. Alex caught the point of the dagger on
his blade, turning it so that the Hollander
was, for a second, unbalanced. His blade had
gone flying, and Alex's iron clasp was impris-
oning his wrist. The dagger, too, fell to the
dust.

"Bind him." Alex pushed van Feinstra into
the eager hands of Captain Dawes and his

crew. His eyes left the Hollander and turned to the veranda where Zanna stood with Kenjuro.

Zanna felt his look. Though she couldn't read Alex's expression at this distance, she felt her pulses leap and a current of love flow between them again—a current so strong that she took a step forward to go to him.

"And so you're running to him, eh, honored miss?"

Kita's mocking voice stopped her where she stood. He was squatting in the dirt some distance away, his arms tightly bound, his face malevolent in the sputtering light of torches and lanterns. "You think you've been clever, don't you?" he went on. "You think you've beaten me and that now all you and your English barbarian lover need do is be happy? Hah!"

Kenjuro let go of Zanna and advanced toward Kita, hands in fists. "You shut up!" he shouted. "Haven't you done enough to her?"

"*I?* I didn't do this to her. She did it to herself!" Kita laughed till he almost choked. "It's ironic, isn't it, Zanna? You've aided in catching van Feinstra and me, and by so doing you've made it impossible for you to ever be with your lover again."

"You lie, Kita-san!" But as she spoke, Zanna felt cold dread. *I must not listen,* she thought. *I must not. I would have given my life for Alex. Surely that is enough to atone for everything.*

"Alex Curtis is the nephew of a great lord who will probably make him the new director general of all the London Company offices in Japan. He will be powerful and rich, your Alex. And can you see such a great lord wanting to associate himself with the daughter of a disgraced criminal?" Kita let the shot quiver for a moment and then added, softly, "But you are clever, Zanna. Your body is beautiful and your face that of an angel. You'll have your way, won't you? You'll make him forget that disgrace, even though it's not to his advantage."

"Don't listen to him, Zanna-san!" Kenjuro urged. He grabbed her arm tightly and said, "Come! Let us go to the Englishman. *He'll* show you how little Kita's stupid words mean!"

"No." Zanna pulled back. Kita was right. Alex couldn't be associated with someone like her. "I can't allow it," she whispered.

Even if Alex loved her enough to overlook the terrible disgrace in which her family had been placed, *especially* then, she could not let him do this. "It would ruin him," she whispered to Kenjuro. "We must go away, go now! I can't bear to see him, talk to him, when I know I must never see him again."

She began to make for the side gate. Kenjuro tried to stop her. "But, Zanna-san! He's looking for you. See?"

Zanna shook her head almost frantically. "I must get away!" she whispered. As Kenjuro unwillingly followed her out of the side gate, she could hear Alex's voice calling her name. She had thought that dying would be terrible. This was even worse.

Chapter Twenty-three

ZANNA WAS HALF-AFRAID THAT ALEX WOULD try to follow her and was relieved when he did not. She ignored Kenjuro, who clicked his tongue and shook his head when the tall Englishman stayed away. "He has realized that this is the only course open to us," she told her old servant firmly. "I won't discuss it anymore, Kenjuro!"

"Then at least think about going back to Isudai and your uncle," Kenjuro urged. He was worried sick for the young mistress, and he hated the great shadows that darkened her gray eyes and the new hollows of her pale cheeks. "Why stay here any longer?"

"I will go when everything that needs doing has been done." Zanna had grown used to living in frost again, in the gently inflexible, self-reliant world she had crafted for herself after Oyuri's death. "There are some things that require my presence, Kenjuro, as you know."

One was Rutledge's funeral. With the permission of Lord Azuma's samurai, the director general of the Katayama London Company was interred honorably at a long and decorous ceremony. Zanna assumed the role of chief mourner, and was joined in this by Alex. She could not help starting when she first saw him, but she would not permit herself to look at him or speak to him, and they exchanged no more than a few words as they accepted the condolences of the merchant community. Only when the funeral was over and when he turned to her, saying, "Zanna, we must talk," did she feel a surge of panic that made her shake her head in an almost desperate way.

"I cannot, my lord. Not now. Please—you must give me time," she had whispered in a choked voice, and then she had hurried away hating her weakness. *I will write to him and say that I will never see him again,* she promised herself. *It is for his good!*

But she saw him again, and quickly, too. Swift-riding messengers had taken news of the Katayama murder to Iwase, and Lord Azuma dispatched his trusted advisers to act as a court of inquiry. Once summoned, Zanna saw not only Alex again, but Kita and van Feinstra, as well. The latter two looked filthy and terrified as they were forced to prostrate themselves before Lord Azuma's justice.

Zanna sat a little apart from Alex. Her testimony against van Feinstra and Kita was called for, and she gave it in a flat, unemotional voice. Then, the confession obtained from the prisoners was read aloud. The verdict was swift. Kita was condemned to death, van Feinstra to be expelled from Japan and placed in the custody of his own country's justice. As soon as the dazed men were led away, the official in charge of the court turned to Zanna.

"There is a matter against you, as well," he told her. "I have heard that you forged an official document and used my lord of Iwase's name. That is a serious offense."

Zanna had expected this, and so, obviously, had Alex. Through a court interpreter he explained that Zanna had thought quickly to save his life, jeopardizing her own. "The Japanese are a just people who must respect bravery and self-sacrifice," Alex pleaded. "Zanna-san should be honored, not condemned for what she did. If she is condemned, I, too, should be held guilty, for it's my life she saved."

He looked straight at her as she spoke, and in spite of her resolve, she felt a melting within her, an aching, desperate longing to be held once more in those strong arms, feel the touch of his lips. *My love*, she thought, *my love*—, and almost hoped that the stern official would sentence her as he had sentenced Kita.

However, this wasn't to be. Lord Azuma's representative pardoned Zanna and instructed her to help Lord Alex all she could. "Lord

WINTER BLOSSOM

Azuma has decreed that until the London
Company appoints a new director general,
Alex Curtis is to take charge of that company
in Japan. Since your father was at the bottom
of this present trouble, it behooves you as his
daughter to do all you can to help the head of
the new company." He paused, and added
sternly, "Remember! It is your solemn duty!"

"It is my duty, Kenjuro. Didn't you hear?"
The sun was bright and warm on Zanna's
back as she and Kenjuro walked toward the
Katayama London Company office. It was
June, and the blue dome of the sky was un-
troubled with clouds.
Kenjuro's bottom lip was stuck out rebelliously. He had hoped for so long that his
young mistress would make her peace with
Lord Alex, prayed that the Englishman would
come to Oshin's small house and try to talk to
Zanna. How well he knew that Zanna-san
wept for him each night! But Lord Alex hadn't
come, hadn't sent for her, or even intimated
he wanted to see her. He was afraid that any
further dealings with this barbarian lord
would only cause her further pain.
"The English lord didn't *ask* you to come
and help him at the office, mistress," he said.
"Suppose he sends you away?"
"In that case I will be released from my
duty and I can leave Katayama." She spoke
with outward composure; inside, Zanna was
close to tears. The day, heavy with the drone
of honeybees and the bright, metallic cry of

300

cicadas, stirred such loving memories. The scent of the earth and flowers was warm; a lacy butterfly danced like a plush black shadow ahead of her, and as she stepped up to the outer gate of the London Company office, she heard wind chimes jingle overhead. She stood silent for a moment, struggling to still a rising panic. *I'm not ready to face him*, she thought, in despair. *I'll come back another day, when I can control my emotions*. But when would that be?

"Honored miss, let's forget this and go *home*," groaned Kenjuro.

His whine so closely matched her own thought that Zanna's pride rose in defiance. Squaring her shoulders, she stepped through the gate and walked calmly through the busy clerks and apprentices in the outer office. A few of them just stared, but one of the apprentices, a lad who'd come with them to Iwase, jumped up and gave her a big, welcoming bow.

"Zanna-san! It's nice to see you," he said. "Shall I tell the master you're here?"

The master—Alex. With an effort, she smiled. "No, I'll go into the inner office unannounced. I don't want to disturb his work," she said.

Leaving the youth bowing, she walked up to the door of the inner office and raised a hand to knock. Instead, she gave the door a little push and looked in. Alex was bending over the familiar lacquered desk, frowning at some figures in an open ledger before him. She watched him hungrily, unobserved. There were indications that he had been working too hard, sleeping too little. There were dark lines under his eyes, the faintest hollows in his cheeks. A yearning filled her to take his face in her hands and kiss away those lines of tension.

She must have made some movement, some sound, for he looked up and saw her. For an instant, their eyes met, and she saw the unguarded leap of excitement in his. Then, she dropped her gaze and bowed deeply. "Good morning, my lord," she said. "I hope I don't disturb you?"

"Of course not." His voice was as cool as hers and as courteously bland. "I didn't know you were coming. Shall I send for some tea?"

"No, please. I've come to work." He looked at her in such surprise that she could not help a sad smile. "At the trial of Kita and van Feinstra—don't you remember? I was told it was my duty to help you."

"To—?" *How can you help?* his face plainly said, and the emotionless eyes were not encouraging.

"Many of the ledgers and the records kept by the company are in Japanese," she explained. "I could translate them for you and make your work easier. I know that there is much to do before you can build up the London Company's business."

He turned away from her abruptly. "I don't think it would be so wise," he told her. It was incredible that she was there, for he had just been thinking of her—when, really, did he not think of her? He needed to discipline himself so that he did not shout out the words he wanted to tell her—words she obviously did not want to hear.

"And why not, my lord? I owe you my assistance."

"Duty!" His voice had a harsh quality, suddenly. "It *would* be that for you, wouldn't it, Zanna? Have you ever done anything for something besides duty, I wonder?" Then, he swung around to face you. "No, I'm sorry. I had no right to say that to you. You risked your life for me—and I have not even thanked you for that."

"Please." A knot was forming in her throat, and she could not look at him.

"No, it's true. You must accept my thanks for that great service. A man's life is a dear possession, and because you gave me back mine you've done your *duty* to me." He stressed the word heavily. "I require no more of you. I can hire an interpreter who can take charge of the books, Zanna. You must not feel obligated in any way."

He was releasing her. She could leave, now, and she could go to Isudai. She would be free of duty, of the strong tie that kept her here. But something inside her forced her to say, "Are you sure, my lord? Are you certain?"

He regarded her gravely, and she met his eyes. *Oh, Alex,* she thought, and all the pent-up love within her seemed to reach toward him in the silence. But he gave her no sign that he felt the same, and she realized that he, too, had decided that the best thing for them would be to separate now and forever. Why else would he want to hire an interpreter to help him with the books?

"What will you do now?" he was asking in that new, abrupt way he had of speaking. "Go back to Isudai?" She nodded. "Are you—do you have money?"

He had thought of this before and had had no way of asking. It had driven him half-mad to think of Zanna living with that old woman in Hamabashi, eating the food of the poor while he could not think of any way to aid her. He had known she would not accept money; but now he attempted to offer it, and she was already shaking her head.

"I have enough. Please don't concern yourself at all. Uncle Yasutomo has sent me enough to come back to the mountains. I told him I'd return as soon as I—as soon as I had finished helping you."

As soon as she'd done her duty. Duty had brought her to Katayama, duty had made her pretend she loved him. Duty had forced her to try to exchange her life for his—and now she was going out of his life for that same duty. "You have nothing left to do in Katayama? Your marriage—."

She winced. "That is over, Lord Alex," she said, hastily. "No, there's nothing to keep me here."

He felt a sinking of heart. As Rutledge had predicted, full disclosure of her father's thieving had ruined Zanna's chances of a good match. Was he to be blamed for that? Alex asked himself, angrily. He pulled open the desk drawer and drew something out, something that glinted icy in the sunlight.

"You recognize this, Zanna?" It was the plum-blossom box Umezono had given Alex long ago. "I gave this to you, and it seems you sold it to raise money to save me. You must at least take this back. A gift is a gift."

She put her hands behind her back, shook her head. "When you presented this to me, things were different. Alex, you *know* the reason why I came to Katayama. You know why I must leave now!"

She was reminding him, and in no uncertain terms, that there had been no love between them, at least on her side. She had done her duty, paid her debts and she was now cutting her losses. He sternly stifled the impulse he had to take her in his arms and crush her to him. "In that case, let me do something for you," he said. "No matter what you say about duty, I feel I owe you something—for my life if nothing else. And I don't think your uncle is a wealthy man, is he?"

"Please!" There was hot flush on her cheekbones, and he took this for embarrassment. "Let's not talk about this any longer, Lord Alex!"

But once started, he was determined. "I want to repay you in some way. How? Shall I build you a home in Isudai? Or, if it's money you could use. . . ."

Her eyes suddenly blazed at him. "I don't want to be paid for saving your life," she said.

He knew he'd hurt her and he was glad. His own personal misery was such that she should suffer, also! "You once told me you had no dowry," he plunged on. "You could use the money to make a good match."

"How *dare* you!"

Her gasping whisper was wrenched from her, shocked them both. She was trembling with anger and hurt, her slender hands curled into fists, her lovely face no longer frozen but full of life and pain. But it was fury and not tears that flashed in her eyes.

"How could you?" she threw at him. "Can you put a price on my honor, Alex? Do you think I'm like *them*—my father and Kita and the Hollander? Did you actually think that it was their command that made me love you?"

He could only stare at her, and when he tried to reach out to her, she stepped determinedly backward.

"I did not *know* that I was their tool! I loved you as much as any woman can love—more! That night when Kita and van Feinstra came to kill me instead of you, I prayed that I would have the courage to die without a cry so that you could be safe to sail back to England and be happy. And yet now you try to give me money, like a true companion bought for cash!"

"Zanna!" But she turned, suddenly overwhelmed with what she had said, and ran from the office and through the staring clerks.

306

Outside, she found Kenjuro had ambled off to buy some refreshments at a nearby stand, and she began to walk toward him as quickly as she could. She realized that she was crying, and she brushed the tears away with the back of her hand, like a child. *He offered me money,* she thought.

"Zanna, listen to me!"

She had not heard him come, and now the hard clasp on her shoulders kept her prisoner. She ducked her head so that he could not see her tears. "Go away, honored lord," she snapped. "Go back to your company and your country and the wealth and power you love. Buy somebody else with your money!"

"Dammit, woman, will you listen?" he roared.

Half of Katayama turned and stared at them as Alex grasped her hands and swung her around to face him. They glared at each other, she with telltale tears wet on her cheeks.

"I am listening," she said, coldly. She tried to pull loose, could not. How warm and strong was the remembered touch of his hands. "Let me go!" she cried at him.

"Never! Never again. I'll hold you here, now, always," he swore, and still angrily, he shouted at her, "I love you, you headstrong woman. You beautiful, stubborn wench whom I will love till I die."

She felt her defenses crumbling within her, and she shook her head so hard that her dark hair tumbled free. "Alex, Alex, don't do this.

We can't—I should not have come! I should not have spoken so. Please, please let me go away."

His voice was gentler now, and he drew her closer, holding only her hands, but forcing her to meet the look in his blue eyes. "I can't," he said. "When you are out of my life, everything is empty. I need you, Zanna."

Then, suddenly, he let her hands go. She knew that she needed only to turn and run away—if she wanted to. She could escape from him and go to Isudai or anyplace else. But she also knew she would not do this. She was like that captured songbird she had freed in the mountains: free and yet unable to escape.

"I offered you money," he was saying, still not touching her. "You were right to accuse me of dishonor. But I was afraid you'd reject what I truly wanted to offer you."

"Alex—."

"Snowflower, I offer my lifelong devotion." His tone dipped, became husky—the voice she knew and remembered from the long, golden magic of Isudai days. "I would be your husband, your lover, the father of your children. We will live here, or in England, or anywhere on this earth that we choose and be happy." She began to speak, but he silenced her, a finger on her trembling lips. "I know you feel that I am unworthy of you—."

"You! Oh, Alex. I stayed away only because —because I am disgraced now, without family. How could you wish to love someone like that?"

His arms around her were answer enough, the touch of his mouth on hers a promise she could not mistake. He kissed her closed eyelids, her cheeks, the corner of her mouth, drew her close, closer still into the sanctuary of his arms as their lips met again in a kiss that mingled their breath, their souls.

"We will go away to Isudai together," he promised her. "This company business will keep. We will be married, and we will go away and be alone. As to what you've just told me, did I not tell you long ago that the riches you bring me are above price? Eyes like gray diamonds, lips like rubies, breasts tipped with coral. . . ."

A loud giggle stopped Alex's speech. Looking cautiously over her shoulder, Zanna realized that they had attracted quite a gathering. Children, bug-eyed, held each other by the hand and pointed. Old ladies clucked their tongues in disapproval. Young people craned their necks avidly. In the near distance, old Kenjuro grinned his contentment like a toothless monkey.

Zanna began a chuckle that ended in her lovely, clear laugh. "My beautiful English lord," she said, "all my riches are yours to claim. But I think not here. Perhaps if we could slip away from this crowd—."

Alex's eyes sparkled with answering laughter and love. Ceremoniously, he bowed to her, lifted her hand and kissed the ring finger of her left hand. "Then let's find a private, crowdless place," he told her, "and I will show you how much I've longed for you and how much I love you. I warn you, Madame Winter Blossom, that will take me a long time. In fact, it will undoubtedly take the rest of our lives."

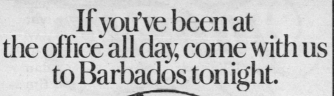

Tapestry

HISTORICAL ROMANCES

WILLOW WIND
Lynda Trent

"CALL ME 'MATT.'
I WOULD PREFER THAT."

"Why?" she asked. "Does everyone call you by your first name?"

"No, but I want you to. May I call you 'Becca'?"

"My name is Rebecca."

"I know. But I want to call you something no one ever has before. We are going to be very important to each other and I want you to know that from the start."

"I don't know you," she protested in a whisper. "And you don't know me."

"We know each other," he told her softly. "We knew all we needed to know from the very beginning."

CORONET BOOKS